VANISHED
If Hitler Had Won the War

A Novel

C.K. LIM

Copyright © 2017 C.K. LIM

All rights reserved.

www.authorcklim.com

ISBN: 1977641490
ISBN-13: 978-1977641496

For Moppet,

who sat by my feet from the beginning till the end.

CONTENTS

1	Annelie	1
2	Gunther	5
3	Jack	12
4	Thomas	18
5	Gunther	22
6	Annelie	28
7	Thomas	34
8	Anna	37
9	Thomas	42
10	The Past	46
11	Annelie	53
12	Gunther	61
13	The Past	70
14	Gunther	72
15	Annelie	77
16	The Past	83
17	The Past	86
18	The Past	88
19	Thomas	94
20	Annelie	100

21	The Past	106
22	The Past	110
23	Gunther	115
24	The Past	125
25	The Past	131
26	Thomas	135
27	The Past	138
28	Gunther	143
29	Annelie	151
30	Thomas	157
31	Gunther	162
32	Thomas	167
33	The Past	172
34	Annelie	181
35	Gunther	183
36	Thomas	188
37	The Past	192
38	Gunther	196
39	Annelie	199
	Epilogue	203
	Acknowledgments	

1. ANNELIE

The hallway of the museum is deathly quiet save the rhythmic ticking of the old clock on the wall.

Annelie sits on the wooden bench, staring at the framed portrait of the Führer gazing back at her. In the glossy, coloured photo the size of a legal pad, he is dressed in his army uniform with a red swastika armband strapped to his left forearm. His hair is neat with a glossy sheen, on his face a stern expression. His cheeks sagged, as if burdened by the mammoth effort he had marshalled to win the war, to create their nation of today – the great German Reich.

For the Reich is indeed great, Annelie mouths silently as she stares at the portrait. All across the land, from the cities of Paris in the west to Warschau in the east, Drontheim in the north to Athen in the south, hallways in every school echo with the chorused chanting of young voices, proclaiming the greatness of the Führer and the greatness of the Reich. For this land would be nothing if not for the Führer. The Europe of today would be a backward, fractured mess if he had not marshalled all its territories into unification when he did.

We owe this great land to our great Führer, our great Father, Annelie mouths silently, recalling the ritualistic chants that marked the start of each school day.

Yet, decades after the war had been won, their great Father remained unsmiling in his portrait and its many replicas that hang in hallways of schools and government institutions. Frozen in time, he watches over everyone and everything like a hawk, ever the stern parent, always dissatisfied. Perhaps if he hadn't passed on so early, the portrait that she now stares at might be a different one – one of a smiling Führer, like a doting father smiling with pride at his child's high school graduation. Somehow, Annelie finds the image of a happy Führer impossible to imagine.

To pass the time while she waits, she plays a game with herself to see how long she is able to hold the Führer's gaze without blinking. She cranes her neck, training her eyes on his. Despite her determination, her eyelids burn with the desperation of an itch. She falters before the second hand on the old clock completes a full rotation. Turning away, she shifts her attention to the wooden door she hopes would soon open. To her disappointment, it remains resolutely closed.

She eyes the clock once again, counting the extra minutes since she last checked the time. One minute and twenty-two seconds have passed since she last looked. Thirty-seven minutes since she arrived, she calculates silently.

She looks away, glancing up and down the empty hallway, desperate for a distraction. The museum is now closed. The quietness that fills the vast halls and high ceilings verge on eerie. The only footsteps to be heard are the ones of the security guard, faint now that he is patrolling the distant west wing of the building.

The wait grows the restlessness within her. With each tick of the second hand, the stiffness in the base of her spine mounts. To nurse the paralysis that is creeping into her backside, she stretches her legs and shifts her weight around, creaking the wooden bench as she does so. That seems to help. But not by much.

As she sits in silence in the musty hallway, the starched white blouse she borrowed from Pavlina feels stiff against her skin. The starched collar grazes the back of her neck every time she turns. The scratch is beginning to bother her. Every few minutes, she tugs at her skirt, stretching it over her kneecaps only to have the hemline stubbornly snapping back to its place on her thighs, revealing the flesh colour stockings hugging the contours of her long legs. She huffs silently, shaking her head in exasperation.

Everything about her feels unnatural that day – her borrowed clothes, her mother's nylon stockings, the compact powder caked on her face, the boxy court shoes squashing her feet – all pieced together in her desperate attempt to impress. She wants to make a good first impression.

She *needs* to make a good first impression.

Annelie glances at the old clock once again. The second hand has barely moved an inch since she last checked the time. She turns her attention to the yellowing bulleted list of Code of Conduct stuck to the corkboard by four rusty thumbtacks. It looks small next to the large map detailing the emergency exits of the building. As she squints at the small dotted line on the evacuation map pointing the direction out of the East Wing, the wooden door creaks open. She shoots to her feet, standing erect as an older man with a receding hairline, thinning scalp and glasses on the bridge of his nose steps out.

"I'm Klaus Müller, Museum Director," he says, holding out his hand. She steps forward and shakes it eagerly.

"Annelie Eckhert," she replies, nodding vigorously.

"Come in," he says, half smiling as he withdraws his hand and steps aside. Beyond the rectangular doorframe, Annelie sees a wall lined with shelves filled with books. The corners of her lips lift instantly. She likes this man already.

She strides forward, hesitantly at first then more confidently. Once she is inside the room, the door clicks shut behind her.

"Have a seat," he says as he walks around her, an open palm gesturing to the empty chair in front of his desk. She does as she is told and soon they are facing each other, with only a wooden desk in between.

"You came highly recommended by the Dean," Klaus Müller says as he relaxes into his swivel chair. "The fact that you speak fluent English helps a great deal. I hope you realise what a great opportunity this is."

Annelie smiles and nods. She has heard that phrase more times than she can count.

I hope you realise what a great opportunity this is.

"I do my best in everything I put my mind to, Sir," Annelie says with a smile, sitting with a straight back, her hands folded in her lap. It is her first ever job interview and she is desperate to impress.

"What we do here is very important," Klaus Müller continues, leaning backwards in his chair, interlacing his fingers over his torso. "We are not just running a museum. We are preserving a part of European history. A *critical* part."

He goes on to rattle off the museum's statistics. Three carefully curated rotating exhibitions. Seven permanent collections. A staff of three hundred people. Five levels of security clearance. Twelve thousand items on display, another two thousand being restored in the basement workshop.

The numbers roll off his tongue with practised ease, punctuated by occasional gulps of saliva and sharp intakes of breath. As she listens intently, Annelie tries to guess how many times Klaus Müller has repeated the same speech.

"We receive about a million visitors a year," he says. "They come from all over to see the Führer's legacy. What we do here is very important." His unnerving gaze meets hers. Annelie does not flinch. Instead, she responds with a nod and a smile.

"*Very* important," he repeats as he leans forward.

"Sir?" Annelie interrupts. "What exactly will I be doing? The Dean was not clear when he mentioned this job to me."

Klaus Müller plucks the glasses from the bridge of his nose, blows on each lens and wipes off the fog with a small piece of cloth. He takes his time, inspecting the clarity of his glasses against the sunlight from the window. When he is satisfied, he carefully replaces it on the bridge of his nose.

"Well." He exhales loudly. "You are not experienced enough to work in Cataloguing or Restoration." Here, he pauses to swallow his saliva audibly before continuing, "We could use an extra pair of hands in Archive but, from what the Dean tells me, I think the best place for you to start is in Guiding."

"And what does that involve?"

"Story-telling, mostly," he says, inhaling loudly. "We receive about a million visitors a year. They are not here just to look at the exhibition. After all, what is the significance of a piece of cloth if there is no story around it?"

Annelie's heart sinks immediately. She had hoped for something more… *glamorous*.

Something more prestigious.

Something that pays well.

Not *tour guiding*.

Despite her disappointment, she smiles brightly.

"I hear you are quite the gifted orator," Klaus Müller adds, the corners of his lips curling into a smile.

Annelie feigns a smile.

"What story will I be telling, Sir?" she asks meekly.

"The story of the Jews. The race that no longer exists."

2. GUNTHER

Gunther beams as the horde of photographers snap photos of him. The bursts of flashes and the orchestra of clicks lift his chin higher. He smiles, occasionally turning this way and that at the requests of the enthusiastic press. With all eyes on him, he puffs up his chest a little bit more, showing off the medals dangling from the front left pocket of his uniform.

The photo session takes longer than anticipated as the photographers instruct him to change his position from one spot to another. Even though he is beginning to tire, Gunther obediently does as he is told, smiling the entire time.

"I feel like a movie star!" he jokes. The press laughs and the clicks fire off incessantly. Standing on the platform facing the crowd, Gunther begins to feel warm. He dismisses it as an adrenaline rush and makes no gesture to loosen the collar that is cutting into the flesh around his neck. The heat from the lamps is making him sweat but he pretends not to notice, and keeps smiling.

Just a few more minutes, he comforts himself, wearing the same big smile that now aches his cheek muscles. It's his moment in the spotlight and he is determined to enjoy it.

The morning event had gone swimmingly well. The celebration of the Reich's scientific progress and the unveiling of the Josef Mengele statue at the Mengele Centre for Genetics Research went without a hitch. There was a huge turnout at the Volkshalle – both by the press as well as by the public – and his speech was met with thunderous applause. A standing ovation like no other.

Gunther is secretly pleased with himself. He has lost count of the number of times he stood rehearsing in front of his bathroom mirror, making sure he pauses at the right moment, raising his voice at the right inflexion and tapering it when he needs to. The same way the Führer used to do. What a great orator he was!

He had watched film footage of the Führer addressing the public and took care to note his facial expressions and tone of voice. Every nuance – from the way he stood to the way he moved his hand – was carefully choreographed into Gunther's delivery. All those hours crafting his speech and rehearsing in front of the mirror paid off. From the approving nods he received from the Chancellor, Gunther is sure he is in line for a promotion very soon.

And about time too.

After the photographs, Gunther is ushered into another room for the ensuing press conference. As he tails his assistant down the quiet hallway, away from the reporters, he pauses to catch his breath, wiping the beads of sweat from his forehead with a folded handkerchief.

"Are you all right, Herr Scholz?" Further, down the hallway, his assistant turns around and asks. Gunther dabs at his forehead twice more with his folded handkerchief and waves him off dismissively.

"Get me some water," he grunts. "Still. Not sparkling."

He finds his way to the room and climbs the short steps onto the platform where he is to be seated next to the Chancellor. A middle-aged lady in an army officer's uniform greets him and ushers him to his seat.

"The Chancellor will be here shortly," she says before retreating. Gunther nods, suddenly nervous by the prospect of that empty chair next to him. He needs to make sure this press conference goes without a hitch. His career depends on it.

Sitting behind the clothed table, Gunther feels everything at once – nerves, exhaustion, excitement, apprehension – they all wash over him like a tidal wave. He runs his forefinger around the damp collar of his uniform and takes a swig of water from the crystal glass that has magically appeared before him. The water tastes sweet in his dry mouth. He guzzles the glass empty and sets it down. Before long, it is refilled to one centimetre below the rim.

The room is a hive of activity. With a quick scan, he estimates there are about two hundred chairs lined up in neat rows in the room, all of them occupied. Some reporters are stuffed in the aisles, others huddle at the back of the room, craning to get a good view. More camera crew are still filing in, scouting for floor space to set up their equipment.

Gunther feels warm and a bit lightheaded but there is no time for rest. He gestures for his assistant to turn up the air-conditioning. The young man scurries off and does as he is told. Before long, gusts of cold air are blowing in Gunther's face.

As Gunther basks gratefully under the blast of cold air from the vents above, the atmosphere in the room shifts. The cacophony of voices hush to a whisper as a tall, formidable figure makes an entrance. Gunther catches his eye and rises to meet him.

"Afternoon, Chancellor," Gunther says as they exchange a firm handshake. The Chancellor takes his seat and Gunther resumes his position.

"Good work this morning, Scholz," the Chancellor says without looking at him. He faces the press, acknowledging familiar faces with a smile and a nod. Gunther immediately feels flushed with pride.

"Thank you, Chancellor. It's an honour to serve our great nation."

"Come by my office tomorrow. There is something I would like to discuss with you," the Chancellor says. Gunther smiles without meaning to.

Chancellor Gunther Scholz.

His eyes sparkle at the thought.

A tapping of the microphone settles the crowd into their seats. When the shuffling of chairs dies down, the Master of Ceremony begins to make the necessary introductions.

"Per the usual protocol, please state your name and the press you represent before asking your question. I now invite the Chancellor of the Reich, Heinrich Wessemann, to commence proceedings," the Master of Ceremony concludes and extends her open palm in the direction of the platform.

Gunther watches with quiet contentment as the Chancellor speaks into the bud of the desk microphone below his chin. The Chancellor's voice fills every inch of the room, captivating the roomful of journalists.

That will be me one day. Gunther beams as his gaze shifts from the Chancellor to the attentive audience. He imagines himself sitting in the plush chair behind the huge oak desk in the Chancellor's office. Outside one window, the gigantic dome of the Volkshalle looms majestically. Beyond another, the Victory Arch beckons. His will be the most prestigious address in all of Germania.

Ah, to be the Chancellor of the Reich! To have the greatest title in all of Europe!

It will be the biggest, most significant achievement of his life. Gunther feels dizzy just thinking about it.

"We will now be taking questions. Let's begin."

The final few words in the Chancellor's address yanks Gunther back from his daydream. Within the room, voices erupt and hands shoot up in the air, demanding for attention. Both the Chancellor and Gunther scan the room, eyes darting over the ocean of outstretched arms, all waving to be called. Gunther's glance lingers over the front row and rests on a fresh-faced female reporter leaning towards him. She has a recorder in one hand, which she eagerly waves in the air. Gunther looks at her curiously. He does not recognise her. In fact, he is very sure he has never seen her before.

She must be new.

"Chancellor! Herr Scholz!" she calls. Her voice is clear and strong.

Something about her draws him in.

As a rule, Gunther does not humour reporters who are unknown to him. The risk with unknown reporters is that he could never be sure what type of questions he will be asked. The lack of control over the interview process makes Gunther uncomfortable. To be safe, he usually picks the few he is familiar with. The ones he knows will ask the type of questions he will gladly answer. The type of questions that will put him in good stead for his promotion.

On this occasion, however, Gunther is not the person in charge of the press conference. To his dismay, he turns to find the Chancellor staring in the same direction, equally enamoured by this young female reporter.

No, not her. Not her, Gunther protests silently.

To his horror, the Chancellor points at the young reporter. The crowd falls silent as all eyes rest on the reporter, waiting to hear her question. Gunther feigns a smile, taking a swig of water from his crystal glass to hide his nervous tick.

"Anna Weiss from Panzerbär," she introduces herself briefly into the microphone. "First of all, what an inspiring address you just gave, Chancellor. If the rumours are true that you intend to retire in the near future, I regret to say that your successor has big shoes to fill."

"I certainly don't doubt that, Fräulein Weiss," the Chancellor says. "I wear a size 48."

The room erupts into raucous laughter.

"And that sense of humour is what we will sorely miss." Anna Weiss smiles. "My question today is for Herr Scholz."

There is a shuffling of chairs. Gunther raises his eyebrows but only briefly. He quickly rearranges his facial expression to form an appreciative smile.

"Herr Scholz, congratulations on today's celebration of the Reich's contribution to the advancement of genetic science," she begins. "I feel proud of what we as a nation has accomplished in such a short span of time. I'm sure you agree with me when I say that our genetic research has helped put the Reich on the map."

Various clusters in the room grunt in agreement.

"As a young reporter starting out, I felt it was necessary to do some homework before coming to today's event. Let's just say that I'm still wet around the ears." She smiles, tugging at her ears, one ear at a time. The crowd erupts into another round of laughter. Amidst the frivolity, Gunther looks over at the Chancellor to gauge his mood. He seems relaxed and visibly amused. The Chancellor watches her with intrigue.

When Anna Weiss begins to speak again, the laughter dies.

"I'm sure you can imagine how surprised I was, Herr Scholz, when I discovered that the original work on blood research was done by a husband-wife pair, Ludwig and Hanna Hirszfeld, during the Great War."

"What is your point, Fräulein…" Gunther scrunches up his brows as he struggles to recall her name.

"Weiss."

"What is your point, Fräulein Weiss?" he asks, unscrewing his bunched-up eyebrows.

"The Hirszfelds were Jews. They were sent to the Warschau Jewish Settlement during the Second War."

A hushed silence descends upon the room. Gunther immediately feels the intensity of the two hundred or so pairs of eyes staring at him, burning a hole into his soul.

He looks over at the Chancellor, who, in turn, is watching him intently. He then glances over at the faces in the crowd. He knows that how he responds next will be the defining moment of his career. He does not want to rush his answer, at the same time, he also does not want to appear unprepared.

"That is a very good question, Fräulein Weiss," Gunther says after clearing his throat. He speaks carefully, making sure to hold a calm and steady tone. "What we should remember is that today is a celebration of scientific and medical advancement made *in* the Reich. The infrastructure we have in place over the last hundred years has enabled us to make extraordinary leaps in scientific research and discovery. If we continue to make great strides in the same direction, we will no doubt be the leader in *all* areas, not just genetics research."

"So, what you are saying is that it doesn't matter if the discoveries were made by the Aryans or non-Aryans? Such as the Jews?"

Anna Weiss' question hangs in the air like the putrid stench of a corpse. Gunther wants to ignore it but knows that he must not. He clears his throat again to stall for time.

"Today's celebration is about scientific advancement, Fräulein Weiss," Gunther says patiently. "The spotlight is on the scientific achievements this nation has made. We are not so much celebrating racial contribution specifically as we are celebrating the progress achieved by the nation AS A WHOLE, generally."

Gunther takes another swig from his crystal glass. He desperately wants this question to be over with but Anna Weiss seems unrelenting. She remains standing, clutching the microphone tightly in her hand, showing no sign that she is satisfied.

"Help me understand this… what you are saying is that, by celebrating ALL discoveries made – including those NOT by Germanic people of Aryan origins – you are acknowledging that the other races are just as, if not MORE, superior than the Aryan race?"

The silence in the room is palpable. Gunther steals a glance at the

Chancellor. The man is clearly interested to hear what he has to say. Gunther has no choice. He inhales deeply and, with a forced smile, replies as politely as he can, "That is not what I meant."

"What do you mean then?"

Gunther doesn't answer immediately. He scans the room, looking at every face present. Every reporter in the room is waiting for his answer. What he says next will either make or break his career, he knows it. He wishes he has a press secretary on hand to advise him on the politically correct way to answer that question. Short of faking a heart attack, he can't think of any other way to get himself out of that bind.

"Are you a Jew-lover, Herr Scholz?" Anna Weiss is first to break the silence. Her microphone voice echoes in the room, her question prompting a few raised eyebrows amongst the press.

"What kind of question is that???" Gunther blasts, his face a contortion of rage. "OF COURSE I AM NOT!!!" He shoots up and slams his fist down onto the table.

"You seem quite defensive about it, Herr Scholz. Is it possible that you might have something to hide? A non-Aryan skeleton in the closet perhaps? Maybe even a Jewish ancestor?"

A chorus of gasps erupts. Gunther's eyes widen with horror. Amidst the shock responses, a chuckle or two can be heard.

"Fräulein Weiss, that is a very serious accusation. Do you have proof of what you're saying?" the Chancellor's voice booms through the microphone, cutting through the escalating murmurs from the floor.

"As a matter of fact, I do."

The entire room watches with baited breath as the young reporter reaches into her handbag and pulls out a folded piece of paper. A few camera shutters click as she unfolds the piece of paper, the rustling of which is amplified by the microphone in her hand.

Gunther can feel his heart pounding hard against his chest.

What does she know that I don't? He is desperate to find out, at the same time, equally terrified of what he might find.

"According to this hidden record from the Birth and Death Registry, your parents – Ludwig and Ava Scholz – only has one son, Pieter. Unfortunately, Pieter died during the Second War," Anna Weiss says, holding up the piece of paper for all to see. "I tried to trace your lineage to the Scholz family but I couldn't find any. In fact, there does not appear to be any record of your birth. So since we're on the subject, why don't you enlighten us on where you've come from? Who are you, really, Herr Scholz? If that is even your real name."

Gunther's jaw drops. He is stunned by Anna Weiss' accusation. Voices of people – all talking at the same time – erupt in the room. Camera shutters click furiously from all directions. Chairs move and topple over as people clamour over one another to take a closer look at the piece of evidence in Anna Weiss' hand.

"Order! Order!" The Chancellor's voice booms over the microphone but no one is paying attention.

Gunther looks around in stunned silence. For the first time in his life, his mind goes blank. Nothing in his imagination could have prepared him for what just happened so he merely stands there, looking shocked, unsure of what to do. In the flurry of activity, his sees that a slew of reporters is hurriedly making their way out of the room, presumably to break the news ahead of the competition. His common sense rushes back to him. He needs to set the record straight before news hit the public. But what can he say?

"Wait! Wait!" he calls. The panic in his voice is drowned out by the chaos in the room. A sharp pain stabs him in the chest. He clutches at his medals and falls over with a loud thud. In the vertigo, Gunther hears a shriek. He cries from the excruciating pain shooting through him when he lands on the ground. Then, his world turns pitch black.

3. JACK

"Jesus Jack, loosen your grip, will ya? I might be old but I'm not a cripple," Thomas grumbles, trying to yank his arm away as the two men cross the cobblestone street after a blue BMW hatchback rattles away on the uneven surface. The younger of the two men loosens his grip on the crook of the older man's elbow once they are safely on the other side.

"Relax, I'm just looking out for you," Jack says with an easy smile, his hand still guiding Thomas' elbow as they walk. "Besides, you're not *that* old. You just think you are."

They climb the stone steps one at a time towards a heavy wooden door. When Thomas pushes it open, the smell of age immediately rushes to greet them. Jack shows the guard at the entrance their tickets and they are waved in without much fanfare.

Inside, Thomas stands in the hallway, his eyes gazing up at the high ceiling and the orange downlights that shine meekly down on them, casting short, stumpy shadows against the floor. He looks around him at the unfamiliar museum interior. The place is a fusion of old and new, with old stones for walls and modern light fixtures illuminating the various installations.

As he stands staring at the images scrolling across the large TV screen mounted on the wall, Jack calls out to him, "Hey, check this out, there is a guided tour in ten minutes. How about we go for that?"

Jack jogs enthusiastically towards him with the pamphlet in hand but Thomas is only half listening. He stares at the black and white pictures taking turns appearing on the screen, unable to tear his eyes away.

"Why don't you go ahead and do that?" Thomas says absently after a moment. "I'll meet you back here in an hour."

Jack wanders off, leaving Thomas standing there, staring at the black and white images of rubble and broken bricks – remnants of buildings that once stood majestically before they became a pile of debris at the hands of the Nazis. He follows the simple map in the pamphlet and, without much difficulty, finds the spot in the museum where the guided tour starts.

As he approaches, he spots a young woman standing in a corner, leaning against the wall with her head down, flipping through a notepad as she mutters to herself. Jack studies her as he walks closer. She is dressed in a white blouse buttoned all the way up to the collar. A baggy cardigan hangs from her frame and a shapeless navy skirt extends from below the cardigan to just above her knees. Her legs are wrapped in white stockings and her feet is gloved by a pair of black flat pumps, functional without being ostentatious. She seems young, Jack notices. She can't be much older than twenty-one or twenty-two, he guesses. He walks over and spies the name etched on the badge pinned to her grey cardigan.

"An-ne-ly, did I say that right?" he says, startling the young woman. She straightens up and quickly composes herself, putting on the most genuine smile she can muster.

"And you are?" she replies.

"I'm Jack. I'm here for the guided tour," Jack says holding out his hand for a handshake. Annelie does not take it. Instead, she nods perfunctorily while exchanging the notepad in her hand for a handheld paddle from her sling bag.

"Wait here, please. The tour will start in… five minutes," she says, looking at her wristwatch. Annelie raises the paddle with the word "Tour" on it high in the air. Stumped, Jack withdraws his hand and stuffs it in his trouser pocket. They wait in awkward silence as visitors begin flocking towards them in droves. When a sufficiently large crowd has gathered around the sign, Annelie puts it away in her sling bag and beckons the group to come closer into the circle.

"Good morning, my name is Annelie Eckhert and I will be your guide today," she says in her loudest, most professional voice as she tries to catch everyone's eye. "We will be spending the next sixty minutes together on this tour and I will be telling you about the history of the Jewish people in Europe." She then switches over and repeats what she just said in German.

Jack watches her from amongst the group. There is something quite comical about the seriousness with which she takes her job. She wears a stern expression, occasionally traded in for an engineered smile at the appropriate moments. It's as though she is acting from a script or a user manual, Jack can't decide. He looks around at the other visitors, whose expressions are of focused concentration, hanging onto her every word.

Geez, this is only the introductions. We are not even on the tour yet!

Jack wonders if he is in the middle of an episode of Candid Camera. The whole experience is just too serious to be real. He chuckles at the thought.

"Excuse me, Sir?" A voice interrupts his train of thought. He looks around to find that all eyes are on him.

"Yes, you," the voice who is speaking to him comes from the guide herself. When their gaze meets, she glares at him imploringly.

"Who? Me?" Jack asks.

"Yes, you. Is there something you find particularly funny?" Annelie asks, like a stern school teacher about to reprimand a delinquent student. Jack looks around and sees the serious expressions staring back at him disapprovingly.

"No, no. It was just something I was thinking about… privately… on my own," he says, shrinking a little.

"If it's not something you are willing to share, please keep it to yourself. Everyone, let's begin!" She exchanges her stern expression for a bright smile, beckoning the group to follow her.

Annelie briskly leads the way down the hall, followed closely by the group of visitors. Their tramping footfall echoes down the hallway, like a poorly coordinated march. They enter the Hall of Origins, the first point on their guided tour, where Annelie begins the story.

Into her second week guiding at the museum, Annelie still suffers from performance anxiety. The script that Klaus Müller gave her was sixty pages long.

"One page for every minute of the tour," he said.

She quickly realised that the text is too wordy to be useful. It reads like a textbook rather than a play, which is what Guiding should be in her mind. At the end of her first day in the museum, she spent three hours combing through each paragraph, highlighting interesting facts with her fluorescent yellow highlighter before copying the sections she needs into a notepad. That notepad has since become a Guiding bible, which she consults religiously, a flimsy pad of paper held together by a spiral binding wire, so well thumbed that the corner of every page is dog-eared.

Two weeks into her new job, Annelie finds herself disliking her work more and more. She finds the chore of maintaining a constant sunny disposition extremely taxing. The small talks with the visitors, the smiling and the nodding when the visitors share their opinions, and the task of answering the same questions three times a day, six days of the week, mind-numbingly mundane.

Where is the toilet?

How do I get to the Old New Synagogue from here?

Where is the nearest tram stop?

For a change, Annelie would like to have an interesting conversation with someone that does not involve directions to the lavatory, the tram or the nearest café.

As she takes the group through the museum on this day, showing them the exhibits and supplying them with factoids, she could not help but notice the American man in the group. He looks around distractedly and can often be found smirking at an artefact or two, sometimes rather disrespectfully.

"Excuse me, Sir." She pauses the tour and speaks directly to Jack. All eyes turn to look at him. "Is there something in here that you find amusing?"

"No, not at all," Jack says, trying to keep a straight face. "I'm learning so much about the Jewish people. You are doing a terrific job. Keep going."

Not satisfied, Annelie continues, "Feel free to leave the tour if you have somewhere else you would much rather be."

"No, no, I'm really enjoying this," Jack says, nodding profusely with a smile. "Please continue."

Annelie looks at the other visitors in the group. They are all looking at her expectantly. A few steal quick glances at their watches but say nothing. She knows there is only ten minutes left on the tour. It's hardly worth the effort to turn this disruptive man away.

Just finish up already, she thinks to herself, inhaling deeply and feigning a bright smile while refraining from rolling her eyes skyward.

"Let's proceed to Festivals and Celebrations," she says, leading the way towards the final section of the tour. The group follows her, the drumming of their footsteps echoing in the high-ceiling room.

When they finally arrive at the end of the tour, Annelie finishes up by recommending a few other exhibitions in the museum and other attractions worth visiting.

"Thank you for coming on this tour today. If you have any questions, I'll be here for the next five minutes or so to answer them," she says. The group erupts into applause and then disperses, scattering off like ants heading in different directions.

As promised, Annelie lingers after most of the visitors have gone on their way. Experience tells her that there will be at least three or four visitors with questions or at least some anecdotes to share. On this day, an older couple rushes up to her, their words stumbling over one another in their eagerness to speak with her.

"That was wonderful! I've never heard the story about the Jewish people told in such a fascinating way! Truly remarkable! What a marvellous tour!" the lady in the couple says with shining eyes. She reaches out to take Annelie's hands, and – with the enthusiasm of a five-year-old being gifted a bag of candy – shakes them profusely. Annelie smiles and nods politely.

"Karl here fought in the war," the lady says, cocking her head towards the man. "We still remember the day the Führer arrived in Vienna. The crowd in Heldenplatz was absolutely *thrilled* to see him in the flesh! What a great man he was!"

Annelie continues to smile and nod, supplementing with the occasional raised eyebrows as her glance alternates between the lady and the man.

"What a brilliant idea it was to set this museum up. Did you know the Führer originally had plans to dedicate this museum to Jewish artefacts? I believe he was going to call it… what was it, Karl? Yes, the Central Jewish Museum," the lady says, stealing a quick glance at the older man.

"But this is even more remarkable, isn't it, Maria? All of the Reich's history in one place!" Karl marvels.

"We had no idea that Bohemia is so beautiful. It's our first time here. What a marvel this place is! Trust the Führer to select such an exquisite spot to showcase the magnificence of the Reich!"

Annelie continues to feign a smile, nodding and agreeing.

"You are doing such a great job here in the museum," Karl says, patting her on the shoulder. "Doing the nation proud. You should be so proud." His broad, genuine smile prompts a guilt within Annelie. She *should* feel proud. She *should* be grateful. Unlike her peers in the Labour Repatriation Program, hers is a vocation that *may* lead to better opportunities. Who knows, she might even get a good government job someday.

"I am." Annelie smiles again, this time, with genuine pride.

Karl and Maria take turns to shake her hands. They bid her farewell and turn to head towards the Adolf Hitler section of the museum. Annelie's glance follows them until they disappear into the room, then she looks at her watch to see if she has enough time to go on a coffee break before her next guided tour.

"That is THE biggest load of bullshit I have ever heard." A man's voice comes from behind.

"Excuse me?" She turns around, forcing a tight smile. The voice belongs to none other than that annoying American man in her group. The one who could not stop smirking. Annelie inhales deeply and tries hard not to roll her eyes.

"You said that Jews were conniving, dishonest people. Do you know that for a fact?" He walks up to her.

"Well, we have historical evidence that the Jews incited the Great War," Annelie supplies with all the politeness she can muster.

"What about the fact that they no longer exist?"

"That is factually correct." Annelie nods indignantly. "There is no citizen alive that is of Jewish ancestry in today's Europe."

"So… you are telling me the entire race died off just like that?"

"That is correct."

"And this… *typhus* that wiped them out conveniently killed off *only* the Jews?"

"Well, they do have weaker immune systems. Their genetic make-up is inferior compared to the Aryans. It's a fact," Annelie replies matter-of-factly.

"What if I told you they are not all gone?" Jack whispers

conspiratorially. Annelie raises her eyebrows. That notion has never occurred to her.

"You have proof of this?" She eyes Jack suspiciously.

The man nods with a knowing smile.

"Tell me everything you know."

4. THOMAS

Thomas makes his way slowly around the museum, looking at the exhibits on display. Under the high ceiling of a room lit by round orange downlights, he stares at the items on the other side of the glass. His reading glasses are perched on the bridge of his nose and, with careful attention, he reads the description on each plaque mounted below the exhibits.

He keeps moving until he arrives before a tall standing wall cabinet containing a shawl pinned to the wall. He presses his face against the glass to take a closer look at the weave. His eyes follow the blue and white threads down to the tassels on each end. Then, he reads the inscription on the plaque. It tells him it is a prayer shawl, one of the many from the collection point in the Old New Synagogue. The date of the collection was 1941.

When he is done reading, Thomas looks back up at the shawl. It had an owner once, of that he is certain. Someone whose familiar shoulders the shawl felt at home with. He might have even known the owner of this shawl, of that he is less certain. Nevertheless, he wants to touch it, to feel it between his fingers. But the thick sheet of glass stands between him and his longing. Reluctantly, he sighs and then moves on.

The next glass cabinet contains three items, numbered accordingly. Thomas leans across and begins reading the plague, straining his poor eyesight on the tiny inscriptions. It tells him that item number 1 is a Torah mantle, item number 2 the Talmud and item number 3, a Torah pointer. All three items had an owner once too, Thomas is sure of it. Whether or not they all belonged to the same person, of that he is less certain. He glosses over the Torah mantle and the Torah pointer but pays careful attention to the Talmud. As he bends over to inspect the foreign letters inked on the opened page of the thick volume on display, a faint memory from a distant past emerges from his memory bank.

He remembers the smell of time. Musty. Stale. The smell of centuries trapped within the confines of the stone walls. He remembers the dimness of the corridor and the burst of light through the oddly shaped windows high up where the wall and ceiling met. He remembers someone singing, the melancholic tune carried by a man's voice, echoing in the cavernous room. The voice lilts and sings words that he does not understand, as if telling a tale of a time long gone. It was beautiful. Mesmerising. Thomas remembers being moved by it even if he did not understand it.

As he straightens up from looking at the Talmud, his memories begin to take on a life of its own. It feels strange being there. Surreal even. Surrounded by things from the past, Thomas suddenly remembers snippets of the old life he had long forgotten. Now, as the picture in his head comes into focus, he remembers his earliest memory of this place. The place where the smell of centuries lingered.

The place where it all began.

It was late morning on a warm summer's day. They were playing hide and seek – Thomas and his friend, Ivan. As his friend clapped his hands over his own eyes and began to count, Thomas scurried down the cobblestone street, looking for a place to hide. Somewhere Ivan would not have thought to look.

He found himself wandering away from home, into the neighbourhood of Josefov, before chancing upon an old building where voices of people singing could be heard. Staring at the brick building from the street, Thomas thought it was curious. His curiosity led him through the heavy wooden front door, down the stone steps into a cool, dim, musty corridor. The place smelled of age – of hundreds of years of existence contained within the stone walls. The corridor was empty of any shadows, the only sounds to be heard were Thomas' tramping footfall as he traversed the short distance between the front door and the wooden door from behind which voices of people singing could be heard.

He stood outside the wooden threshold, an ear pressed to the door, listening – with his eyes closed – to the strange melody coming from the other side. He had never heard anything like it before. It was… magical.

"Aha! Found you!" A hand slapped him on the shoulders, jolting him from a spell.

"Shhhhh!" Thomas turned and hissed at his friend, bringing a forefinger to his lips. Then, beckoning for him to join in, he replaced his ear against the wooden door. Both boys stood there quietly, listening until the singing stopped. Then murmurs and sounds of people shuffling could be heard. When footsteps could be heard coming towards the door on the other side, they scampered off.

Thomas felt a rush when they both burst through the door into the sunlight out on the street. It was there that they split off – Ivan to the left and Thomas to the right. When he reached the corner of the street, when he turned around to see if his friend was behind him, people were spilling out of the stone building into the street.

In the swarm of bodies filing onto the sidewalk, a pair of eyes met his. The iris was a light brown. The gaze was unyielding. He stood there, staring. The pair of eyes stared back knowingly. As if realising he had been caught witnessing something forbidden, Thomas turned around and ran. The sunlight blinded him but he kept running, away from the stone building, away from the unyielding gaze and out of the neighbourhood of Josefov.

His lungs were burning for air by the time the familiar door of his apartment building came into view. His legs were aching but he kept running. He burst through the main entrance and did not stop until he was at the top of the fifth flight of stairs, his tramping footfall echoing as he circled up the staircase.

"Where have you been?" his mother asked when he bolted through the front door, desperately out of breath.

"Must be lurking around the Jewish town again." His father lifted his eyes from the small motor he was fiddling with over the sheets of old newspapers, his fingers stained with black grease.

"How many times have I told you never to go there?" His mother stood over him with a frown, lips tightened in a straight line, arms akimbo. "You might catch something."

"I… I'm sorry, Maminka," Thomas mumbled as he bent over to catch his breath, his hands on his knees. His face felt hot from all that running and his chest was heaving violently, desperately sucking in the air around him. In between gulps of breath, he added, "I… I won't do it… a-again."

"If I find you there again, you will be in a lot of trouble," his father piped up, lifting his eyes once again.

"Yes, Táta," Thomas replied obediently.

When both his parents had shifted their attention back to what they were doing before, Thomas went to his room, closed the door behind him and climbed onto the windowsill.

He twisted the handle on the windowpane and lifted it open. From there, he looked out at the sea of orange shingled rooftops and the many spires that graced the city skyline. A light breeze blew and caressed his face. His gaze flitted over the horizon, scanning the undulating sea of rooftops until he eventually spotted the old stone building nestled amongst the many buildings in a distance. He could barely see it and yet there it was.

Thomas stared at it, craning his neck, listening hard. Beyond the noises from the street, he waited to hear the enchanting voice sing again but none came. He closed his eyes to the sunlight. Underneath the red brightness of his eyelids, he saw the pair of haunting brown eyes staring back at him. It

made him smile.
    It was 1932.
    He was twelve years old.

5. GUNTHER

Gunther heaves a huge sigh of relief as he sinks onto the bed.
Finally, he is home.
What bliss it is to be lying in his own bed, in his own room, in his own house. He lays there, not uttering a word, savouring the sound of… nothing. No beeping machines, no clanging of metal rails, no squeaking of rubber soles on the shiny cement of the hospital floor all hours of the day. More importantly, Gunther relishes the prospect of not having to listen to the incessant chatter of the nurses who come in to change his bag of IV drip every so often throughout the day.

"How are you feeling today, Herr Scholz?"
I would feel a whole lot better if I didn't have to be here.
"How did you sleep last night, Herr Scholz?"
Well, let's see. Between the hourly IV drip check, the machine beeping and the old geezer right there, I managed to get about five seconds of shut eye. How do you think I slept?
"Why so glum, Herr Scholz? You should be happy you're still alive!"
I'll be happier when I get out of here.

Lying very still in his own bed, Gunther shuts his eyes and savours every morsel of the silence. He never knew he could enjoy silence as much as he does now. The quietness is so calming and soothing, he imagines that is what paradise must be like.

Gunther sinks deeper into the cushiony softness of his mattress, surrounded by duck feather pillows that yield to the curves of his limbs. He sighs another deep sigh. A sigh of contentment.

The past two weeks in the hospital had been utterly dreadful, Gunther recoils. For starters, the hospital room he was put in was a twin-share, which meant he had to *share* the room with another patient. To make matters worse, that old geezer snored like a choked exhaust pipe. By the third night of his stay, Gunther was wide awake in his narrow hospital bed, nerves frazzled from lack of sleep, staring at the ceiling, picturing his fingers clasped around the old geezer's throat. He could choke him to death and make it look like an accident. No one would suspect a thing.

More than anything else, Gunther is still fuming over being put in the bed closest to the door. All hours of the day, the room door was propped wide open by a doorstop. While the other geezer got the window view of the beautiful garden, he had to settle for a door-shaped view of the busy hospital corridor.

To while his idle hours away, he watched doctors in white lab coats looking at charts as they walked past, patients lying prostrate on hospital beds being wheeled somewhere, nurses walking by – almost always in pairs, orderlies in protective gear pushing metal carts holding bins marked with the biohazard waste symbol. He was most envious of the patients who were well enough to wander, parading up and down the corridor in their hospital gowns, holding onto the mobile IV rod like a fateful companion. Every slap of their slippers against the floor is like a dagger to his heart, reminding him of his mortality. And his advancing age.

Lotte refused to bring him the daily newspapers when she visited. Even his daughter, Eva, could not be persuaded to smuggle a magazine in when she dropped in from time to time.

The press must still be talking about me, he lamented.

The evenings were the longest, Gunther found. After his wife left when visiting hours were over, Gunther found himself staring at the white ceiling of his hospital room, with only the choked exhaust pipe snores of his sleeping neighbour and his own thoughts for company.

His room door was always wide open. Even when all the lights in the room had been switched off at night, there was always a luminous door-shaped box penetrating the darkness. The harsh, white light from the fluorescent tubes in the hospital corridor never faltered. Deep in the night, when most residents were fast asleep and the corridors were empty of shadows, the lights could be relied on to keep the hospital illuminated, a beacon in the black night.

It also meant that he could never get to sleep.

It was always cold in the hospital, Gunther discovered. It didn't help that the hospital gowns were thin and the blankets never quite warm enough. The cold air made being indoors feels like standing in a middle of a perpetual blizzard, with no respite from the cold. He tried wrapping himself up in the winter jacket Lotte had brought in but the nurses always made him take it off. They couldn't check his IV tube and take his blood pressure with all those layers bulking him up so he was always shivering. Never warm enough.

Lying in the comfort of his warm bed, Gunther feels his lids heavy with sleep. He is looking forward to a night of restful slumber – one free from choked exhaust pipe snores, blinding white fluorescent lights and the sterilised scent of antiseptic. The pillowy softness luxuriously coaxes him into slumber. He almost dozes off when the door opens and a shuffle of footsteps wakes him.

"Gunther…," Lotte grumbles when she spots his shoes still laced to his feet. She wanders over – a glass of water in one hand, his pillbox in the other – and hands him his medication. He sits up begrudgingly and accepts the water and pillbox without a word.

"Is it true?" she asks as she bends over to peel his shoes off, one at a time. Gunther pops a handful of pills into his mouth and guzzles half of the water. The water makes a gurgling sound as it travels down his throat.

"Is what true?" he feigns ignorance, hands the glass and the pill box back, fluffs a pillow and rests back on it.

"Don't play dumb with me. You know what I'm talking about."

Gunther thinks for a long time without saying anything.

Is it true?

That question has been haunting him since waking up in the hospital bed two weeks ago. Never mind that the doctor said he had had a heart attack, is what that reporter from Panzerbär said true?

Gunther doesn't know.

During the time he was confined to the hospital bed, Gunther had a lot of time to think about what happened that day.

Who was she?
How did she know?
Why did she bring it up?
More importantly, is it even true?

Gunther knew he had to find the answers to all his questions but he was bed bound and, to be honest, too tired to give a damn. While the scandal around this newly unearthed information played out beyond the hospital walls, Gunther lay meekly in bed, unable to muster the strength to contest his innocence. He was shocked to find that, for the first time in his life, he felt really weak. Physically weak. Unable-to-move kind of weak. His heart attack took a toll on him in a way he could never have imagined. Every ounce of strength seemed to have been sapped from his muscles. His limbs lay limply, his breathing laborious. Shrouded by a perpetual blanket of exhaustion, Gunther had never been more grateful for rest even though he was never one to sit still and do nothing.

None of his colleagues from the Ministry had visited him, he noted dismally. His assistant stopped by once with a fruit basket, hovering around the bed for all of ten minutes, humming and hawing as Gunther fired out instructions.

"I need you to call Joseph Fischer from the Birth and Death Registry to see if that reporter's document is authentic. And then I need her files pulled up. Anything you can find – her family history, school records, medical records – whatever you can get your hands on. I want to know everything about this Anna... what's her name?" Gunther snapped his fingers.

"Weiss."

"Yes, yes. Anna Weiss. I want to know who I'm dealing with. Find her weak spot. Her vulnerability. Any debts she has, speeding tickets, parking infringements, anything I can use for leverage. You understand, Dietrich?"

"Umm... Sir? It's against the Code of Conduct to carry out an investigation against a free citizen without Ministry approval," the young man replied timidly.

"You have my approval."

"Umm... Sir? You've been stood down from service...you no longer work for the Ministry. Hasn't anyone told you?"

The news came as a shock to Gunther. Staring at the ceiling, he was immediately silenced. His mind momentarily went blank before the long years of his military service flashed before his eyes. Overnight, the skyscraper of his career – the one he spent decades building, laying one brick on top of another – crumbled into a pile of rubble at the hands of that young reporter. Gunther could hardly believe it himself. Confined to the narrow hospital bed, unable to move, his already battered ego took another pummel.

Stood down from service?

He stared wide-eyed at the ceiling in disbelief.

No one had told him. Not even his wife.

Those few minutes, without a doubt, were the most awkward minutes of Dietrich's life, Gunther was sure of it. As the young man hovered uncertainly at the foot of his hospital bed, Gunther decided to relieve him of his misery.

"Just do what you can, ok?" Gunther said meekly without looking at him.

Dietrich left soon after and Gunther was left pondering the fate of his own career – or what was left of it.

"Did you know my father was a General in the Luftwaffe?" Gunther says now as he stares at his own ceiling.

"Of course I did," Lotte says quietly. Gunther turns to look at her. She stands uncomfortably a few feet away, eyes not meeting his gaze.

"He was a fine soldier. A *very* well-respected army officer," he continues to say, turning back to look at the ceiling once again. "And the coldest man I have ever known."

He remains quiet for a long time, remembering a distant childhood and an absent father. For reasons unclear to Gunther, his father was always very hard on him. Maybe he was just that little bit wild, that little bit more defiant, not at all like the well-behaved, obedient children of the other army officers. Of that, he was certain. He can still see it – that impatient look on his father's face, and something that resembled disdain in his eyes when he caught Gunther misbehaving in ways that no obedient children were wont to behave. In a desperate bid for his father's affection, Gunther eventually joined the Nazi Youth – to both his parents' relief.

"You must be tired. Get some rest," Lotte says eventually, interrupting his reverie.

Gunther doesn't turn when she leaves the room. Instead, he waits until the door is firmly shut before sitting up and reaching for the day's papers. With one hand, he puts on his reading glasses. With the other, he picks up the paper on top of the pile. On the top fold of the front page – in big bold print – a menacing headline lassos Gunther's brows together in a flash. He scans the article quickly, picking up phrases that calls for him to be denounced.

"Impostor"

"A tarnish to the nation's purity"

"The Führer must be rolling in his grave"

Gunther rolls his eyes skyward and tosses the newspaper aside. Running a hand through his tousled hair, he peels off his reading glasses in exasperation. He had hoped the entire saga would die down by the time he left the hospital but the public would not let up. Here is a scandal that is bigger than anything anyone has seen since the war. The press is not about to let him off the hook that easily, he knows that.

I'm ruined, Gunther thinks as he exhales loudly. *What am I to do?*

He cups a hand over his mouth and drags it down his chin, pulling his cheeks down as he ponders his fate. Then, with a sharp intake of breath, he reaches for his phone and dials for the operator.

"Panzerbär, please," he says, clearing his throat. "Anna Weiss."

When the line connects and a woman's voice greets him, Gunther pauses, suddenly unsure of what to say.

"Hello? Anyone there?" Anna Weiss' impatient voice fills the silence. Gunther inhales deeply and then announces his identity.

"Don't hang up," he begs. "I need to know what you know. I need to know the truth. Will you be willing to meet with me?"

There is a pause on the other end of the line. Gunther can hear voices of people talking in the background, none of them belongs to Anna Weiss.

"I've had a really rough couple of weeks," he adds, shaking his head at no one. "I just need to know what you know. I just need to know the truth."

The sigh on the other end of the line is audible. Still, no answer came. Gunther waits patiently, listening for cues.

"Where and when?" When she finally answers, Anna Weiss sounds weary.

"How about tomorrow? 10 am? My place?"

She agrees. Gunther gives her the address.

After he hangs up the phone, Gunther feels spent. He sighs loudly and sinks back onto his pile of duck feather pillows, relishing the cushiony softness submitting to the contours of his body. He relaxes further onto his bed and shuts his heavy eyelids, falling into a very deep sleep.

6. ANNELIE

Annelie looks at herself in the full-length mirror. Her critical eye spots the freckles on her cleavage. She tugs at her dress, trying to pull the plunging neckline to a respectable height but it snaps back to its original position as soon as she releases her grip. She draws in a deep breath and tries again. The neckline stubbornly snaps back into place, revealing the deep indentation between the pale mounts of her breasts.

She sighs loudly, silently wishing she had a different dress. The one she has on she borrowed from Pavlina. A velvet dress in dark burgundy, it hugs her body tightly, drawing too much attention to her feminine contour. The hemline sits high on her thighs, revealing the pale flesh of her long, bare legs.

"I look like a prostitute," she murmurs unhappily as she examines her reflection sideways in the mirror.

"Don't be ridiculous," Pavlina says, watching her from her vantage point on Annelie's bed. She lays on her belly, propped up by her elbows, her legs swinging in the air, alternating backwards and forwards like the pendulum in a grandfather clock. "You look nice. *Sexy.*"

Despite her friend's assurance, Annelie is doubtful.

"I should let my hair down, shouldn't I?" she says, her attention now on her ponytail. Without waiting for a reply, she reaches up and pulls off the rubber band holding her hair together. Her long blonde tresses fall around her neck and shoulders in a cascading wave. She runs her fingers through them and scrunches her hair up in various spots.

"Here, I got this from Zuzka, put it on. Men go crazy over women in red," Pavlina teases as she hands Annelie a tube of red lipstick.

"I'm just meeting him for… research. It's strictly for work," Annelie says as she takes the tube, twists it open and glides the lipstick on. She purses her lips and then presses them together, rubbing the petals of her lips together to smooth out the sticky, shiny coating. She is nervous about meeting Jack but she tries not to show it.

"Is he rich?" Pavlina says, ferreting through a jewellery box.

"He must be. He's from America," Annelie replies distractedly as she takes a final look at herself.

"That's your meal ticket right there, you lucky bitch!" Pavlina exclaims with a laugh. "You'll get to move to America! Imagine that!"

Annelie smiles a tight smile. Between the two of them, she knows she is the luckier one.

Annelie with the Midas touch, Pavlina's mother used to call her. *Everything she touches turns to gold.*

Her friendship with Pavlina hasn't always been an easy one, Annelie reflects as she watches her friend through the reflection in the mirror.

Pavlina the bright and quick-witted girl, by far the smartest, most clever person Annelie has ever known. Given the chance, Pavlina could easily beat all the students in Annelie's class in mathematics, physics and chemistry. She could have been an excellent engineer or doctor or whatever she set her sights on. Instead, the bright and quick-witted Pavlina spends her day sitting in front of a sewing machine in a factory, hunched over pieces of fabric, piecing them together, running them through the machine and then repeating it all over again with the next piece from the pile of freshly cut pattern.

Annelie, on the other hand, gets to finish high school and go to university. She gets to pick the subjects she is interested in and attend the lectures of her choice. Annelie gets to graduate with a degree and go on to do bigger and better things while Pavlina faces a lifetime of servitude in the factory – the only vocation available to her under the Labour Repatriation Program.

Between the two of them, Pavlina is the smarter one. Unfortunately for Pavlina, between the two of them, Annelie is the luckier one. Unlike Pavlina, Annelie has the right name on her papers. And that makes all the difference.

We make our own luck in this world, Annelie, her mother has always said, *If anyone should feel sorry for Pavlina, it's her own mother. It's her fault for not making their own luck.*

Annelie turns around and looks at her best friend.

Is it Pavlina's fault that she was born into the wrong lineage? Or is it her mother's fault for bringing her into this world, knowing fair well the fate that awaits her child? Annelie wonders.

"This ought to do it." Pavlina looks up with a wide grin, holding up a silver necklace with a pearl pendant. She climbs off the bed, goes over to Annelie and drapes the necklace around Annelie's neck. They both face the mirror while Pavlina adjusts the pearl pendant until it rests perfectly between Annelie's breasts.

"If this doesn't make him go nuts over you, then he must be either blind or gay."

The two friends laugh. Annelie looks at her friend and feels only love for her. She takes a final look at herself, adjusts her dress and slips into a pair of high heels Pavlina has managed to borrow from another girl in the factory.

"Papa, Mama, I'm off!" Annelie calls as the two girls scurry past the kitchen and out the front door.

"Call me tomorrow, I want to know everything!" Pavlina says when they hug each other goodbye once outside the apartment building.

"Try to keep your clothes on!" her friend calls out to her when she is half way down the street, teetering on her heels. Annelie blushes without intending to.

I'm just meeting him for research, Annelie tries to convince herself. As much as she hates to admit it, she has grown to like Jack. During the forty-five minutes they sat together having coffee in the museum's coffee shop, she discovered that he was actually quite… nice. As she walks towards the underground station, self-consciously tugging her dress, she can't help but feel nervous. A voice catcalls her from across the street but she pays no attention and keeps walking.

Before she left Jack at the coffee shop that afternoon to start her next tour, they had agreed to meet in front of the museum that evening. When she arrives, she sees that he is already standing there, looking smart in a dinner jacket, a small bouquet of flowers in his hands. He smiles when he sees her. Annelie can't help but smile back.

"For you," he says, handing her the bouquet and kisses her on the cheek. Annelie immediately feels hot around her cheeks and ears. Her heart pounds heavily against her chest but she tries to hide it by burying her nose into the bouquet. The flowers smell faintly of spring and feel awkward in her hands as they head towards the restaurant a short walk away.

"You look beautiful," Jack says. Annelie suddenly feels self-conscious once again. She tugs at her dress with her free hand and carefully balances on the high heels she is unaccustomed to wearing. Her eyes lack the courage to meet Jack's so she keeps them fixed on the cobblestones right in front of her, treading carefully so as not to trip over the cracks.

When they are seated across the small table from each other in the restaurant, Annelie wishes she had asked Pavlina for some advice.

What should she do? Should she say something clever? Or should she be flirting?

Speaking of flirting, how does one do it?

Sitting there, Annelie feels like a fish out of water. So inexperienced is she in the matters of men, that she finds herself staring at the glass of water to her right, not at all sure where to look.

"You're nervous," Jack speaks first.

Annelie doesn't reply.

"It's ok. I don't bite."

The smile in his voice makes her smile a little.

"See? That wasn't so hard, was it?" he says.

When she finally lifts her eyes to meet his, she sees that Jack is grinning. *God, he's handsome.*

After a stuttering start, the evening progresses smoothly. The wine arrives and she sips it slowly. Jack does most of the talking, regaling her with tales of his travels. Annelie's eyes shine as she listens about the places he has been to and the things he has seen. She has never travelled much, having lived most of her life in Bohemia. Apart from a few summer holidays spent at the Tatras, Annelie's travel stories can be counted with one hand.

"The air in Tibet is so thin that for the first day, I was gasping every time I take a step. I told my dad that when I get home, I'm hitting the gym. He laughed and then passed out!" He laughs. She studies him carefully, taking in his easy smile and his effortless confidence. He speaks with a matter-of-factness that can only come from an upbringing devoid of fear. Only someone who never has to look over their shoulders can carry themselves with such ease and confidence. How she envies him.

Their food arrives and Annelie teases him for having ordered the wrong thing from the menu. They laugh, eat, drink some more and talk into the late hours of the night.

When the last chair has been turned upside down on the nearest table, the Maître D' comes over and regretfully informs them the restaurant is closing for the night. Jack settles the bill and they both walk out of the restaurant, flushed with a rush of oxytocin.

"Let me walk you home," Jack offers in high spirits.

"I can't let you do that. It's miles from here and you'll have to walk back later," Annelie protests mildly.

"That's even better. I'll have more time with you. Besides, I need the exercise anyway," he says, reaching out to take her hand. Their fingers interlace comfortably like long lost lovers finding familiarity in each other's hands. Annelie smiles at how good it makes her feel.

As they walk down the street hand-in-hand, she feels as light as feather. Under the orange glow of the street lamp, she turns and studies Jack's handsome profile, feeling completely content.

By the time they arrive in front of her apartment building, the streets are quiet and empty of shadows.

"Tonight was a complete disaster," Jack says as they hover on the steps, catching Annelie by surprise. She thought the night had gone swimmingly well.

"I promised to tell you everything I know about the Jewish people but I barely told you anything. Will you forgive me?" Jack adds as he holds her gaze. The way he looks at her makes her face feels hot. She watches attentively as he brings her hand to his lips and plants a kiss on the inside of her wrist. It makes her skin tingle. Annelie smiles.

"I would like to make it up to you," he says in half a whisper, pulling her closer to him. Annelie is suddenly aware of his hands around her waist. She relaxes and leans into him, feeling his hands move to the small of her back. His warm breath brushes against her cheeks, sending her heart racing as she waits nervously for what is to come.

"How about dinner tomorrow night?" he whispers.

"Yes, that would be nice," she whispers back, her eyes lacking the courage to meet his. When she finally looks up at him, he gazes at her tenderly, and then leans forward and presses his lips on hers. Annelie closes her eyes and holds her breath, allowing herself to be kissed. His lips feel soft and moist, nibbling hers gently.

When their lips part, she opens her eyes and sees that he is smiling. She smiles too. Without another word, he leans in for another kiss. And then another. His arms tighten around her svelte figure while her hands caress the back of his neck, their lips constantly moving, never parting.

When they finally come up for air, they are both smiling. Somewhere from a window above them, someone wolf-whistles, breaking the spell. They laugh and untangle from each other.

"Same time tomorrow?" he whispers.

"Same time tomorrow," she whispers back. Reluctantly, she lets go of his hand and opens the front door.

"Goodnight, Jack," she says, glancing over her shoulder at him.

"Goodnight, Annelie," he says, standing on the pavement, his eyes never leaving her as she disappears behind the narrowing sliver of the doorway. With a fluttering heart, Annelie closes the door and skips up the flight of stairs with wings on her feet, humming in the echoing stairwell, all the way up to the third floor.

The apartment is drowned in darkness when she finally jostles the key into the lock. Gingerly, she opens it and closes the door behind her. With the grace of a practised ballerina, she removes her high heels and tiptoes on the creaking floorboards.

"Annelie," a voice calls out in the dark. A finger flicks a switch and a light bulb springs to life, instantly illuminating the entire living room.

"Mama." Annelie huffs. Standing in the doorway in her dressing gown, her mother frowns with arms akimbo. Annelie's shoulders drop. So do her feet.

"It's way past midnight," her mother says icily.

Annelie does not answer.

"Were you out with Pavlina?" her mother presses on as she walks past. "You went out dressed like *that*? You look like a whore."

Annelie stops in her tracks. She can feel her mother's gaze burning into her back. Slowly, she turns around.

"No, Mama, I did not go out with Pavlina. Even if I did, what's wrong with that?" she says, braver than she feels.

"You went out with a boy then?"

Annelie does not answer. Instead, she stares back at her mother. Neither of them flinch.

"Does he know?" her mother is the first to break the silence.

Despite her mother's stern bravado, Annelie can see a flash of terror in her eyes. She does not reply immediately. Instead, she holds her gaze, relishing in the deliciousness of taunting her mother, staring at the fear that dances between them in silence.

"No," she finally says. Her answer is met with an audible sigh of relief.

"Keep it that way," her mother says brusquely.

"May I go now?" Annelie asks through gritted teeth but does not wait for the answer.

"Not just yet," her mother says as she turns away. "Pavlina cannot come over here anymore. You have to stop fraternising with the likes of her if you want to have any prospects in life, you hear me?"

Annelie listens with her back to her mother but she does not say a word. Every cell in her tense body wants her to turn around, to scream at her, to tell her to fuck off and stop telling her what she can and cannot do. Instead, she stands very still, grinding her teeth, careful not to say anything she might regret.

"What are you still standing there for? Don't you have work tomorrow?"

Without even a backward glance, Annelie marches off in the direction of her room. In the small hours of the night, when all in the building are fast asleep in their beds, a door slams shut in Unit 3B, echoing up and down the empty street.

Thanks for ruining my night, Mama.

7. THOMAS

Thomas walks slowly along the winding cobblestone lane. Old buildings flanking either side of the narrow street tower over him. He surprises himself by remembering his way around the old city but his eyes betray his memories. Many of the shops he once knew are now gone. In their places are institutions he does not recognise – two trendy bars, a vinyl record shop, a place that resembles a crèche, a vegetarian café, a sign pointing towards a car park underneath what seems to be a discotheque for the underage. A part of him feels sad, the other part indifferent.

Daylight is gradually disappearing. Street lamps flicker and come on. As he passes by shop windows that line the street, he peers first into the shop and then up at the sign overhead. He is looking for something. He hopes he recognises it when he sees it.

Thomas keeps walking until he spots a small stone statue of the Madonna hanging over the arch of an ageing wooden door.

This is it, he thinks. He hovers on the footpath and looks around him, scanning the quiet laneway before opening the door and descending the stone steps into a basement. The stench of cigarette smoke rushes towards him, making him cough. The temperature plummets several degrees as he reaches the bottom, his footsteps echoing along the way.

The place is packed with people. A cacophony of voices having unintelligible conversations fills the basement bar. Through the hazy dimness lit only by orange halogen bulbs, Thomas spots an empty table in the far corner of the room. As he weaves through the ocean of warm bodies, catching whiffs of stale cologne, he overhears snippets of conversations. People are speaking words he has not heard in a long time – words of his mother tongue, a language he is convinced had disappeared when his homeland fell under German occupation all those years ago. A sour sensation rushes to his nose but he does not allow himself to get sentimental.

The table he finds is a small round wooden table with two mismatched wooden chairs. No sooner has he sat down, a waitress swoops in to take his order.

"Slivovice," he replies. She raises one eyebrow and studies him briefly.

"Not from around here?" she says.

"Been out of town for a while," Thomas replies, not looking at her.

"Figures," says the waitress. "No one's asked for a slivovice in a long time. Where have you come from?"

"Do you have it or not?" Thomas is getting impatient. He just wants his drink, not a Spanish Inquisition.

"I'll see what I can find," she says and disappears.

Thomas sits and scans the roomful of people. He is looking for someone. He hopes he recognises him when he sees him. More than anything else, he hopes the person he is looking for shows up.

A broad figure blocks his view. A block of silhouette towers over him while two filled shot glasses – one in each hand – appear at his eye level.

"Slivovice?" Thomas raises his eyes to the silhouette.

"Becherovka," comes a reply in a deep, gruff voice.

"You remembered," Thomas says, taking one of the shot glasses from his thick, calloused hands. The man sits down without being invited.

"You came," comes another reply in the deep, gruff voice.

The two men bring the rim of the shot glasses to their lips and tip them back with one swift flick of the wrist. Their Adam's Apples bob as the drink finds its way down their throats.

"I was expecting Jan," Thomas says after wiping his mouth with the back of his hand. He coughs and grimaces from the burning sensation at the back of his throat.

"Well, Jan's not around so here I am," deep, gruff voice replies calmly.

"What happened to him?"

"He died. Got killed by the Gestapo."

There is a long pause. The noise in the bar fills the empty space in which there are no words.

"Have you got the package?" Thomas is first to break the silence, his eyes never stop scanning the room the entire time.

Deep, gruff voice grunts, reaches into his front shirt pocket and pulls out a folded slip of paper.

"You can find it here," he says, sliding it across the table to Thomas.

Thomas takes the slip of paper and shoves it into his trouser pocket.

"Now give me a *real* slivovice," he says. "What was that you just gave me? It's disgusting."

"The kind of crap we've been drinking since after the war," snorts the deep, gruff voice.

"What does a man have to do to get the good stuff around here?"

"Come with me."

Deep, gruff voice rises and walks to a small side door, barely noticeable in the dim, smoky room. Thomas waits for a few moments before following discreetly. After the burly man has disappeared behind the door, he makes his way across the threshold. As he turns around to close the door behind him, his eyes chance upon a steely gaze. A distant memory flashes before his eyes. Time comes to a standstill and the noise in the bar dissipates into complete silence as a familiar fear shoots through his nervous system like a jolt of electricity.

No, it can't be.

Thomas shuts the door quickly but he knows it's too late.

"Is there another way out of this place?" he asks when they are in a dimly lit passageway. His hands are trembling but he tries not to show it.

"Yes. Why?"

"I have a feeling we are being watched."

8. ANNA

Anna Weiss taps her foot manically. The clacking of her right sole against the marble floor echoes in the high-ceilinged room. She looks around, at the opulence that is Gunther Scholz's parlour. A seven-tier crystal chandelier hangs from the ceiling in a cascading wave, like an upside-down wedding cake, reflecting scintillas of the morning sun against the walls and the polished wooden furniture.

A gleaming black grand piano sits in the corner of the room, next to it an imposing harp. Her gaze flits around the room, taking in the antique buffet, the regal high-back chairs (*Edwardian*, she notes), the pair of blue Ming Dynasty vases on each end of the mantelpiece and a large Japanese style painting hanging on the burgundy colour feature wall.

She rises from her seat on the ottoman and approaches the painting, studying the delicate yellowing paper with its faded watercolour of women with slanted eyes in kimonos.

"That painting was a gift from Emperor Hirohito," a man's voice makes her turn around. The butler who ushered her in earlier now stands at the doorway.

"Herr Scholz is ready for you in the sun room," he adds. "Please follow me."

Anna does not argue. She walks across the expansive room and tails the middle-aged man down a long corridor, passing by framed paintings punctuating the walls at precise intervals. She recognises one of them as a painting by the Dutch artist, Vincent Van Gogh. Starry Night Over the Rhone, she believes it's called. On the opposite side, a larger than life painting towers over her. She immediately recognises it as The Night Watch by the Dutch Master, Rembrandt. In stark contrast to the gaudy ostentatiousness of the parlour, the long corridor is beautiful and regal. Anna's earlier reservations over the Scholzs' tastes in design are quickly replaced by a quiet admiration for their good taste in fine art. She wants to stop and admire the collection – so obviously carefully curated, but the butler walks briskly ahead. Anna tries to keep up but only just.

"Anna Weiss," Herr Scholz sings cheerfully, rising to greet her with expanded arms when she enters a sun-drenched room with floor-to-ceiling white French doors. "Thank you for coming. Sit, sit." He takes her hand and pulls her in for a quick peck on each cheek as if they were old friends reuniting after a long time apart.

The warm reception confuses Anna but her attention quickly turns to the well-manicured English garden beyond the French doors. The neatly trimmed hedges, the vibrant blooms of the roses and the elegant water features spread majestically before her, stretching beneath the clear blue sky for as far as her eyes can see. The view of the garden is breathtaking, and for a moment, she forgets where she is and why she is there.

When her senses finally return to her, Anna tears her gaze away from the garden to meet Herr Scholz's, and – with a forced smile – sinks onto the chair gestured by his open palm.

"Tell Adele to bring us some coffee," he says brusquely to the butler, who nods and then disappears.

"You didn't have too much trouble finding the place?" Herr Scholz says with a faint smile.

I can't miss this huge monstrosity even if I tried, Anna thinks but does not say out loud.

"No, not at all. Your instructions were very clear," she replies politely, eyeing him suspiciously.

"What do you think about the paintings?" He cocks his head in the direction of the corridor. She spots a glint in his eyes.

"They are wonderful," she marvels genuinely.

"Did you know the Führer was a big fan of Fine Art?" he says dreamily.

"No, I did not."

"Well, he was. He was an aspiring painter. A very good one at that," Gunther speaks, gazing into the distance. "Luckily for us, he ventured into politics. Imagine where we would be if he hadn't!"

Herr Scholz laughs heartily. His laugh echoes within the high walls of the sun room but Anna doesn't respond. She studies him carefully, noting his good spirits in spite of all that has happened.

"The Führer collected many beautiful paintings during the war, some of which, he gifted to my father," he says with a glint of pride.

You mean he STOLE many beautiful paintings during the war.

Anna raises her eyebrows, keeping her thoughts entirely to herself as she looks around the sparsely furnished sun room. A faint ticking draws her attention to a clock on the mantelpiece. Gunther follows her gaze.

"I see you've spotted the mirror clock," Gunther says, pleased with himself. "It belonged to Empress Elisabeth of Austria. The clock has two faces, you see. The back face shows the time in the reflection of the mirror. It's quite clever, isn't it?"

"Yes, very," Anna replies politely, feigning interest.

At this moment, a lady with a white apron tied over her frock appears with a gleaming silver tray, followed by another bearing a three-tier cake stand. Gunther says nothing while the ladies set the trays down and begin to lay the table with all its contents – a teapot made from bone China, two matching tea cups and saucers, a delicate milk jug, a sugar bowl and silver teaspoons to match. On every tier of the cake stand, Anna can see morsels of pastries and cakes arranged neatly in concentric rings around the centre of the stand.

"What do you think about the China and the silverware?" Gunther asks, raising his eyebrows in the direction of the crockery.

"It's... nice," Anna replies uncertainly.

"It was a gift from the Hofburg Palace," Gunther explains. "The Austrians are very generous people. We have a fine ally in them."

"Is there anything else you need, Sir?" the lady with the white apron asks once the table is set.

"That will be all." He waves them away. Anna watches as the two ladies disappear as quickly and as silently as they appeared.

"Help yourself, don't be shy," Gunther says nonchalantly, reaching for an apple tart from the cake stand.

Anna returns her attention back to him. On her way there that morning, she had imagined a vision of a dishevelled man, unshaven, dressed in a wrinkly dressing gown, pale and weary after a debilitating heart attack. She thought she might even take pity on him, after what the media had done in recent weeks. To her surprise, the man before her eyes is cleanly shaven and immaculately dressed, smelling faintly of aftershave, generously helping himself to the sweets on the cake stand without a care in the world. If she did not know any better, she would have thought he had just returned from a vacation. That sight puzzles her.

"Excuse me, Herr Scholz," Anna says with a frown. "I was under the impression that you wanted to talk to me about your... *real* family?"

"Hmm, about that," Gunther mumbles with a mouthful of pastry. "There is another matter that is more pressing." He sets down the half-eaten apple tart onto his plate and dusts the crumbs off his fingers first, then the corners of his mouth, in no apparent hurry.

Anna's frown deepens as she waits.

Gunther swallows audibly before continuing, "It's about another piece of journalism I wanted your opinion on." He turns away, his outstretched arm reaching for something outside her field of vision.

Anna's gaze follows as he pulls something out from underneath the table, revealing a crisp brown manila folder. She watches as he takes out his reading glasses and sets it on the bridge of his nose. Then, carefully, he fishes out four sheets of printed paper from the folder.

"Tell me what you think about this title," he says, eyeing her from behind his reading glasses. Clearing his throat, he announces dramatically, "VANISHED! The Truth about the Missing Six Million Jews. By Anna Weiss."

Anna's eyes widen with horror.

"Where did you get that?" she asks in a panic. "It's an encrypted file stored on a secured server."

"Nothing is as secured as you believe it to be, Anna Weiss," Gunther says coldly, shoving the folder with the sheets of paper onto the table. "Now, I read your piece. You are quite the talented writer. It's too bad that you chose to write about this… *topic*. Does your editor know about this? I can't imagine a reputable paper like the Panzerbär allowing this FILTH on the front page."

"This is not FILTH. It's the truth," Anna protests. "The public needs to know THE TRUTH. They need to know about Project Cyclone B and what REALLY happened to the Jews!" Her raised voice echoes in the room, filling every inch of the space.

"DO YOU THINK THEY CARE???" Gunther shouts as he shoots to his feet. His voice booms in the cavernous room like a loud clap of thunder. "LOOK AROUND YOU! Look at what we have! Every German is gainfully employed. We have food. Shelter. Clothing. We have all the fuel we need to power the grids. We have an abundance of arable land to grow all the food we will ever need. No one. NO ONE. Has gone without ANYTHING after we won the war. Do you really think they care about what happened to the Jews?"

His outrage stunned Anna into silence.

"That doesn't make it right," she replies in a small voice, her eyes still trained on him.

"You are a naïve little girl, Anna Weiss," Gunther says, narrowing his eyes. "Nobody wins a war by doing the right thing. A war is won by doing what needs. To. Be. Done." He rests his palms on the edge of the table, glaring at her like a predator ready to pounce on his prey. Then, just as quickly, he straightens and snaps his fingers. To Anna's bewilderment, two uniformed men march in. The grey uniform and the double lightning bolt insignia on their collars give them away as the SS. For the first time since the fateful press conference, Anna is terrified.

"I'm afraid your idealism has gotten the better of you, Anna Weiss," Gunther says, sitting back down. He reaches for the half-eaten apple tart and puts it into his mouth. Without looking at her, he adds as he chews, "We can't allow rogue reporters such as yourself threaten our way of life."

"What are you saying?" Anna looks at the uniformed men on either side of her, panic rising in her voice. "You have no authority to do this."

"You know damn well what I'm saying. I can do whatever the hell I want," he spits. "Take her away." He flicks his fingers as if slapping a fly away from his face, and the two men grab Anna by the arms.

"No! You can't do this!" Anna shrieks as she struggles to break free. "I have done nothing wrong!"

"Yes, you have!" Gunther barks viciously. "You have malicious intent to leak classified information to the public. You are a threat to our nation's peace. THAT is treason! A crime that is punishable by DEATH. I don't know who your source is but I'm sure a few hours with these gentlemen will make you sing like a bird."

Impatiently, he waves the uniformed men away. Anna is dragged, kicking and screaming, towards the door.

"Fräulein Weiss," Gunther calls out after taking a sip of his coffee. The men halt. "How does it feel to have your career destroyed right before your eyes?" He narrows his eyes at her before saying to the men, "Exterminate her. And then wipe her files clean."

Anna's protests continue to echo down the corridor but Gunther is no longer paying any attention. Instead, he picks up his phone and hits the speed dial.

"Bring the car around," he says. "I have a plane to catch."

After he hangs up the phone, he takes another sip of coffee and pops a small square of cheesecake into his mouth. The salty sweetness melts on his tongue, bringing a satisfactory smile to his lips.

Revenge is indeed sweet.

9. THOMAS

The humidity in the morning sprouts tiny beads of sweat on Thomas' forehead. Walking the two blocks to the central train station, dark patches begin to form beneath his armpits and his back. When he arrives, the cool air in the train station is a welcomed relieve.

As he stands beneath the blast of the vents, feeling the gusts of cool wind blowing down on him, Thomas surveys the interior of the station. Aside from the glittery new shops peddling postcards and fridge magnets, not much has changed. The kiosk selling newspapers and magazines still stands on the same corner, lit by the same tired fluorescent tubes. The only thing different is the newspapers and magazines it carries on its stands. He walks past it, catches a glimpse of the headline on the day's Panzerbär but pays no attention to it. He has a train to catch and he doesn't want to miss it.

He stops in front of the large LED signboard hanging from the ceiling, announcing the arrivals and departures that morning. A woman's voice comes over the PA but he is barely listening. His glance flits down the board until he sees his destination on the screen. He looks at his watch and then at the board again to be sure. His train is leaving in seven minutes from platform 12. He needs to hurry or he will have to wait another hour for the next one.

Before advancing in the direction of the platform, Thomas looks around the station while discreetly patting the pocket of his shirt. He knows the slip of paper is still there but he checks just the same – just to be sure. His gaze darts around the cavernous space of the station, noticing people riding up and down the escalators, some in groups, others on their own. At the main entrance, he sees a young mother pushing a pram, exchanging a quick peck with a man in a suit before he hurries off. He sees backpackers with their rucksacks strapped to their back, necks craning, checking to make sure they are on the correct platform. His glance skips over a bunch of teenage boys in school blazers and shorts, play-shoving each other and then jogging briskly as they make to catch their trains. The station is a hive of human activity. People are coming and going in swarms, mostly in a hurry.

Out of habit, Thomas scans the station carefully, looking for something out of the ordinary. Something peculiar that doesn't quite belong there. In between stealing quick glances at his watch, he spots three men who seem out of place in that station. Two of them look young, probably in their late twenties or early thirties. The other is visibly older – around middle-aged. Dressed in civilian clothes, they seem ordinary enough but Thomas isn't fooled. He knows they are watching him even if they pretend not to be.

The two young men are amateurs, Thomas thinks to himself, watching them as they move chess pieces around on the board by a small table outside a grimy coffee shop.

Only old men with no jobs to go to play chess in the coffee shop at the train station in the daytime, he observes, raising his eyebrows. When he spots the Bishop and the Knight trading places in the wrong direction, Thomas' suspicion is confirmed.

He turns his attention now across to the other side of the station – to the middle-aged man. He looks sharp in his suit, cleanly shaven with his hair neatly slicked back – like a man out of a Brylcreem ad – concentrating on the folded newspaper in his hand. At first glance, he looks ordinary enough but as the minutes tick by on the giant clock over the wide entrance, he seems content to just stand and read – folded newspaper in one hand, briefcase in another – with no apparent hurry to be anywhere else.

Thomas is still watching him when he glances up. Their eyes meet across the busy train station. Time seems to slow down as the bustle around them comes to a standstill and the cacophony of noises fade into a faint muffle. The flicker in the man's eyes tells him he knows Thomas has seen him, the same way he had spotted him in the basement bar the night before.

The bustle resumes and Thomas is first to look away, pretending not to have seen the man. He casually makes his way towards the escalator under the sign that says Platform 12, glancing over his shoulder as he rides down towards the platform. The man in the suit also begins to move, marching towards the escalators, heading for the same platform as Thomas.

When he arrives at the bottom of the escalator, Thomas notices the two young men have left their post outside the coffee shop. At that moment, the train rattles in, slowing to a halt as it pulls up to the platform. The waiting passengers rush forward as the doors slide open and people begin to spill out from the carriages.

Thomas takes the opportunity to weave his way through to the far end of the busy platform, glancing over his shoulder every so often to see where the men are. Amidst the noisy station, a woman's voice comes over the PA system, announcing that his train is departing in one minute. He looks around, spots the men trapped by the gridlock of human traffic, and picks a carriage at random to get on. Once inside, he shuffles behind a line of passengers who are busy matching seat numbers to the numbers printed on their tickets, stealing quick glances out the window every so often.

As the crowd on the platform thins, he hears a cry.

"He's on the train!"

The voice belongs to one of the young men. They've spotted him.

Thomas hurries down the carriage. When he looks out the window again, he sees that the man in the suit now joins the two young men. The three congregate briefly before dispersing, each alighting a different door on the carriage. Thomas knows that once the train starts moving, he will not be able to lose them. They have him cornered like a rat in a trap.

Damn Krauts.

A whistle pierces through the cacophony of noises on the platform and the train begins to move slowly. Hurriedly, Thomas pushes his way back out of the aisle, forces open a door and makes a leap out of the moving train onto the platform. He lands in a roll and feels the brunt of the fall in every cell of his body. He is still seeing stars from the pain that shoots through his limbs when an angry voice rushes over to him.

"What are you doing??? Are you crazy???"

When his vision comes into focus, he sees first a pair of legs clad in navy blue trousers then the long face of a stern woman frowning down at him.

"I got on the wrong train," Thomas croaks as he tries to sit up, wincing with pain. By now, the train is pulling away from the platform at high speed, rattling noisily on the tracks, rapidly disappearing from view. He turns his attention to the sting on his arms and legs, spotting a tear in his trousers and red lacerations where the skin lay bare. One side of his arm is bleeding.

"Sir, next time you get on the wrong train, wait till you get to the next station. Get off there and take another train back," the woman with the long face scolds as he brushes the dirt off his clothes. Thomas apologises some more and allows himself to be helped onto his feet by the elbow. He refuses the woman's offer to call an ambulance, instead settling for a wad of gauze to clean his wounds with. Once satisfied, he limps his way towards the escalator, riding it back up.

As he limps off at the top, he scans his surroundings to make sure he is not being followed. He then exits the station and hops on the next available tram.

VANISHED

They must have men watching the flat as well, Thomas thinks as the door folds shut and the tram begins to roll noisily down the track. He scans the passengers in the tram warily before finding a seat and sinking gratefully into it. For the first time that morning, he exhales loudly – half out of relief, the other half out of exasperation. He needs a new plan. And a place to hide while he figures out what to do next.

Damn Krauts, he curses silently, his face crumpling from frustration as he thinks of the three men and his foiled plan.

The tram turns a corner and travels further down the street. Thomas gazes absently out the window, looking – but not looking at the same time – at the buildings that pass him by. After the tram makes two more turns, he decides to get off. Someone presses the buzzer, the tram screeches to a halt at the next stop where Thomas and a few others get off. He looks left and right before crossing the busy road. Then, absently, he begins to walk, guided only by his fading memory of the old city.

He walks for some time, passing by baroque buildings now shabby with age. He walks down quiet cobblestone streets, passing unfamiliar shop windows until he finds himself in a familiar place. At the spot where the old neighbourhood of Josefov begins, he sees a shiny new shopping complex where old apartment buildings once stood. The betrayal on his memory shocks him. Before he knows it, Thomas begins to cry.

10. THE PAST

1933

Her name was Sarah Barová. She was in the year below Thomas in school. Kind, bright, always with a ready smile, Thomas wondered why he had never noticed her before.

Thomas sometimes wondered too if it was fate that brought them together. After all, in all the years they had been in the same school, he had never seen her. They had never met on the playground nor walked past each other in the corridors. Neither knew of the other's existence even though, day after day, for many years, they had both walked the same streets, entered the same gate, and perhaps even had the same teacher – though not necessarily at the same time. Yet, of all the people who were spilling out onto the street after the prayer service in the synagogue that summer's day, she was the one Thomas saw. Her intelligent brown eyes captivated him. In her, Thomas saw something that made him feel altogether light and warm at the same time.

"Maminka says I shouldn't be hanging around you," Thomas said as they were walking home from school one day. His shoes chanced upon a pebble. Absently, he kicked it, sending it flying a few feet ahead.

Term was almost over. The summer holidays loomed ahead. As the school days numbered, Thomas began to fret. Once school was out, he would be hard pressed to come up with excuses to see Sarah.

"Why not?" Sarah asked lightly. By then, they had caught up to the stray pebble, and it was Sarah's turn to kick it.

"She thinks I might catch something."

Sarah stopped walking. Thomas followed suit. A look passed between them.

"Do you think you might catch something?" she asked, staring at him. Thomas shook his head.

"Then, that's settled then," she said brightly, resuming her steps.

They continued to take turns kicking the pebble until they arrived at the junction where Sarah would turn right and Thomas would turn left. They waved each other goodbye and went their separate ways home.

On the last day of school, when they were again walking side-by-side on their way home, Sarah had asked him, "I'm having a birthday party, would you come if I invited you?"

"I'll have to ask Maminka," Thomas said pensively even though, deep down, he was elated that she had thought to ask him. "But I would love to come."

His answer had delighted her. In her smile, Thomas caught himself smiling too. They were close to the junction now and he began to walk slower, stretching out the remaining minutes he had left with her before the summer holidays put an end to their daily walks.

"I'll ask Grandfather to send an invitation out in the post," Sarah said brightly as their steps came to a halt at the junction. "Have a wonderful summer!" She smiled happily, waved and turned to walk the remaining three blocks home. For a long time, Thomas merely stood there, watching her as she walked further and further away, her figure shrinking until she completely disappeared. Then, with a happy sigh, he turned and walked the rest of the way home with a spring in his step.

A few weeks later, on a humid day in July, the Marz family returned home from their family vacation at the Tatras to a pile of envelopes. By then, Thomas had forgotten all about Sarah's birthday party. When Maminka handed him an envelope from the small pile of letters in her hands, both she and Táta looked on curiously.

"Go on, open it," Táta nudged. Under both Maminka and Táta's watchful eye, Thomas gingerly peeled opened the envelope. In the inside was a card printed in beautiful cursive calligraphy on heavy, embossed paper. Thomas' eyes shone as he admired the elegance of the card. He slid it out carefully and read it quietly, all the while not meeting Maminka and Táta's gaze.

"Well?" Maminka asked impatiently when he didn't speak for a long time.

"It's an invitation to a birthday party!" Thomas replied brightly as he looked up from the card in his hands.

"Whose is it then?" Táta asked, cocking his head in the direction of the envelope. Thomas looked thoughtfully, first at Táta, then at Maminka.

"A girl from school, Sarah. Sarah Barová," he said. "Can I go, Maminka? Táta?"

"Let me look at that," Táta said, snatching the invitation from his hand. Thomas watched with baited breath as Táta's brows bunched together while he read the invitation.

"It's an invitation to a Bat Mitzvah," he said, looking imploringly at Thomas. His frown deepened. A darkness passed his face. "This Sarah Barová, who is she? She's a Jew? Why has she invited you?" Táta shot questions at him brusquely and Thomas' heart began to sink. He glanced from Táta's face to Maminka's and then back at him again. Both their lips tightened in straight lines.

"Sh... she's a girl I know from school," Thomas replied in a small voice.

Maminka and Táta exchanged tensed glances. Finally, Táta said tersely, "No."

Thomas began to protest but Táta wouldn't hear of it.

"I said NO! NO. MEANS. NO!" he shouted, his face scrunched up in anger. Thomas shrank. With a sinking heart, he watched as Táta huffed and scrunched the elegant invitation card into a ball and tossed it into the wastepaper basket in the kitchen.

"And stop fraternising with the Jews," his father warned, raising a forefinger in Thomas' face. "If I catch you anywhere in that Jewish town, I will beat you myself."

Thomas bit his lip angrily but said nothing.

That night, when only sounds of snores could be heard coming through the walls in the quiet apartment, Thomas cracked open a narrow sliver of his door and padded softly out of his room. He fumbled into the kitchen through the darkness, looking for the wastepaper basket. Having found it, he rummaged through it and fished out the crumpled invitation from underneath the balls of scrunched up brown wax paper previously used for wrapping meat. Then, stuffing the crumpled ball underneath his pyjamas, he padded softly back to his room, quietly shut the door and sat on his bed, smoothing out the crinkles in the paper one by one with the aid of the faint light from the street lamp outside his window.

When he was finally done, he sat back to admire the beautiful calligraphy and smiled in satisfaction. Already, he had a plan on how he would attend Sarah's birthday party. He already knew what he would give her as a birthday present.

On the day of the party, Thomas waited for Táta to leave the apartment for cigarettes before he snuck out. In his school bag, he had a clumsily wrapped present and his best clothes folded neatly over it.

"I'm going over to Ivan's, Maminka," Thomas said casually as he poked his head into the kitchen. His heart was thumping in his chest as he waited for her to answer. She grunted without a backward glance and waved a hand without turning to him. Hurriedly, Thomas shot out of the apartment, running down the flights of steps before anyone could stop him.

By the time he got to Ivan's, he was desperately out of breath. Once they were in Ivan's room, he quickly got changed into his best shirt and trousers, and borrowed a comb to make himself look presentable.

"Here, put some of this on," Ivan said, handing over a half-filled bottle made of heavy glass.

"What is it?" Thomas looked at him suspiciously.

"It'll make you smell nice," Ivan said, arms outstretched, waving the half-filled bottle in Thomas' face.

Thomas took it hesitantly, removed the stopper, sniffed it and instantly screwed up his nose.

"That smells like women's perfume!" he protested, scrunching his face in disgust.

"Don't be daft, Petr puts it on himself before he goes out to kiss girls," Ivan said, wandering over to him. "Here, you do it like this." He pulled out Thomas' hands, turned them over so his palms were facing skyward and carefully tipped some of the liquid out. Too much came out at once and splashed onto his shoes. Thomas scowled.

"Don't be such a sissy, it's not that bad," Ivan said, putting the stopper back into the bottle. "Now, slap it on your face, like that." He slapped his own hands to his cheeks and neck as demonstration, and Thomas followed suit, mimicking him uncertainly.

"There, you smell much better already," Ivan gloated proudly as he leaned in for a sniff.

"I hate it," Thomas said with a scowl as he sniffed his own hands. "I want to get it off."

"Stop fussing, you're going to be late!" pestered Ivan.

Hurriedly, Thomas grabbed the clumsily wrapped present and made for Sarah's address. The thought of seeing her again made him smile. His feet moved quicker when he spotted her building not far away. Suddenly, he felt nervous and unsure of himself.

As he stood outside the apartment building, Thomas stared at his own reflection in the shop window downstairs, inspecting himself with a critical eye. He smoothed his hair and straightened his shirt. Then, with a sharp intake of breath, he pressed the doorbell and waited.

As he waited, his heart pounded furiously in his chest. When the front door of the apartment building opened and he was let in, Thomas felt his knees wobble. His palms began to sweat – a fact that embarrassed him no end. As he stood uncertainly in the entrance hall, looking up at the stairway, a cacophony of people's voices echoed from above. The click-clacking of a pair of lady's heels could be heard from one of the floors. Then, a head poked out over the banister.

"You must be Sarah's friend," the lady called out to Thomas. "Come up!" Her head disappeared and the click-clacking faded away.

Thomas climbed the steps uncertainly, his stomach in knots. When he arrived at the landing where a front door gaped open and voices of people talking and laughing could be heard coming from the inside, he inhaled deeply before making his entrance. As he stood in the doorway, the present in his hands, he stared uncertainly into the roomful of strangers.

"Sarah, your friend's here!" Somewhere in the apartment, a voice could be heard calling out. Thomas stood perfectly still, looking around at the grown-ups who were talking to each other.

Then, as he turned, his eyes met Sarah's. She smiled. His heart skipped a beat, then he smiled back. She floated towards him – a vision in a long cream colour dress, cinched at the waist with a pink satin ribbon, her short sleeves made from lace. Her dark hair was swept back in a neat bun. In her face, Thomas sees a radiance he had never seen before. If it was even possible, she looked lovelier than ever.

"I brought you a present," Thomas said when he finally gathered himself. The clumsily wrapped package exchanged hands.

"What is it?" she said, eyes shining.

"It's a book," Thomas said. "It's called The Good Soldier Švejk. Have you heard of it?"

She shook her head, looking at the package in her hands.

"You'll like it. We can read it together if you like."

He can see that her cheeks quickly turned a tinge of pink. It made his heart soar. They stood staring at each other, smiling, until a tall figure appeared by Sarah's side. Thomas looked up to find a pair of smiling eyes and long, scraggly grey beard bearing down on him.

"You must be Tomáš," the man said, holding out his hand. "I'm Grandfather."

Thomas took his hand and shook it politely.

"I've heard a lot about you," Grandfather added with a wink.

Thomas couldn't help but smile wider. When his eyes fell back on Sarah again, her cheeks were a deep shade of crimson.

"Come, Tomáš, you're just in time for the exciting bit – FOOD!" Grandfather said, placing a gentle hand around his shoulder, bringing him in.

The front door shut behind him, chairs were moved and feet shuffled. Soon, they were all seated around the dining table and a hushed silence fell. Thomas eyed the platters of food that were laid out in the centre of the table as Grandfather addressed the guests, thanking them for coming, especially those who had made the trip from abroad.

Then, the lady who had called out to Thomas in the stairwell earlier spoke briefly, her eyes misting when she mentioned that Sarah's father would have been really proud of her if he was still alive. There was a brief silence in which eyes were lowered around the table. Then, as if on cue, a little voice piped up and said, "Can we eat now?" The solemn silence was instantly broken. A peal of laughter erupted and the mood in the room lifted instantly.

Grandfather went on to recite something over a cup. Hands were washed. Thomas mimicked uncertainly, encouraged by Sarah's nod. More recitation followed before Grandfather removed a cloth covering two loaves of braided bread. The guests fell in complete silence as the bread was sliced, salted and handed around the table.

As the entire ritual unfolded, Thomas watched in raptured fascination. He accepted his portion of the bread and ate it quietly, savouring the salty taste that danced on his tongue. Then, as if awoken from a spell, people began to talk as they helped themselves to the food laid out on the table. The atmosphere was once again festive.

Surrounded by unfamiliar faces, Thomas was grateful to be seated next to Sarah. He looked around the table, counting the eleven guests seated there – six grown-ups and five children – including himself.

"Where are your other friends?" Thomas asked when it became evident that they weren't expecting any more guests.

"I only invited you," she said, passing a bowl of ladled soup in his direction. "Everyone else is family." Thomas' heart skipped as he accepted the bowl. She was smiling. He couldn't help but smile back.

As the grown-ups talked amongst themselves, Sarah began pointing out each of them to Thomas.

"That's Aunt Anja and Uncle Ludvik. Uncle Ludvik is my father's younger brother. He moved to Berlin when I was very little. That's where he met Aunt Anja. And that little boy in the blue shirt is their son – Lukas. That little girl is their daughter – Lucie. They only arrived two days ago," she whispered. Thomas nodded thoughtfully as he stuffed a spoonful of soup into his mouth.

"And that's Mrs. Spegielová and her husband. They are good friends of Mother's. Mother and Mrs. Spegielová went to school together. They've been friends for thirty years! Imagine that!"

They both paused and sipped a spoonful of soup.

"Do you think we will be friends for thirty years?" Thomas asked, after they have both swallowed their soup. He studied her profile intently, taking in the shape of her nose and chin.

"I think we will be friends for much longer than that," Sarah said buoyantly. Her answer made him smile.

"And that little boy over there," Sarah continued, pointing to a small face sitting next to Grandfather. Thomas immediately identified him as the little voice who piped up earlier. "That's my brother, Amos."

They both paused and sipped another spoonful of soup. By now, the grown-ups were engrossed in a heated conversation around the table. Both Thomas and Sarah stopped eating and began to listen attentively.

"He's a mad man!" Uncle Ludvik said, glancing first at Grandfather and then at the others. "Goebbels incited a massive book burning in

Opernplatz. They were burning mountains of books – all by Jewish authors. It was pure madness!" His voice rose as he waved his hands animatedly.

"Rumour has it that Hitler intends to strip influential Jews of their passports and citizenship," Aunt Anja added gravely. "We think Ernst Toller could be one of them."

There was a collective sigh amongst the grown-ups around the table before someone else spoke. This time, it was Mr. Spegiel.

"Who is this Hitler person?" he asked, looking first at Uncle Ludvik then at Grandfather.

His question hung in the air, innocent yet probing. A look passed between Grandfather and Uncle Ludvik. Then both men looked around the table, suddenly aware that the children were all listening. Finally, it was Grandfather who spoke.

"He's a man who loves his country very much," he said quietly. Then breaking into a smile, he added, "But he's not our concern today. Today is Sarah's day so let's eat up and celebrate!" To that, every person around the table cheered. The gaiety returned and they all ate lunch in a festive mood.

Later that afternoon, when it was time for Thomas to leave, Grandfather placed a gentle hand on his shoulder once again and said, "We want to see more of you, Tomáš. Come by for a visit anytime." He clapped him gently on the back. Thomas responded with a grateful smile.

"Yes, Sir," he said, beaming.

After saying goodbye to everyone, Sarah saw Thomas all the way down the three flights of steps to the front door of the apartment building.

"I forgot to say," Thomas said, suddenly shy as he hovered over the threshold. "You look really pretty today." She lowered her eyes, smiling. When she lifted her eyes again, Thomas could see that her cheeks were, once again, a deep shade of crimson.

"Thank you for the present. It was really thoughtful," she said. Then, leaning in, she planted a soft kiss on his cheek. "I'll see you in school then?"

"Yes… yes," Thomas mumbled, feeling his face turning hot. They smiled uncertainly at each other before she turned around and made her way back up the staircase. His eyes followed her as she ascended, her long dress making a swishing sound as each step echoed in the stairwell.

When finally, she waved and disappeared from view, Thomas sighed happily. After a door could be heard creaking shut from one of the floors above, Thomas turned and stepped out of the building. He couldn't remember walking back to Ivan's place or that he changed back to his day clothes and somehow found his way home. All he could think of was that kiss on his cheek.

And her smile.

And the fact that she said, *I think we will be friends for much longer than that.*

11. ANNELIE

"Where were you last night?" Klaus Müller asks within the morning silence.

Sitting in his office, her hands in her lap, Annelie notices a strand of loose thread straying from the hem of her skirt. She instinctively reaches over and tugs at it with focused concentration. As the thread snaps and comes away between her fingers, she flicks it satisfactorily away before looking up at him.

"I was home," she replies carefully as she smooths out the crease in her lap.

They both stare at each other in silence – Klaus in his chair, Annelie in hers – the two separated by a desk in between. Yet, the chasm could not be wider. Beyond the wooden door, the hallway is quiet. The day is young. The main doors of the museum won't open for another half an hour, after which, a steady stream of visitors will arrive and Annelie will be dutifully called to her post, Tour sign in hand, while Klaus busies himself with… whatever it is Museum Directors do.

As the clock continues to tick, Klaus Müller rises from behind his desk and walks around to where Annelie is sitting. Her gaze follows him until he is planted on a corner of his desk, facing her. His long build looms over her, one leg dangling at an angle. His polished shoe catches a ray of the morning sunlight, the beam of dancing dust casting a strip of orange against the jet-black of his shoe.

"Annelie," Klaus Müller says very quietly, his arms folded across his chest. He draws in a deep breath before continuing, "I'm not the enemy here. You know that, right?"

Annelie's brow crinkles briefly then she nods, feigning a smile.

"You and I, we are on the same team," he says.

Are we? Really?

"If you are in any kind of trouble at all, you know you can always come to me," he adds, unfolding his arms, placing them sidelong on the edge of the desk.

There is a brief pause in which nothing can be heard save the rhythmic ticking of the clock.

"Are you in trouble?" he says when an answer is not forthcoming. He raises his eyebrows, looking at her expectantly.

Annelie frowns in confusion before shaking her head slowly.

"I received a visit earlier," he says. "From the Gestapo."

It is Annelie's turn to raise her eyebrows. Her heart begins to beat hard against her chest. If she is alarmed, she tries not to show it.

Today could be the day I get found out. She swallowed hard.

"To what do we owe the... *pleasure*... of his visit?" Annelie says, feigning brightness.

"He came to personally keep me updated on a... *situation* we had yesterday."

"What kind of... *situation* are we talking about here, Sir?"

He pauses momentarily, studying her with narrowed eyes. When he finally speaks, it is with firm conviction.

"A Code Yellow."

Annelie looks down at her lap without replying immediately. She knows what a Code Yellow is. Page 9 in her museum employee handbook clearly spells out the criticality level of each colour on the spectrum. Code Yellow is a high-risk threat. What that risk is, Annelie waits to find out.

"There is a man on the prowl," Klaus Müller says as he straightens himself. The desk creaks from being relieved of his weight. As he walks back to his position behind the desk, his shoes clap gently against the floor. Annelie's gaze follows him as he reaches for a brown envelope and pulls out a grainy picture. He looks first at the picture in his hand before looking over at her.

"He was spotted in the area yesterday morning. This picture is from the CCTV at the entrance."

When he flips the picture over to show her, Annelie leans in and squints for a better look. She sees two men on the front steps – the younger man in front, the older man behind him. They are mid-step, and the younger man has something in his hands – tickets to the museum presumably. Klaus Müller watches her carefully as she takes in the details of the picture. The flicker in her eyes does not escape him.

"Have you seen him?" he asks, pointing to the older man behind Jack.

"No, Sir. I have not," Annelie replies firmly as she shakes her head, leaning back against her chair. "Why is he a Code Yellow, Sir?"

A sharp intake of breath punctuates their conversation.

"This man is very dangerous," Klaus Müller says. "He is a known terrorist. A very cunning man. The Gestapo believes he's been... *in hiding* for the last few decades. For some reason, he has decided to resurface now."

"What is his crime?" Annelie asks.

"He is with the Resistance," Klaus Müller explains. "He tried to sabotage our war efforts on several occasions."

"Sir," Annelie says. "So much time has passed, surely he must be a changed man? Look at him." She points to the older man in the grainy picture. "You can see for yourself, age has caught up with him. How dangerous can he be?"

Her question hangs in the air, supplanted by another sharp intake of breath.

"Never underestimate a terrorist, Annelie. You know what the English would say about this man?"

"No, Sir."

"They would say a leopard cannot change its spots," Klaus Müller replies.

Annelie looks at her superior. His gaze is firmly trained on her, stern and unyielding.

"And a tiger cannot change its stripes," she adds, unflinching.

"Ah, that I have not heard before," the corners of Klaus Müller's mouth curve into a smile. "See, you *are* a clever girl. We can do so much with you. In the meantime, for the safety of our employees, I have cancelled all guided tours until further notice. You have been transferred to the Archive Department as of today. Helga will show you what to do." Klaus Müller lifts his trousers and sits down. Without looking at Annelie, he reaches for the pile of paper on his desk and begins to flip through it, signalling the end of their conversation.

Annelie rises to leave.

"Oh, and one more thing," he says without looking up. She pauses on the threshold of his office door. "I wouldn't stay out too late if I were you. The young man in the picture is his accomplice."

Annelie flinches, this time a little too obviously.

"Thanks for the caution, Sir," she says, steadying her quivering voice.

"You will tell me if you see either of them, won't you, Annelie?"

"Of course, Sir," Annelie replies. "Is that all?"

"That is all."

Annelie marches out of Klaus Müller's office and shuts the door behind her.

*

"You can sit over there." Helga points to an empty wooden desk in a bank of four. "Marcus will show you what to do."

She leaves Annelie standing in the cramped doorway and disappears back into the hallway, the click-clacking of her shoes receding rapidly until it becomes confused with the other noises of a museum about to open its doors for the day.

Annelie surveys the room despondently. The room is windowless, lit only by the harsh light from two fluorescent tubes. Everywhere she looks, boxes stack upon boxes, making the already small room even smaller. Her gaze falls on a bespectacled man sitting behind a desk, his brows furrowed in deep concentration as he scribbles furiously away on a pad of paper. He looks up from a pile of yellowing sheets of folded paper strewn over his desk, sees Annelie and then resumes what he was doing, completely uninterested.

Dismayed at the lacklustre reception, Annelie inhales deeply. Behind her, the cacophony of voices coming from the front entrance wafts down the hallway into the room.

"Shut that door, will you?" says the bespectacled man without looking up. Annelie does as she is told. Then, without another word, she walks past him and goes to sit down behind her desk.

"Here." A silhouette casts a shadow over her. A heavy book drops onto her desk with a loud thud, startling her a little. She looks up to find the bespectacled man looming over her, a hint of boredom in his eyes.

"That's the policy and process manual," he says. "Read that. That will keep you busy for the rest of today." In no time at all, he is behind his desk, once again scribbling furiously away on the pad of paper.

Meekly, Annelie takes the book and flips to the first page. She tries to read the first row but none of the words register in her mind. The only image that burns in her retina is that grainy picture. The one where Jack is seen holding two tickets, with the older man closely behind him.

Jack – an accomplice to a terrorist? That notion shocks her to her core. She sits very still, hunched over the big book of policy and processes, pretending to be deeply engrossed except that she is anything but. For the first time since leaving Klaus Müller's office, Annelie begins to grapple with what she has just heard. After the initial shock has worn off, disbelief hits her. Then anger.

Her mind draws a blank as she struggles with the currents of her feelings. Then, as she begins to reflect on the night before, dissecting every moment of her time with Jack, what she feels is a deep sense of betrayal.

Can someone fake all that? she wonders, suddenly wounded.

When she arrives at the memory of their kiss in front of her apartment building at the end of the night, her face contorts into a grimace.

What a fool I've been! she thinks ruefully, biting her lip, her eyes quickly filling up with hot tears. She wants to pound the desk with both fists, to punch something – *anything*, and to throw something at the wall. But she doesn't. Instead, she froze in her hunch, silently staring at the words that crawl like tiny black ants through a curtain of blur, wishing for time to speed by so that she can run home to cry into her pillow.

When she can no longer contain her tears, Annelie watches as drops fall onto the page in tiny splashes. Discreetly, she reaches to wipe the corners of her eyes with the crook of her fingers, stifling a whimper. The nib of Marcus' pen continues to scratch furiously against the pad of paper. Beyond the closed door, muffles of people's voices reverberate down the hallway, tramping footfalls advance and then recede. All around her, life is unfolding with each passing second and yet, deep inside her, time has come to a standstill.

"*An-ne-ly, did I say that right? I'm Jack. I'm here for the guided tour.*"
"*That is THE biggest load of bullshit I have ever heard.*"
"*You are telling me the entire race died off just like that?*"
"*What if I told you they are not all gone?*"
"*Same time tomorrow?*"
"*Same time tomorrow.*"

*

Daylight is fast receding, casting a film of grey over every object in the living room. But Annelie does not move to turn on the lights. Instead, she sits alone on the couch, staring sourly into space, her arms tightly folded over her chest as she taps her foot pensively. Her parents have gone to the movies. In their absence, the silence keeps Annelie company as she waits for Jack.

All day, she has been thinking about him. About what she would do. What she would say. She plays through the scenario in her mind of the moment she sees Jack again – the buzzer rings, she opens the door, he is standing there, all smiles. She slaps him before he has a chance to say anything and then slams the door in his face. When he begs her to open the door, she will give him "the speech".

She had spent the afternoon carefully selecting the words she would say to him. She had rehearsed those words over and over so that when the moment arrives, they will not desert her. She will not falter. When the moment arrives, she will give that son of a bitch a piece of her mind. He wouldn't know what hit him.

I hate him. Annelie huffs angrily as she uncrosses her legs, recrosses them the other way and continues to tap pensively against the floor. Her face is scrunched up so tightly she can feel the crease of her brows begin to hurt.

Two minutes before seven, the buzzer rings. Annelie leaps to her feet. Her courage deserts her before she manages to get to the intercom. As she stands over the little black box on the wall, she contemplates not answering. On the other side of the intercom, three floors below, beyond the green front door is Jack – the man she desperately wanted to see. The same one she now desperately wants to avoid.

Maybe if I don't answer, he will go away, she thinks as she hovers over the intercom. As if reading her mind, the buzzer rings again. It keeps ringing until the desperation to make it stop forces her to answer. Drawing in a deep breath, Annelie presses the button. It crackles to life and Jack's voice bursts into the apartment.

"Hi, it's Jack."

He sounds bright. Happy. Even without seeing him, she can already see his smile. That image softens her but only for a moment. She quickly remembers her mission and regains her iciness.

"Third floor. Apartment on the right," she says stonily into the intercom. The door on the other side clicks open and then shut. Now, she waits.

A wall away, the light thuds of Jack's footsteps circle up the three flights of steps until, finally, they stop just outside the front door. A knock comes over but Annelie does not answer immediately. Instead, she leans against the wall next to the front door and shuts her eyes, searching for the courage that is no longer there.

"Annelie?" Jack's voice comes through the door. She does not answer.

"Annelie, you there?" Another set of knocks comes over the door. Again, she does not answer.

"Annelie, open up. I know you're in there."

The knocks are unrelenting. As with the ringing of the buzzer, Annelie desperately wants it to stop. When she finally caves and opens the door, she is greeted first by a bouquet of red roses, then that charming, easy smile.

"What's the matter?" Jack frowns the moment he sees Annelie's long face. She pulls him into the apartment, looks into the stairwell and then shuts the door.

"What's going on, Annelie?"

"Why don't YOU tell me what's going on?" Annelie snaps, poking a forefinger at his chest.

"What are you talking about?" He stares at her in confusion.

"Who are you, really?" She narrows her eyes. "Do you have weapons on you? A gun perhaps?" She reaches out to pat his shirt and trouser pockets, to which, he responds by tossing the flowers aside and grabbing hold of her arms.

"What is this about, Annelie?" he says, more seriously now.

She tries to wrest her arm free. "Let me go!" she protests.

"Annelie, why are you behaving like this?" Jack retorts in exasperation, releasing his grip. She breaks free, backing away instantly, a pained look on her face.

"What do you mean why am I behaving like this???" she snaps. "YOU LIED TO ME!!!"

"When did I lie to you? What did I lie about?"

"Yesterday. Last night. Everything. ONE BIG. FAT. LIE! ALL OF IT! The tour, the date, the kiss. ALL LIES!"

"Annelie, stop it!"

Jack tries to come near her but she backs away further.

"Stay away from me!" she yells.

"Annelie, look at yourself! You are being ridiculous!"

"ME? RIDICULOUS??? HOW DARE YOU??? YOU LIAR!!!"

A loud slap crackles through the air. A wave of shock stuns them both into silence. Annelie stares at her own hand in disbelief. It quivers in mid-air, a tingly sensation lingering in the wake of the slap. She stares at Jack, at the pained look on his face, and regrets it instantly. Neither of them speaks as Jack draws in a deep breath, slowly reaching up to nurse his throbbing cheek. The pain burns through his flesh but he does not respond. He merely stands there, looking at her, confused and unsure. In the stunned silence, the only sounds to be heard are their shallow breathing and the rhythmic ticking of the grandfather clock.

Then it happens quickly – he steps forward and gathers her into his arms. She struggles at first, trying to break free but she relents eventually, burying her face in his chest.

"Breathe, Annelie. Just breathe," he whispers into her hair as his hand strokes her comfortingly on the back. The tenderness softens her and she begins to cry.

"Tell me what's wrong," he says quietly, gently squeezing her heaving shoulders. She straightens to look at him, her cheeks slippery with tears.

"I had the worst day," she whimpers. "Klaus Müller called me into his office this morning and showed me a picture of you and this other man from the CCTV. He said that the older man is a terrorist and you are his accomplice. And I should report to the authorities if I see either of you."

He searches her gaze before asking, "Do you think what he says is true?"

"I don't know…," Annelie says in a small voice, looking down.

"I'm not an accomplice to any terrorist," Jack says, lifting her chin up so that their eyes meet. "And the old man in the picture is not a terrorist. He is my dad. He's the kindest man I know. He wouldn't even hurt a fly."

"Then why are they hunting you?"

"I don't know," Jack says. "We have some business to attend to. That's why we are here."

Annelie looks down once more, remaining quiet for a while. When she looks back up at him again, it is with tears of relief.

"I don't think we should go out tonight," she says. "We might be watched."

"I'm perfectly happy to stay right here," Jack says, stroking her cheek before planting a kiss on her lips.

They stand there, arms around each other, kissing in the middle of the living room. Daylight continues to recede, but neither of them is paying any attention. They kiss softly at first, slowly. Then as their bodies press closer, they kiss more urgently, fumbling their way towards the couch. She sinks onto the couch first, gently pulling him to her until she is lying prostrate on the cushions and he is leaning over her.

In the dimness, a look passes between them but no words are exchanged. Instead, Jack moves in closer and begins to kiss the crook of her neck. That sensation makes her skin tingle. She whimpers softly. Her heart pounds hard against her chest when she takes his hand and guides it towards the zipper of her dress. She is hardly breathing when he looks at her uncertainly. Then, encouraged by her smile, he glides the zip down. Her dress peels away, revealing first her shiny shoulders, followed by the freckles on the pale mounts of her breasts. They undress each other silently, their clothes falling into a heap on the floor before their skin touches.

They kiss first, their bodies settling into each other's grooves before Jack presses himself into her between her thighs. The sharp, alien sensation shocks her at first, prompting a small gasp. Then, when he begins to move, her skin begins to tingle in places she never knew existed. The sensations slowly rob her of all her sensibilities until all she is aware of is the feeling of him hard inside her.

With fingers interlaced in a tight clutch, their bodies rock in tandem to the rhythmic creaking of the couch. She throws her head back, moaning softly. They kiss and caress each other's body, melding and moving together, until there is no telling where one body ends and the other begins. They make love into the encroaching twilight, their moans of pleasure punctuated only by their shallow breaths. When his movement becomes more urgent, her moans become louder, until eventually, she begins to scream.

Outside, in the apartment building across the street, a pair of binoculars peer out from behind the curtains of a window on the same floor.

"Are you taping this?" a voice says.

"Yes. Every minute of it," the other replies.

12. GUNTHER

Sometime just after three p.m., a sleek black car pulls up in front of the revolving door of The Jagiellonian Hotel. The windows are tinted but it does not stop the doorman from rushing forward enthusiastically to open the door.

"Welcome back, Herr Scholz," the doorman says as Gunther climbs out of the car. "Travelling light this time?" He eyes the leather bag in Gunther's hand and then the empty carriage behind him.

"I'm only here for the night, Chris." Gunther hands the bag over absently.

"Shall I make the usual arrangements for dinner?"

"There will be no need for that." Gunther waves. "I'm going for a walk. Send my bag up to my room, will you?"

The sun is glorious and the sky a clear blue, Gunther could not think of a better day to make this visit. He has always liked coming to Krakau. The medieval charm of the old town square with its winding cobblestone streets is a nice change from the modern, grand architecture of Germania.

Germania – with its wide roads and majestic Volkshalle – represents the Reich of today, the modern and progressive Europe that was the Führer's vision. The Victory Arch – undoubtedly the largest man-made arch in Europe – dwarfs the once-famous Arc de Triomphe in Paris. As a child watching the arch being constructed in the centre of Germania, his father had said to him, "Gunther, do you know how big this arch will be when it's finished?"

"No, Papa," Gunther replied. "How big will it be?"

"It will be so big that the Arc de Triomphe in Paris will easily fit into its archway. That's how big it will be. It will be magnificent."

Little Gunther had yet to see the Arc de Triomphe in Paris but when he looked over and saw the glint of pride in his father's eyes as he watched the men pouring concrete and cement, Gunther knew that this monument is of great significance to the nation.

Germania – the future of Europe. Everywhere else – the past.

Secretly, Gunther likes visiting the past. There is something romantic about it. A form of escapism, like walking into a cinema theatre, sitting in the dark for two hours, being carried away to a completely different world by the actors on the silver screen. Even if he hates to admit it, Gunther has a soft spot for the simplicity of life outside Germania. Maybe, when he retires, he will move into a cottage somewhere in Krakau or Bohemia. He has a list of books he still wants to read but could never find the time for them. Also, it's probably time for him to write his memoir, get his memories down on paper before age creeps up on him. Lotte has been complaining that the city is getting overcrowded. An idyllic life in the countryside will be just the thing for them.

As Gunther now walks through the older part of Krakau, his thoughts travel back to the present – to the slip of paper in the inside pocket of his jacket. He stops momentarily and takes it out, unfolding it to reveal an address. He knows the neighbourhood. It's not far from here.

Gunther keeps walking. He walks past old buildings, coffee shops, restaurants and small blue carts parked on street corners selling braided ring-shaped bread. On a different day, he would stop to get one. His favourite is the one dusted with poppy seed. But not today. Today, he has business to take care of. Until it has been taken care of, Gunther could not allow himself the luxury of being distracted.

He crosses the park and finds himself in a part of town he rarely frequents. The poorer part. The streets become unfamiliar but that does not deter him. He looks at the address on the slip of paper again and finds the nearest street sign. The names match. He is on the right street, he just needs to find the right building.

He walks slowly, his hands in his pockets. The graffiti on the walls and the broken windows make him frown. Empty beer bottles scatter on street corners, some lying in a puddle of sour-smelling liquid. Here and there, dried vomit cakes the pavement, like little pots of landmines. He covers his nose away from the lingering putrid stench – the kind found only on the homeless (which he had not seen in Germania in decades) or in tunnels under bridges where the drunk lay unconscious in their own urine.

The neighbourhood is dilapidated, that much is obvious. Even as he walks down the street in his smart jacket, polo shirt, neatly pressed trousers and well-polished shoes, Gunther stands out like a sore thumb amongst the scruffy locals.

He looks around him at the lingering gazes obviously fixated on him. In their eyes are questions he knows they want answers to.

What is he doing here?

How much money does he have in his wallet?
How easily can we get it?

He knows he does not belong there. So too the locals. The more they stare, the less sure of himself he becomes. As he nears the address on the slip of paper, he wonders if he should turn back and just go home. Put it behind him. But a big part of him refuses to – the part that wants to know. The part that wants to see for himself if what the papers said is true.

He arrives in front of a grey building. It has tall iron gates that reaches all the way up to the next floor. He peers through the bars and sees the caretaker's hut not far away. Beyond that, his eyes catch sight of gravel, an untamed garden and concrete blocks of flats. He looks around for a doorbell but finds an intercom buzzer instead. Confidently, he presses it twice. Just to be sure.

"Name?" a gruff voice crackles through the intercom.

"Gunther Scholz."

"I meant who are you here to visit," the gruff voice crackles again.

"Helena," Gunther replies. "Helena Svobodová."

The name rolls off his tongue with practised ease. Ever since the slip of paper was handed to him in the hospital, Gunther has looked at that name more times than he can remember.

Helena Svobodová, he mouthed silently over and over as he stared at the drab hospital ceiling during his sleepless nights.

Helena Svobodová.

The owner of that name holds the key to the truth about his identity. The name on that slip of paper is one he unwillingly memorised. One he hopes he can forget soon enough.

"Helena Svobodová doesn't live here anymore," the voice crackles back.

Gunther is taken aback. He fishes out that slip of paper and looks at it again. The address is current, he was told that much. He has not prepared for the possibility that it is not. There he stands, in front of the iron gate, peering through the bars at the blocks of flats in a distance, unsure of what to do next. Then the intercom crackles to life again.

"She's moved next door. Above the grocery store."

Gunther thanks the gruff voice and slowly walks over to the grocery store next door. Outside the shop window, plastic buckets of salad heads, carrots, onions and potatoes encrusted with dirt line the pavement. The prices written in loopy handwriting on the brown cardboard sign tell him that they are on sale. He fingers the wilted lettuce leaves and the rotting onions, unable to hide his disgust.

"You gonna pay for those or what?" a shout comes from inside the shop. He turns to find that it belongs to a dumpy woman with a triple chin, a light moustache and caterpillar-shaped monobrow.

"Not today," Gunter says sternly, silencing the woman.

He turns his attention up to the window above the shopfront, at the few blouses hanging from the sagging laundry line beneath the windowpane.

That is Helena Svobodová's window, he thinks.

He finds the right door – a grimy collapsible iron rail – and inhales deeply before pressing the buzzer. As he waits, Gunther does not know what to expect. Does he really want to meet this Helena Svobodová? He is suddenly unsure.

After a long pause and another press of the buzzer, the window above him creaks open. A voice calls out, "Kto to jest?"

These bloody Slavs, Gunther mutters impatiently to himself. *Still speaking their bloody Slavic language.*

"I'm from the Ministry of Internal Affairs. Open up!" He bangs at the iron rail.

The window above him clicks shut. Gunther waits as a heavy thumping travels across the ceiling, followed by the squeak of a door hinge in desperate need of oiling. Somewhere at the top of that flight of staircase – the one behind the iron rail – Helena Svobodová's shoes clack noisily down the steps one at a time, slowly but surely.

Gunther sees her feet first – a pair of wooden clogs. Simple, unassuming and hideously ugly. Then he sees her legs – short and fleshy, covered with a network of purple and green veins. The hem of a frumpy floral-patterned frock is next to appear. Gunther waits as her shapeless dress reveals itself a few inches at a time until he is able to see Helena Svobodová in all her glory – a wrinkly old lady with a broad face and short grey hair. Not quite what he imagined.

"Are you Helena Svobodová?" Gunther asks even though he already knows the answer.

"Who are you and what do you want?" she growls from behind the iron rail.

"I work for the Government. I'm here to ask you a few questions," Gunther says, taking in the details of her appearance.

"Show me your papers. I want to see your papers!" demands the old woman. Under her breath, she mutters, "Swinia."

The word does not escape Gunther but he chooses to ignore it. Drawing a deep breath, he reaches into the inside pocket of his jacket and produces his ID. Helena Svobodová squints from behind the iron rails, studying it for a long time. She looks first at the square photo on the ID, then at Gunther, and finally back at the ID again. After satisfying herself that his is an authentic government official identification, Helena unlocks the padlock and jiggles the iron rail open. Without a word, she turns around and makes her way back up the staircase.

Gunther parts the flimsy gate. It rattles noisily. After wiping the grime off his hands with a handkerchief, he follows her up the stairs. Neither of them speaks until they get to the top.

"I have no tea," Helena Svobodová says as she slams the door shut once Gunther is in her dingy flat. She stands firmly by the door, ready to show him out as soon as the requisite number of minutes has passed.

"What do you want?" she asks impatiently. "The reporters have been hounding me for the last two weeks. I've told every single one of them what I know. It's all in the papers. GO. READ. IT. YOUR. SELF."

She picks up a stack of newspapers by the foot of the door and shoves it at Gunther's chest.

Helena Svobodová, as he is beginning to realise, is quite a feisty woman.

"Remind me again what you told the reporters." Gunther takes the newspapers and cast a cursory glance at the front pages before tossing them aside.

"How many times do I have to repeat this story? Can't you swines from Germania leave me alone???"

"Madam, this is serious government investigation. If there is anyone you should be talking to, it's me, not the press."

Helena Svobodová huffs exasperatedly, shakes her head and rolls her eyes skyward.

"Always with the investigation! Always!" she says as she waddles towards a corner where a small sink, a hotplate and an iron kettle sit. She fills the kettle with tap water and puts it on the hotplate to boil.

"I thought you said you didn't have tea?" Gunther says.

"I don't."

"Then why are you boiling water?"

"So that I can throw it on you if you create any trouble," she replies with narrowed eyes. Then, with a huff, she waddles past Gunther towards a shabby armchair by the window and sinks gratefully into it.

Gunther follows and finds himself a seat in the other armchair on the opposite end. It creaks when he sits down and he sinks deeper than expected, his glutes meeting the hard coils of broken springs underneath the threadbare upholstery.

"You're that Minister, aren't you?" Helena looks at him slyly. "The one in the papers. The one they are asking me about."

"It's all a mistake," Gunther says as he adjusts himself in the armchair.

"Damn right it is," Helena Svobodová spits as she rubs her calves. For the first time since meeting her, Gunther notices the different colour skin on Helena's calves – like a quilt of mismatch patches of skin. The sight makes him squeamish. He tries not to stare but, at the same time, he cannot help himself.

"I've told them," she says. "I've told them this swine cannot possibly be my brother. My brother wouldn't do all the things this swine has done. That's right, you know what I'm talking about."

Her steely gaze meets Gunther's. They glare at each other, neither of them flinching.

"I said to those reporters, there is no way this man could be my brother. My brother and my mother were killed by the Nazis during the invasion. The damn Nazis. You lot murdered my entire village. You see this?" She points to the patches of different colour skin on her calves. Gunther cannot help but stare. "THIS. Is what happened in my village. I still remember that day. I can't forget it even if I tried," Helena spouts.

"Tell me what happened to your mother and your brother," Gunther says.

"Oh, you need me to tell you what happened? Can't find it in your military files?" she sneers.

Gunther draws an impatient breath but does not answer.

"All right then, I'll tell you what happened," she says, narrowing her eyes.

"It was afternoon. My mother, my brother and I were in the shop getting food. That's what we were doing – getting milk and bread. My brother wanted sweets but my mother wouldn't let him have them. We didn't have much money. Everything we had went into getting the basics – milk, bread, flour, sugar, butter. That was it. We didn't have money for extras, like sweets. But my brother didn't understand that. How could he? He was only a little bit more than two. So, on this afternoon, my brother asked my mother for some sweets. My mother tried to explain to him that after paying for milk and bread, there isn't any money left to buy sweets with-"

"Is there a point to this story?" Gunther interrupts.

"Do you want to know what happened or not?"

"Just get to the point quickly, Goddammit."

Helena Svobodová rolls her eyes skywards and huffs. "Swinia," she mutters under her breath before continuing. "It was about two o'clock in the afternoon when the tanks rolled in. Those Nazis. There were soldiers everywhere. On foot. In trucks. Everywhere. They were smashing windows and banging down doors, yelling at us. Telling us to get outside."

She pauses to swallow her saliva and her eyes begin to shimmer.

"Three men came into the shop. One yelled at us to go out, the other two fired shots at random things in the shop. A bullet hit the glass jar holding the sweets. It shattered and the sweets spilled out onto the floor everywhere. My brother was so happy. He got to his knees and started picking up the sweets. My mother tried to stop him but he wouldn't listen. There were tiny bits of the glass mixed in with the sweets. He was nicked here and there. On his knees. His hands. Legs. He was bleeding and he started crying. My mother tried to comfort him but he wouldn't stop."

She pauses again, staring blankly into the distance. When she speaks again after swallowing the lump in her throat, her voice trembles.

"The officer who was yelling before yelled louder. We couldn't understand what he was saying so nobody moved. When none of us did anything, he pulled out his pistol and fired a shot."

A whimper threatens to escape but Helena Svobodová stifles it. When she speaks again, her voice is paper-thin.

"My brother fell to the floor and instantly went quiet. He was dead. My mother shrieked. Blood was spreading out from underneath his body. So. Much. Blood. Everyone in the shop began to cry. The officer fired another shot. This time my mother fell to the floor. She went quiet too. I can still see it. Her eyes were wide open when she died. Two bodies in a puddle of blood right in the middle of the shop. Everyone went quiet immediately."

At this point, she stops speaking. Gunther can see that her eyes are glassy and her lips are trembling. He makes to get up but she presses on, and he is forced to sit back down.

"I was all alone now. I wanted to cry but I didn't dare. The officers were yelling for us to get out. A stranger took my hand. Told me to stay close to her. Before we left the shop, I took one last look at them. My brother still had a fist full of sweets in his hand, lying in a puddle of dark red blood. My mother's eyes were wide open. I knew then that I would never be the same again."

She sniffs, wiping her nose with the sleeve of her dress before continuing.

"We were all rounded up. Everyone in the village. We were told to gather in the town hall. All of us crammed into that tiny hall. Then those swines boarded up the door and threw torches into the place. People were screaming and crying. There were flames everywhere. Black smoke so thick it was choking us. I had too much sense to jump out of a window. I was the only one to have escaped alive. My clothes were still on fire when I was running away. I had burns all over my body. I could have died. I should have died. If I had known this would be my fate, I would rather have died that day than live all these years under you swines. You filthy pigs."

When she returns her attention back to Gunther, Helena's face is sour.

"Listen old hag," Gunther sneers, leaning forward. "That kind of talk can get you killed."

She purses her lips and spits into Gunther's eye.

"Do you think I'm afraid of death?" she hisses. "Do you think ANY ONE of us are afraid of death? I have lived a thousand deaths. The death of my country. The death of my people. The death of my freedom. I would rather DIE than be a slave for another day. Do you think I'm afraid of death?"

She stares hard at Gunther as he wipes his eye with his handkerchief. In the far corner of the kitchenette, the kettle whistles, breaking the tension.

She rises with much difficulty and waddles over to the kitchenette. Gunther watches her every move as he straightens.

"I need to look at your papers," he commands as he strides towards the door.

She turns around to face him – kettle in one hand, kitchen knife in the other – a crazed look in her eyes.

"Get. Out. Of. My. House," she hisses. "I'm sick and tired of you swines barging in here like that. GET OUT! NOW!!!" She bares her teeth, snarling like an animal.

Gunther backs away, patting his jacket pockets only to remember that his revolver is tucked between two polo shirts, resting at the bottom of his leather overnight bag, which now sits in his hotel room.

Damn!

He takes a few steps back before turning around, making a run for the door.

"AND DON'T YOU EVER COME BACK HERE AGAIN!" Helena yells as she chases Gunther out the front door.

Gunther descends the staircase two steps at a time, his shoes clacking against the cement. When he gets to the bottom and spills out onto the sidewalk, Helena Svobodová is still yelling.

He exhales loudly, shaking his head in disgust. Then, a gush of hot water comes tumbling down the upstairs window, narrowly scalding him. He looks up to find her leaning out the opened window, an empty kettle in one hand, the knife still in the other.

"SWINIA!" she yells, hurling the kitchen knife at him. Gunther ducks. The knife misses him and lands with a loud clang on the concrete pavement. People walking down the street are stunned. They stop to watch as Helena Svobodová hurls more expletives at the smartly dressed man. Gunther sneers at her before dropping to one knee, wiping the splash off his shiny black shoes with his handkerchief. When he rises, he casts a final glance at the angry face before reaching for the mobile phone in the inside pocket of his jacket.

"Helena Svobodová, Krakau," he says into the phone as he walks away. "Exterminate her. Which one? I don't care which Helena Svobodová in Krakau, exterminate all of them. They are bloody Slavs. None of them are worth saving."

When Gunther hangs up, he is smirking. He knew it. The papers were wrong. He knew he wasn't related to Helena Svobodová. Right from the beginning, he knew he wasn't Slavic. How could he be? He looks nothing like them. Nothing.

Gunther chortles as he catches a glimpse of his reflection in a shop window. His jaw line, his eyes, his face – none of it remotely carries a hint of Slavic origins. Gunther couldn't be more pleased.

On his walk back to the hotel, Gunther stops by a blue cart parked on a street corner and buys a braided ring-shaped bread. One dusted with poppy seeds. He bites into it satisfactorily, savouring the chewy texture and the hint of saltiness on his tongue. Then, he takes his time meandering through the old town, marvelling at its medieval charm.

He pays a visit to the bustling Cloth Hall, then into the tranquillity of St. Mary's Cathedral. When he is done, he walks back to the hotel, whistling his favourite tune. With a spring in his step, Gunther passes the doorman, and then, as if remembering something, doubles back.

"Christopher, make the usual arrangements for dinner," Gunther chirps. "The best of everything. I'm in the mood to celebrate tonight."

"Certainly, Sir," the doorman replies with a smile.

"One more thing." Gunther pauses to reach into his wallet and pulls out a crisp note. He shoves it into the front shirt pocket of the doorman's uniform and pats him twice. "You're not bad for a Slav."

13. THE PAST

1936

"Uncle Ludvik wrote to us," Sarah said gravely as she smoothed out a crease in her dress. "He said things are getting worse for the Jews in Berlin. They intend to emigrate to France after the Olympics is over. He said Hitler is using the Olympics as propaganda for Aryan supremacy. For all the world to see. Grandfather got a little upset after he read the letter."

"Why doesn't he just come back here?" Thomas asked, his brow creasing as he squinted into the sun.

Sarah shrugged and then sighed, absently fiddling with the hem of her dress.

"What does it matter if he moves back here or to France? He still has to move," she said, looking up in the direction of the hill.

They both fell silent.

It was late afternoon on a warm summer's day. A gentle breeze blew, rustling the leaves on the trees. The late afternoon sun cast scintilla of gold and diamond specks on the river. On the banks of the Vltava, their shadows stretched long and slender on the ground. They were sitting on a patch of grass, their knees side by side – almost touching – as they looked up at the castle perched on top of the hill.

"I have something for you," Thomas said after a while. He reached into the satchel resting next to him, rummaging noisily. Sarah turned to face him when he pulled out a small box.

"Happy birthday," he said, handing the box to her with a smile.

Her eyes shone as the box exchanged hands.

"What is it?" She looked at Thomas expectantly.

"Open it," he said.

She did as she was told. When she lifted the lid and peeled away the delicate tissue paper inside, she saw that it was an intricate flower motive hair comb studded with crystals. The same one she saw in the shop window a while back. Her face lit up and she broke into a wide smile.

"Oh, Tom, you shouldn't have!" she said as she gingerly touched the sparkling crystals. "It must cost a fortune!" she added, looking from the comb to him in disbelief.

He shrugged and smiled. For close to a year, he spent every weekend working in Mr. Spegiel's shop, saving every crown he earned. He had seen the way Sarah's eyes shone when she saw it in the shop window several times, and he had been determined to gift it to her ever since.

"Here, let me help you," he said, picking up the comb and scooting closer to her. She sat perfectly still as he carefully wove the comb into the crown of her hair. When he leaned over, Thomas became suddenly aware of how close they were. His heart began to beat a little faster. Touching her soft hair with his fingertips, Thomas inhaled the faint scent in her hair. She smelled of roses and soap at the same time. Absently, he reached over to sweep a stray lock away from her face and tucked it behind her ear. Their eyes met and her cheeks turned a shade of pink. When he leaned in closer, she did not shy away. It was there on the banks of the Vltava that they kissed for the first time.

When their lips parted and their eyes opened, Thomas could see that she was smiling. He was smiling too. He reached over to take her hand, lacing their fingers together. There they sat for the rest of the afternoon, their hands clasped together, both unable to stop smiling. As the breeze blew and the river shimmered, Thomas' heart was so full he didn't think he could ever be unhappy again.

14. GUNTHER

"What the hell is going on?" Gunther mutters under his breath as the car pulls up into his driveway. Curving all the way up to the front porch, on the shallow slope of the tarmac, a fleet of army trucks park in a neat line.

"Were they there this morning?" he asks the driver as the car grinds to a halt, unable to move an inch further up the blocked-up driveway.

"No, Sir."

The driver kills the car engine and Gunther gets out. As he walks past the trucks, Gunther examines the license plates and credentials on each vehicle. The one on the tail end carries the emblem of the War Office, the middle three belong to the Heer while the remaining truck parked right at the top of the fleet carries no emblem. It must belong to the SS.

The bonnets are still warm. They haven't been there that long, Gunther deduces. He walks the remaining stretch of the driveway until he arrives at his front porch. On either side of the front door, two uniformed men stand in attention, backs straight and eyes forward.

Gunther climbs the short steps slowly. Through the wide opened front door, he sees men in uniforms moving around in the house. His brows immediately crinkle with disapproval.

During his time in the Wehrmacht, Gunther personally oversaw more than fifty raids – almost all of them on homes and offices belonging to the Resistance. It would never have occurred to him that someday he would be on the receiving end of one.

"What is the meaning of this?" he asks calmly when the two uniformed men move to block his path into the house.

"I'm sorry, Sir, but we are under strict orders not to let anyone past this point," the one on his right answers. Gunther sizes him up – tall, strong built, very young – most likely not much older than twenty-five. He inhales deeply before saying, "This is MY HOUSE. I am the highest-ranking

VANISHED

officer present. I command you to let me in."

When the two men do not move, Gunther begins to lose patience.

"I said. LET. ME. IN," he says, louder now. Again, the men do not move. Gunther moves to push them apart but the men's reflexes are quicker. In a flash, he finds himself trapped in a bind, his arms twisted in an awkward position behind his back, unable to move.

"THIS IS MY HOUSE, GODDAMMIT!" Gunther yells in agony. "I demand to be let into my own Goddamn house!" He writhes, struggling to break free, cursing and swearing the entire time but the men are stronger and even more relentless, barely breaking a sweat as they held him in a dead lock.

"Listen, punks. My uncle wrote the manual for this entire operation before you were even conceived in your mother's wombs." Gunther huffs, beads of sweat forming on his forehead. "Let me go or you will be sorry you were even born."

"Now, now, Scholz. There's no need for that kind of talk around here," a voice calls from inside the house as a silhouette approaches the front door. Before his face emerges from the shadows, Gunther already knows who the voice belongs to.

Reichsmarschall Schmitt – his rival for the succession to the Chancellery.

"Ah, Scholz, you must be really uncomfortable right about now," Reichsmarschall Schmitt says with a condescending smile. Stuck in an awkward position, Gunther manages only a grimace. He waits as Reichsmarschall Schmitt calmly instructs the two men to release him, which they obey immediately. When Gunther finally breaks free, he scowls at the two men before straightening his clothes.

"Schmitt, what is the meaning of this?" Gunther asks as he smooths his tousled hair. "Why are you raiding my home?"

"It's a beautiful day, Scholz," Reichsmarschall Schmitt says as he lifts his eyes to the sky. "Come, walk with me." He places a hand on Gunther's back and guides him down the steps. Gunther frowns but acquiesces nonetheless.

"What's going on, Schmitt?" Gunther asks once they are out of earshot. They walk side-by-side, around the house towards the back garden.

"I've always thought the garden is the best part of this house, don't you agree?" Reichsmarschall Schmitt replies without looking at him. They walk down the steps into the well-manicured garden where Reichsmarschall Schmitt fingers the neatly trimmed hedges and stops to inhale the faint whiff from a rose bush.

"Schmitt, what the hell is going on?" Gunther barks.

"Now, now, Scholz, no need to raise your voice. We don't want you to have another episode here in the garden now, do we?"

Gunther watches impatiently as Reichsmarschall Schmitt mills around the garden with his hands behind his back, pausing to examine a rose bush here and there as though he was a judge at a flower show.

"You must tell me who your landscape architect is. This place is remarkable," Reichsmarschall Schmitt marvels, turning around to face him.

"Why don't you tell me what the hell is going on first and then I'll tell you all about my landscape architect."

To which, Reichsmarschall Schmitt laughs.

"Scholz, we have the best intelligence force in all of Europe! You, of all people, should know that!" He laughs. "All I have to do is pick up the phone. Information is literally at my fingertips."

He mills around a bit more, inhaling deeply, making a show of enjoying the fresh air and the outdoors.

"Now, let's get down to business, shall we?" When he is done enjoying the garden, Reichsmarschall Schmitt turns to face him, altogether business-like. "This... *situation* with your... *identity*... has become a bit of a, how shall I say it... *problem*." His lips purses and then tightens into a straight line.

"What do you mean *problem*?" Gunther frowns. "You don't seriously believe what the papers are saying, do you?"

"It's not that...."

"I went to Krakau to see Helena Svobodová myself," Gunther spouts.

"I know."

"I don't even know WHY I have to justify this but I am. NOT. Her. Brother. We are not related in any way. At all," Gunther says defensively. "She says so herself. Her entire family died during the war."

"This is not about Helena Svobodová. We know that story is not true."

"Then why didn't you stop the press? Why did you let them print all that garbage?"

"Scholz." Reichsmarschall Schmitt exhales loudly, looking him squarely in the eye. "There are questions being asked about your ancestry. The public wants answers so we let the press give it to them while we conduct our own investigation."

"What did you find?" Gunther raises his eyebrows, his heart beating faster.

"Science is a magnificent thing, Scholz." Reichsmarschall Schmitt smiles.

"Oh, come off it, Schmitt! What did you find?"

"While you were in the hospital, we had your DNA tested."

Of course.

"And?" Gunther scrunches his brow, barely breathing.

Reichsmarschall Schmitt pauses to examine another hedge. When he finally speaks, his tone is icy.

"There is no match between yours and your father's."

The pronouncement is like a loud clap of thunder on a sunny day, sending shock waves to Gunther's core. He finds a step and sinks onto it, his mind drawing a blank as he wrestles with his own disbelief.

"The DNA analysis shows that you are only 18% Aryan," Reichsmarschall Schmitt adds as he mills around the garden, touching the vegetation absently. "That's less than minimum requirement to qualify for public office."

"18%? How can that be?" Gunther looks up at him, aghast. "Look at me, Schmitt!!! My eyes are just as blue as yours!"

"I don't argue with science, Scholz. The facts are the facts. As it turns out, you happen to be a… how shall I say it… *mongrel*." At this word, Reichsmarschall Schmitt's face twists in disgust.

"It must be a mistake," Gunther says after a brief pause. "I can explain it. I just need time. Just give me some time to get to the bottom of this." He looks pleadingly at the Reichsmarschall.

"There will be no need for that, Scholz," Reichsmarschall Schmitt reaches into his trouser pocket and pulls out a folded white envelope. When Gunther's eyes fall on the emblem of the eagle on the top right-hand corner of the envelope, his heart sinks immediately.

"Schmitt, I just need time," he begs, voice cracking.

"The DNA results are conclusive evidence. Nothing else will disprove that," Reichsmarschall Schmitt holds out the white envelope but Gunther does not take it. He stares at it then at Reichsmarschall Schmitt before staring back at it again.

"Take it." Reichsmarschall Schmitt waves the white envelope in his direction but Gunther does not move. He sits resolutely still on the step, fear flickering in his eyes. Without even opening the white envelope, he already knows what is inside.

Dishonourable Discharge.

Two simple words to strip him of everything he has worked for. Decades of service reduced to obsolescence. A single sheet of paper to banish him into obscurity.

Dishonourable Discharge.

There is no escaping his fate.

Gunther draws a sharp intake of breath before taking the white envelope with trembling hands.

"I'm still the same man, Schmitt," he says quietly. "Nothing's changed."

"Everything's changed," the Reichsmarschall replies, obviously bored. "My men are taking all government property back into custody. You have 24 hours to vacate this house."

"But Schmitt, this is my home." Gunther's face crumples in pain when he looks at him.

"Not anymore, it isn't."

"You can't do this to me," Gunther says.

"I can do whatever I want," the Reichsmarschall replies with a final glance before walking away, his boots crunching the dried twigs on the ground.

Gunther's eyes follow him as he makes his way up the steps, back in the direction they came from. A wave of exhaustion sweeps over him, followed by a mounting frustration. Sourly, he scrunches the white envelope into a crumpled ball.

Dishonourable Discharge.

His father would be rolling in his grave right now.

"One more thing, Scholz." Half way back to the house, Reichsmarschall Schmitt turns around. Gunther glances up at him disinterestedly. "There is another letter for you on the table in the entrance hall. I think it's from Lotte."

It dawns on Gunther then that he hasn't seen his wife in two days.

15. ANNELIE

The sound of two abrupt buzzes prompts Annelie to look up from the stacks of old newspapers piled high on her desk. She rises slightly, peers over the top of the piles to find that the desks are empty. She looks up at the clock on the wall, surprised to discover that it is already lunchtime. Another short buzz draws her attention to the back door. A few sharp knocks follow, beckoning her out of her chair.

As she stands behind the closed door, Annelie peers hesitantly through the frosted glass panes on either side. Through the murky glass, she makes out a figure of a medium-height man in brown uniform and a matching cap, holding a clipboard in his hand. Hesitantly, she opens the door a sliver – wide enough to see the man's face.

"I have a delivery for the Archive Department?" The young delivery man glances first at the clipboard in his hand then at Annelie.

"I'll take that," she says, opening the door wider. The clipboard exchanges hands and Annelie signs her name next to the consignment number on the piece of paper. She stands aside and waits by the door, watching the delivery man wheeling a trolley stacked high with cardboard boxes through the doorway.

"Just put them in that room," she points in the direction of the storeroom.

She remains standing as she watches the man navigate the trolley, its wheels squeaking noisily as it made the distance. He disappears momentarily into the storeroom and then re-emerges with the empty trolley. When he walks out the door to head for the truck, Annelie reaches to close it.

"Wait, there's more," he turns and calls out. Annelie freezes, watching him curiously as he disappears behind the delivery truck and reappears again with a trolley stacked high with boxes identical to the ones he just deposited into the storeroom.

"How many more are there?" she asks as he wheels the load through the doorway. The man pauses thoughtfully to check the clipboard before answering, "46 more."

She raises her eyebrows but says nothing.

The trafficking of the identical looking boxes takes a good part of twenty minutes as the delivery man moves between the truck and the storeroom, and then from the storeroom back to the truck again, loading and unloading stack after stack of cardboard boxes.

When finally, the last stack of the boxes has been deposited, the delivery man doffs his cap at Annelie as he wheels his empty trolley out.

"Thank you," she says, closing the door behind him. Outside, the truck engine revs to life, its noisy engine receding as it speeds off.

Back in the storeroom, Annelie checks to see if the consignment is in order. She sees that the boxes are dumped haphazardly in the small room, making a huge mess. With crinkled brows and a huff, Annelie sets about sorting them into the right order.

In the stuffy, musty smelling storeroom, under the poor light of the only naked bulb dangling from the ceiling, Annelie pulls the box closest to her and lifts the lid. Her hand fumbles over the content, fingering the demarcation marked by the blunt folds of thick folders. She removes the top most folder, careful not to tip the box over. When she pulls it out, she sees that the brown manila folder is secured tightly with a piece of string. On the front, the familiar stamp of the eagle and the symbol of the Wehrmacht tells her that they are military documents.

Absently, Annelie unties the string. The brittle knot comes away easily and she soon finds herself flipping through yellowing sheets of paper decorated with smattering of ageing brown spots. She skims the neatly typed out pages, noting the date of the file.

March 1942.

The files are from during the war. Annelie raises her eyebrows. Her interest is piqued. She leaves through the brittle sheets, looking at the identical columns in each of them, trying to discern a pattern. Many of the names in the first column are unfamiliar to her. Next to them is a sequence of four-digit numbers. In the column next to that are more names, followed by another sequence of four-digit numbers.

She flips back and forth between the pages, noticing the regularity of the names repeating themselves before it finally dawns on her.

"It's a timetable," she mutters under her breath.

Of course!

The pages contain departure and arrival destinations and times.

"It's a train timetable!" Her gasp echoes slightly in the room.

She flicks through the remaining sheets and begins to recognise names of towns and cities she has only heard of and read about but has never been to.

Budapest. Welsch-Leiden. Warschau. Danzig.

The tentacles of the rail network are far-reaching. As she scans the timetable, Annelie tries to conjure up a map in her head. She manages only to form a scant picture, not recognising other names on the sheets.

"Bergen-Belsen… Treblinka… Buchenwald… Theresiensiadt…," mutters Annelie distractedly.

What are all these places? Why are there so many trains travelling back and forth to these places?

Annelie's frown deepens the deeper she ventures into the folder. She keeps flipping until she arrives at a page where only one name repeatedly appears in the destination column.

Auschwitz-Birkenau.

She studies the timetable, noting that only trains from a certain set of stations headed for this place at different times of day and then headed back out where they came from soon after. Annelie pauses to consider before flipping back to the first few sheets, retracing her train of thought.

"The trains pick up cargo from the towns and cities… bring the cargo to the closest point…," she murmurs, tapping on the destinations typed out on the paper. The crease on her forehead deepens until it hurts.

"And then they forward the cargo to this place… this *Auschwitz-Birkenau*," she mutters to herself, tracing a path down the paper, as if following an imaginary railway line.

What is this place? What are they transporting to and from there?

Annelie flips through the rest of the sheets quickly, searching for more clues. She sees more train timetables in the remaining pages, repeating the same names in the same columns. Satisfied that there is no new information to be uncovered, she shuffles the sheets back into place, shakes them into a neat stack and re-ties the string over the folder. Then, she sits the folder on the floor and pulls out the rest of the folders from the box, thumbing through the corners of the sheaf of papers, hoping to find something else. Instead, she catches glimpses of more of the same.

Nothing new here. She huffs as she puts the folders back in the box, replaces the lid and pushes the box aside. Undeterred, she quickly moves on to the next box and sees that it contains folders with similar train schedules.

"No wonder we needed so much fuel during the war, the trains are running all the time…," Annelie mutters to herself absently. She pauses to listen for any sound of oncoming footsteps. When she hears nothing, she pokes her head out of the storeroom just to be sure. When she sees that the room is still empty, she ducks back in to continue scrounging through the next stack of boxes.

The boxes in the subsequent stack contain stacks of yellowing sheets the size of postcards secured tightly with rubber bands, vastly different from the timetables. She picks one up. As she unties it, the rubber band snaps between her fingers and fall away. On the cards, she notes the neat typeface spelling out names, birthdays, occupations and a number sequence.

She flips through them quickly, noticing nothing out of the ordinary with the cards, except that there are many of them. Bundles after bundles secured with old rubber bands that stick to the cards, stacked on top of one another, shoved in every available space within the box. She finds another rubber band to re-tie the stack in her hands and puts it back into the box with the others. She then moves on to another stack of boxes, where in the first one, she comes across yellowing monochrome portrait photographs. Annelie flips through them, noticing the subjects all wore similar outfits – striped uniforms. Whether they are men or women, young or old, their heads are shaved, and none of them are smiling.

She looks through the photos, noticing the number sequences stitched to the front of the uniforms and remembers the stacks of cards in the previous box. With one hand still holding the photos, she goes back to the earlier box, rummages through the stacks and finds a card with a sequence number that matches the one in the photo. Then it dawns on her.

These people are prisoners!

With furrowed brows, she now flips through the cards with new eyes, suddenly noticing details she hadn't noticed before.

Bergen-Belsen.

Treblinka.

Buchenwald.

The names on the train schedules are also on the cards.

The trains weren't transporting cargo. They were transporting prisoners!

Annelie pauses as she computes the magnitude of the operation in her head. Hundreds of thousands, maybe even into the millions.

So many of them. What did they do?

She pauses to consider what she has just found and decides she isn't quite done just yet. Gingerly, she puts the photos back in their box and returns the stacks of cards where they came from. Unsure of what to expect, she reaches for the next box.

When she lifts the lid off the next box, the scent of old leather wafts up her nostrils. Within the rectangular confines of that box, she finds a stack of thick leather-bound books. On the front cover of the top most volume, she sees the date inscribed neatly in cursive calligraphy.

1942.

She hesitates before reaching for it. The volume feels heavy. Its impossible thickness begs to be handled with both hands. Carefully, Annelie removes it from the box. Kneeling on the floor, she sets the book down in her lap, the weight bearing down on her thighs. Before flicking it open, she peers out the door to make sure no one is around. The office is still empty.

As she inhales deeply, she lifts the leather flap carefully. What she sees instantly widens her eyes. The leather-bound volume isn't a book.

It's a photo album.

As she flicks through the pages, bombarded by images in the yellowing black and white photos, Annelie's face turns pale. The neat inscriptions below the photos tells her the names of the places and the dates the photos were taken.

Lidice. June 1942.

Lezaky. June 1942.

Auschwitz-Birkenau. 1942.

As she continues to flip through the pages, Annelie's hands begin to tremble. She sees limp bodies hanging from gallows. Bodies lying in a puddle of blood on the ground. Men blindfolded with black cloth, standing in a forest at gunpoint, their hands bound behind their backs. The images horrify her, making her eyes prick with hot tears.

What is this? What is this madness? Her face crumples in pain.

When she arrives at a page with only a single picture on it, her hand shoots up and claps over her mouth in horror. The photo album falls onto the floor with a loud thud, still opened on the same page. What she sees shocks her to her core, and tears begin to fall from her eyes.

"So many... so many...," she mutters with heaving shoulders. Her quivering voice comes out in a thin whisper, echoing lightly within the four walls of the storeroom as her trembling hands reach to retrieve the album.

Through a blurry curtain of tears, Annelie stares at the picture — at the wide dirt trench and the soldier who stands over it, wielding a long black gun in his hands and a smirk on his face. She stares at the pile of bodies in that wide dirt trench, so obviously lifeless, completely naked, so thin that every bone in every ribcage painfully curves out, arms and legs so skinny that they are merely bones wrapped in a thin film of dirty skin. They are piled haphazardly on top of each other, necks and limbs bent at awkward angles, like rag dolls carelessly tossed in a heap — a river of unnamed bodies with no past worth remembering and no future to speak of.

"So many... so many...," Annelie whispers with trembling lips. Unable to keep looking, she slams the album shut and tosses it back into the box.

At that moment, voices of people talking in the distance snaps her sensibilities back in place. She stands up hurriedly, puts the boxes back where they belong and wipes the tears from her eyes before rushing out of the storeroom back to her desk.

The door flings open just as she sinks into her chair. Helga and Marcus immediately stop talking when their eyes fall on her red, watery eyes.

"What's the matter, Annelie?" Helga asks with a frown. "You look unwell."

Marcus nods thoughtfully, creasing his forehead.

"You're not... infectious, are you?" he says.

Annelie does not answer immediately. She sniffs quietly, rubbing her nose. Her eyes lack the courage to meet either of theirs.

"You should go home," he adds. "We can't have you spreading your germs in this small office."

"Yes, Annelie. Go home and get some rest," Helga says, placing a comforting hand on her shoulder.

Annelie nods obediently, fighting back the fresh tears that are threatening to fall.

"The delivery man came by earlier," she croaks. "The boxes are in the storeroom."

The flicker in Marcus' eyes does not escape her. Marcus and Helga exchange a quick glance before Marcus looks at her.

"Did you look at what's inside?" he asks.

"No, I didn't," Annelie answers quickly. "Why? Is it important?"

"No," Marcus replies with a tight smile. "They are just some old files from the War Office. We're keeping them safe while the office gets fumigated."

Marcus continues to speak but Annelie is no longer listening. She gathers her handbag into her arms and excuses herself. Under Helga's watchful gaze, she stumbles out the back door into the quiet alleyway.

Once outside, Annelie breaks into a run, fresh tears falling from her eyes. Her legs struggle to carry her to the end of the street, and she stumbles, dropping to her knees. In amongst the pile of junk that litters the dirty alleyway, she manages to find a garbage bin just before she falters and begins to throw up.

Crouching over the stench of garbage, Annelie retches noisily. Her belly lurches violently, pumping out a watery vomit, leaving a burning sensation in her throat and a trail of sourness in her mouth. As she heaves over the garbage bin, the images from the photo album burn at the back of her retina.

So many.... so many....

Hot tears fall from her eyes as she wipes her mouth with the back of her hand. Paralysed from the shock of the images, she kneels in the quiet alleyway and cries, rocking back and forth as her shoulders heave violently. She cries until her legs lost all feeling, until her eyes sting and her throat turns dry. Then, with much difficulty, she climbs to her feet. She needs to tell someone but she doesn't know who. All she knows is that she will never be able to un-see what she has just seen, and that the memory of those photos will haunt her every waking moment until the day she dies.

16. THE PAST

1938

"Have you heard? Hitler has plans for acquiring living space for Germans in Europe," Mrs. Albrecht's voice travelled from the kitchen through the opened door into Thomas' room. Thomas stopped reading, quietly shut the book and moved closer to the doorway. Outside the window, snow was falling in soft flakes, landing on the windowpanes in a small white bank.

"Hmmmph," amidst the chink of cutlery, a grunt came in the form of Maminka's voice.

"Don't tell anyone but my cousin knows somebody who works in the Reich Chancellery in Berlin," Mrs. Albrecht's voice lowered conspiratorially. Thomas craned his neck to listen more closely. There was a pause where a faint sound of slurping was followed by the chink of cup meeting saucer. "He told her that Hitler had a secret meeting with his military officials last November about his new foreign policy."

"Why do you bother yourself with matters of politics, Maria?" Maminka could be heard saying. "Leave that to the menfolk. Besides, how is that any of our concern here?"

"Erna Marz!" A gasp came from Mrs. Albrecht. "You really should pay more attention to current affairs!" she scolded. "With the way things are going, things won't be the way they are now. There will be changes in Europe. Big changes. You can be sure of that!"

There was a brief silence where the only sounds to be heard were the gentle slurping of coffee and the chinks of cups meeting saucers.

"Anyway, as I was saying," Mrs. Albrecht's voice resumed its conspiratorial tone. "My cousin told me that her acquaintance in the Reich Chancellery told her that Hitler has plans to take over Austria and Czechoslovakia."

"What does that mean for us?"

"Well, it's obvious, isn't it? Czechoslovakia will become part of Hitler's empire. It can only be a good thing for us," Mrs. Albrecht said, a hint of glee in her tone. "The Jews here will have a hard time, that's for sure." Another faint slurp followed, after which the same voice added, "If they know what's best for them, they better start packing and leaving soon. Before Hitler's army arrives. The Jews in Berlin have had their property confiscated. I hear quite many of them are emigrating. And about time too. It was because of them that we lost the last war. Good riddance!"

"For God's sake, Maria. You weren't even born there. What have the Jews ever done to you? Besides, we are all Czech nationals, not German."

"Well, my parents were. I'm every bit as German. So is your husband. With the way things are going, you should thank your lucky stars for that. Very soon, every single person here will be speaking German. You better get Tomáš to brush up on his vocabulary. It will put him in good stead. Maybe even get him to join the Nazi Youth. There's no harm in that."

Thomas frowned as he listened. A dark cloud passed across his face. As Mrs. Albrecht began to tell Maminka about the diamond necklace Mr. Albrecht gave her for Christmas, Thomas hurried out of his room and reached for the coat that hung from the coat stand. He slipped it on hurriedly, pulled on a cap and rushed out the front door, banging the door in his wake. As he circled down the five flights of staircase two steps at a time, his tramping footfall echoed urgently in the stairwell all the way down, until he was out of the apartment building and into the snow-covered street, hardly stopping to catch his breath.

Hitler is coming! He thought, his pulse racing.

He ran down the street, feeling the cold air gazing his cheeks as he ran into the wind. Wisps of white fog blew from his nostrils with every breath. He ran past shop windows, turned at street corners, darting around pedestrians carefully making their way down the slippery sidewalk covered in white snow, until he arrived in front of Sarah's apartment building in Josefov. Panting hard, he pressed the doorbell downstairs urgently. The door opened and he dashed in. When he finally clambered up the stairs and through the front door, he was flushed and out of breath.

"Hit... Hitler is com...coming!" he said as he inhaled rapidly, sucking in the air around him. "Hitler is coming! You... you have to leave. Before... before it's too late." His eyes darted about wildly, from Sarah to Grandfather, then to Mother and Amos, and finally back to Sarah again. They stared at him blankly. No one said a word.

"Didn't you hear me? You have to leave!!! Hitler is coming!!!" Thomas said in exasperation, shaking Sarah by the shoulders.

"Slow down, Tom," Grandfather said as he walked over and placed a reassuring hand on Thomas' shoulder. Thomas was still panting when their eyes met. In Grandfather's eyes, he saw a serenity and calm he could not comprehend.

"Grandfather, Hitler is coming," Thomas said, almost pleading.

"So, let him come," Grandfather said quietly.

"Aren't you afraid of what he might do to the Jews?" Thomas asked with a pained look on his face.

"Tom, this is not the first time in history that the Jews are being singled out as the enemy," Grandfather said quietly. "It's only temporary. It'll pass."

Thomas could not believe what he was hearing. He glanced over at Sarah, then at Mother and Amos. On their faces, he saw only a blank indifference that troubled him deeply.

"Look what happened in Berlin! To Uncle Ludvik!" Thomas wailed. "The same thing will happen here!"

No one said a word. They merely stared at him like he was a raving lunatic.

"Come, Tom, you must be cold," Grandfather finally said, clapping him on the back. "Come in and have some coffee. Sarah just baked us a cake. Let's have some while it's still warm."

As the entire family headed to the dining room, Thomas stared at their backs in disbelief. He wanted to believe that what Grandfather said was true but something in Mrs. Albrecht's sinister tone convinced him otherwise.

As he stood unmoving by the door, Thomas saw a future where the world was divided by a wall – on one side lived the Jews, on the other lived everyone else. A shiver ran down his spine.

What would that mean for him? For Sarah?

Thomas didn't know. The unknown troubled him, so much that he was unable to move.

Not two months later, Hitler's army marched into Austria. A sea of people congregated at the Heldenplatz in Vienna, cheering as he delivered his speech. Soon after, the border posts between Austria and Germany were dismantled. Austria officially became part of the German Reich.

In October the same year, Hitler's army entered and occupied the Sudeten region of Czechoslovakia to the cheers of Sudeten Germans.

Four days later, President Eduard Beneš stepped down from office.

Two weeks after that, he left the country.

Hitler was coming and there was nothing anyone could do to stop him.

17. THE PAST

March 15, 1939

Snow fell over the city. Gusts of icy wind blew. The sky was heavy with grey clouds when German tanks rolled into Prague that morning.

On the slippery roads, boots drummed and engines roared. The soldiers' motorcycles and their sidecars revved in a single file as they entered, followed by jeeps with their opened tops and the loud trucks with their menacing tyres. Soldiers marched in a neat column, their long rifles leaned against one shoulder, boots thumping in unison as they made their way into the city.

Echoing throughout town was a confused mix of cries of anguish and cheers of welcome. Somewhere in a corner, a marching band played, their drums beating gaily to the drones of the soldiers' tramping footfall. Here and there, hands raised in high salute as the fleet of vehicles passed by. The soldiers looked pleased with their victorious entrance. No doubt, the people have come out in droves to see their great Führer, who would be making an appearance at the castle later that day.

Thomas was amongst the people banked on the side of the street, watching but not celebrating. Somewhere in the jubilant pocket of the crowd further up the road, someone started passing out small rectangles of red flags bearing the swastika. Very soon, everywhere he turned, all he could see was little red rectangles waving enthusiastically on that bitter, cold March day.

Red flags hung over tall buildings, more flew from poles erected by uniformed men standing in attention. Overnight, the city turned into a sea of red and black. The swastika sign was everywhere. The sight of it made Thomas sick to his stomach. His city was being defaced right before his very eyes and yet all he could do was to stand quietly by.

Amidst the noises in the town square, he pulled a long face when he spoke into Ivan's ear, "Let's go. I can't stand this any longer." They both left, weaving their way out of the crowd, away from the military procession that was unfolding during the morning rush-hour.

As he made his way to the university, passing by a scant crowd of locals, Thomas spotted a woman not much older than himself dabbing her red, watery eyes with a handkerchief. She was crying desperately, her shoulders heaving with grief, her desolation communicated in a string of hiccups. Thomas slowed his steps, noticing the anguish worn on every face that passed him by – men and women, young and old, who had all woken up to the shock announcement over the airwaves that Hitler's army had taken over their city.

A pervasive sense of helplessness swept over him. Melancholia descended on him silently. Somewhere in a corner of his mind, Mrs. Albrecht's words came back to him. He glanced over his shoulder at the jubilant crowd behind him. In a distance, he thought he saw her beaming face, her gloved hand frantically waving the small red rectangle bearing the swastika sign in the air.

That was only the beginning.

The very next day, the only homeland he knew disappeared from the map of Europe. In its place was a smaller region renamed the Protectorate of Bohemia and Moravia. Slovakia became a nation of its own with the Catholic priest, Jozef Tiso, at the helm.

Of the Czechoslovak Republic, there was no more.

18. THE PAST

1940

"No! I won't allow it!" Táta's heavy hand banged on the table, rattling cups and saucers as he shouted within the tiny confines of the kitchen. "You will not marry that Jew! I forbid you!" His face was scrunched up in anger, the corners of his mouth curved downwards as his chest heaved heavily.

"Why are you doing this to us, Tom?" Another voice supplied, thin and teary. Thomas' eyes moved from his father to his mother. In the dimness of the kitchen, the sourness of both their faces carried a darker shadow. It was still early in the morning, their breakfast lay half eaten on the table, rapidly turning cold. Thomas sat very still, his face expressionless as he absorbed his parents' outburst.

"What have we done to deserve this? Why are you bringing shame to this family?" Maminka began to cry. In her crumpled face, Thomas witnessed an anguish he had never seen before. It pained him in a way he could not describe.

"Why are you so against this?" After what seemed like an eternity of not speaking, Thomas finally said. He stared at them both, his eyes full of pain.

"Because it's unnatural and it's wrong!" Táta shouted on his feet, banging on the table once again. "Why, Tom? Why? Of all the girls you can choose to marry, you chose a Jewish girl? Why???" His voice rose with exasperation.

"What will people think???" Maminka wailed in between chokes of sobs, wiping her eyes with the corner of her frock.

Thomas looked first at his mother, then at his father. She sat meekly in her chair, cocooned in her own grief, her thin shoulders trembling uncontrollably. She seemed suddenly small and feeble, as if she had suffered a great blow. His father stood over him, his angry eyes trained on Thomas, unflinching, the corners of his mouth twitching.

Quietly, Thomas said, "I am not asking for your permission. I'm only asking for your blessing."

"You don't have my permission! And you don't have my blessing!" his father barked, spit flying in his direction.

"Táta, I am going to marry her whether you like it or not!" Thomas raised his voice as he shot to his feet.

"No son of mine will marry a Jew. If you are so set on marrying that girl, go ahead! Once you set foot out of this house, don't you dare come back!" Táta shouted at him, his big voice reverberating through the entire apartment.

"Werner!" Maminka protested in disbelief, placing a hand on Táta's arm. He shrugged it off and told her to be quiet. With a forefinger raised at Thomas' face, he growled, "You listen to me, you brat. I'm going to say this only once. If you marry that Jew, you are dead to me. You hear me?"

Thomas glared first at him then at his mother. Then, without a word, he kicked back his chair and stomped out of the kitchen. A loud crash followed, sending his father into a frenzy.

"YOU GET BACK HERE, YOU BRAT! I'M NOT DONE WITH YOU YET!" His father shouted at his back but Thomas didn't stop. He wasn't even listening. He marched to his room, flung the door open and began to gather his things.

"Werner!!! Why did you say such a thing??? He's our only child!!!" Maminka's desperate cry could be heard from the kitchen. He heard Táta barked back. A loud slap followed. His mother went quiet. Then a faint whimper took the place of the silence.

Huffing, Thomas pulled a suitcase from the top of the cupboard and flung it onto his bed. As drawers and cupboards were opened and banged shut, he grabbed his things, stuffing them into his suitcase until it was overflowing.

"Tom! Your father didn't mean what he said," Maminka's footsteps scurried from the kitchen, tears leaking from the corners of her eyes as she pleaded at the foot of his bed while he forced the suitcase shut. Thomas steeled himself, paying her no attention.

"Of course I did! Why would I say it if I didn't mean it?" Táta shouted, stomping in behind her.

Thomas gathered his coat and hat in one arm, and with the other, lifted his suitcase off the bed, and marched out of his room.

"Tom, PLEASE!!!" his mother pleaded, tearily grabbing onto the crook of his arm.

"Maminka, I have to go," he said quietly, yanking his arm away, all the while not looking at her. He walked past his father without a glance. Then, without another word, he was out the door.

As he walked down the flight of staircase, suitcase in one hand, coat and hat in the other, his mother's voice and footsteps followed him.

"Tomáš!!!!!!" she shrieked.

He did not answer. He did not even look back.

"Tomáš!!!!!!"

He kept walking.

"Tomaaaaaaaaaaaaaaaaaaaaaaaaaaas!!!!!!!"

Her cry turned into a desperate howl, stabbing Thomas in the chest but he did not stop.

With eyes filled with hot tears, Thomas kept walking until he was out of the building and into the street. Behind him, Maminka's howl was drowned out by the noisy street. He kept walking, putting one heavy foot in front of the other, until all he could hear was the sound of a city carrying on with life.

*

"Are you sure about this, Tom?" Grandfather asked, his eyes trained on Thomas as they sat in the dining room that afternoon. The apartment was quiet. No one else was home. Thomas stared at him momentarily before nodding resolutely.

"You could wait till you finish university," Grandfather added gently.

"The university has been closed since last November," Thomas said with a frown. "It won't make a difference. I've made up my mind."

"Have you talked to your parents?" Grandfather prodded. Thomas looked away, his eyes lacking the courage to meet Grandfather's. Then, slowly, he nodded.

"They won't agree to it," he sighed, staring at the floor. "My father has just as much disowned me."

"And you still want to do it?" Grandfather's calm voice came over him. "That is a big sacrifice, Tom. We are in for some hard times, are you sure you want to be part of this? It's not too late to change your mind."

There was a brief silence in which neither of them moved. Then, Thomas lifted his eyes and nodded resolutely.

Just then, the front door of the apartment burst opened, prompting both Thomas and Grandfather to look up.

"They treat us like animals!" A shout came from the front door. They got to their feet and hurried to the living room. There, Thomas found Amos stomping around, a scarlet face scrunched up in anger as he cursed and swore at no one in particular.

"How can they do this to us?" he shouted, the veins on his forehead pulsing menacingly. In his eyes, Thomas saw a flicker of pain and desperation — a sight that had become more and more common with each passing day.

Thomas turned his attention to Sarah and Mother, who had only just entered the front door, their expressions meek as they quietly closed the door behind them.

"What happened?" Thomas was the first to ask.

Mother and Sarah exchanged glances. A small sigh escaped as Mother placed a hand on Sarah's arm, giving her a squeeze as if to say, *you tell them*. Then, without looking at anyone, she retired to the kitchen, bearing the bag holding their provisions for the week, her eyes lowered to the floor. She had been crying, this Thomas was sure of.

"It's nothing," Sarah said quietly as her gaze met Thomas' quizzical stare.

"It's not nothing!" came another shout from Amos. "Why do you say it's nothing? We are not NOTHING!"

"Amos, we do not shout in this house," Grandfather said quietly. "Shouting resolves nothing, you know that."

"Why are you on their side, Sabba? We can't do this. We can't do that. We can't be here. We can't go there. Tell me, what is it that I am allowed to do? What kind of liberties do I still have if I can't even speak my mind in my own home???" Amos pulled at his hair in utter frustration.

"Aaaaaaaaarrrgggggghhhhhhhhh!" he shouted. His loud voice reverberated through the entire apartment, silencing even the noisy creaks from the neighbouring walls. Like a petulant child, Amos stomped off to his room. With a loud bang, the door slammed shut behind him.

Grandfather sighed softly, shaking his head slowly. In his slumped shoulders and restless stoop, he seemed altogether spent and helpless. It had been a year since the Nazi's decree forced him to give up his jewellery store. Before then, it had stood at that street corner for fifty years, doing a roaring trade. And, just like that, it was taken from him.

He didn't even put up a fight.

For the purposes of Aryanisation, the Nazis called it.

Thomas noticed that Grandfather hadn't been the same since his store was taken over by the Germans. Overnight, old age descended on him swiftly. His silver hair turned white. His sprightly steps turned into hesitant shuffles. He hardly left the apartment anymore, preferring instead to keep his own company, perched in his olive green high-back armchair by the window, gazing blankly into the distance.

Thomas noticed too, that each time he visited, the apartment seemed to be missing yet another piece of furniture. Prized antiques were no longer in their usual spot. Instead, their ghosts could be seen in the walls of the apartment, lingering in the fading wallpaper around their silhouette. He made no mention of it and, instead, discreetly smuggled tins of canned food he looted from Maminka's pantry into Mother's kitchen. It was the least he could do.

"We had another incident today," Sarah explained quietly, glancing first at Grandfather then at Thomas. "The tram was packed, we couldn't find any space in the second car, so we went into the first car."

She paused, swallowing hard as a shadow crossed her face.

"A lady spoke to us. Told us we were in the wrong car," her voice began to tremble, prompting Thomas to take her hand. When she continued, it was with a thin voice.

"She said that all filthy Jews should go to the back end of the second car. Everyone stared. It was horrible, Tom. Just horrible."

As she began to cry, Thomas wrapped his arms around her trembling shoulders and brought her in for a hug. A look passed between Grandfather and him, ending with an exchange of nods.

"Sarah," he whispered into her hair. "There's something I want to ask you."

Her shoulders stopped trembling as she lifted her eyes to meet his.

"What is it?" she asked, wiping her eyes.

"Will you marry me?" Thomas asked with a small smile. His question was met with stunned silence. When an answer was not forthcoming, the smile disappeared from his face. He watched intently as Sarah's expression changed from stunned to disbelief, his heart beating furiously in his chest. She looked over at Grandfather, who nodded encouragingly. When she turned back to face Thomas, her face broke into a wide smile.

"This wasn't the way I wanted to propose but it's as good a time as any. So, will you? Be my wife?" Thomas added hopefully.

"Yes! Oh, Tom! Yes!" she squealed, bouncing up and down in his arms. Thomas was instantly filled with relief and ecstasy in equal measures. The mood in the apartment lifted when both Mother and Amos re-appeared in the living room to learn the happy news, the gloom on their faces traded in for smiles. For a brief moment, they put their troubles aside and rejoiced over Thomas and Sarah's impending nuptials.

A week later, in a simple civil ceremony in the Old Town Hall, Thomas and Sarah were married. Thomas wore a borrowed suit and Sarah a pale-yellow dress, a matching hat and white cotton gloves. She looked radiant, holding a small bouquet of flowers Mother had arranged from flowers cut from their garden box on the balcony. Thomas could not stop smiling as he stood there, Sarah's gloved hands in his.

Afterwards, when they were posing for the photographer outside the Old Town Hall, Grandfather and Ivan stood on one side of Thomas while Mother and Amos stood to the other side of Sarah. The sun was in their faces. Everyone was dressed in their best clothes, joking and laughing. For a brief moment, Thomas thought of Maminka, sitting by herself in the kitchen of his old home, the way she usually did after Táta had gone to work and all the breakfast dishes had been washed and dried. That moment filled Thomas with bitter-sweetness.

That very same afternoon, after they had had lemonade and cake at the Hotel Fiser, Thomas moved into the Bars' apartment in Josefov where the newly-weds began their lives as husband and wife.

19. THOMAS

"They disappeared," deep, gruff voice said. "All of them Jews. Put on the train. No one knows where they went and what happened to them."

Thomas looks out the car window, watching – in deep concentration – the acres of green field passing by. Outside the city, away from the new buildings and foreign signage, Thomas finally sees the homeland of his memories. He gazes at the trees and the hills, at the part of his past that is still untainted, remembering a time when he was still innocent and happy. His heart suddenly aches with a poignant longing for what once was, before the war came, before everything changed.

The car speeds down the quiet country road, a cloud of dust in its wake. The narrow road is flanked by miles and miles of meadow on either side, stretching as far as the eye can see. Now and then, a farmhouse looms in a distance, surrounded by a clump of trees. Apart from the occasional bicyclist pedalling on the shoulder of the road, theirs is the only car traversing the countryside.

They have been driving for over an hour – deep, gruff voice on the wheel and Thomas riding shotgun. The car is a rental Thomas borrowed from two English tourists – a dusty Volkswagen hatchback in gun metal grey. They drove out of the city before the first light streaked across the sky, hoping to avoid being followed as they make their way into the countryside.

"They died, Karel," Thomas says quietly. "That's what happened to them."

Apart from the monotonous hum of the air conditioning, the silence in the car is companionable. Staring out the window at nothing in particular, Thomas remembers whispers about a place in Poland. No one knows for sure what happened there except that the trains ferrying human cargo all headed to the same place – a place outside a town known by the old name of Oswiecim. The same one the Germans called Auschwitz. Rumours had it that the Jews were sent there as slave labour for a German factory.

That must be one hell of a giant factory, Thomas thinks silently. He knows better. The trains went there full and always came back empty. No one who enters that place ever leaves.

In the years when he first arrived in America, Thomas had heard stories of prisoners who escaped this place.

"In this place, it's not a matter of *if* you will die but *when* you will die."

Behind the barbed wire fence that ringed the perimeter, terrible things were done to the prisoners – almost all of them Jews. The stories the runaways carried with them to America were so horrific that people found them hard to believe.

"Surely that can't be possible. Hitler was Time Magazine Person of the Year!"

But Thomas knew better.

"They introduced the Labour Repatriation Program after the war was over," Karel pipes up, pulling him back from his reverie. "If you ask me, it's just a fancy name to enslave the Slavic people. Labour Repatriation my ass...."

Thomas listens without saying anything. His mind is far away, remembering a time long gone when his people did not have to carry papers on them when they travel between towns, when they were free citizens of their own homeland, coming and going as they pleased without fear of recrimination. Things are so different now that he worries the passage of time will normalise this slavery. With each passing year, as people of his generation gradually dies off at the hand of age, the memory of their once free land disappears with them, leaving the younger generation with the belief that *this* is normal. *This* is their fate.

He turns and looks at Karel, at the callouses on the hands that now sit on the steering wheel, and the permanent black grease underneath his fingernails. The Karel of his memories was no more than a boy with a glint of mischief in his eyes, brimming with a youthful optimism and an eagerness that was both admirable and infectious.

Years of hard labour have aged him beyond his years, Thomas laments silently as he takes in Karel's tanned, leathery face and the deep lines on his forehead.

The remaining hour of their journey ticks by in silence. As the car moves further and further away from the city, it moves closer and closer to the town of Iglau – once known as the town of Jihlava before the war. From a distance, the cluster of stone buildings beckon to Thomas through the windscreen. He leans forward, his eyes greedily taking in the old churches and monuments that grace the town skyline as they draw closer and closer to their destination.

When finally, the car stops rattling down an uneven cobblestone street, they pull up in front of a row of shophouses on the outskirts of town. Karel kills the engine while Thomas peers up at the shop sign from inside his side of the car window. Without a word, they both climb out of the car, shut the doors behind them and make for the white front door of the hardware store.

A bell tinkles when they push the door open, prompting the lady in a black t-shirt behind the counter to turn and look at them.

"Can I help you?" she says, putting down the catalogue gun in her hand. They march up to the counter, Thomas glancing surreptitiously around and then over his shoulder.

"We are after some slivovice. Do you have any?" Karel asks. Thomas lingers in an aisle, looking – but not looking at the same time – at the green coils of garden hose hanging from the hooks of the metal shelf. He catches the eye of the lady, who studies them briefly before replying, "Wait here, I'll see what I can find."

She disappears behind a door and Thomas busies himself looking through rolls of brown duct tape. Minutes later, the same door opens and the lady in the black t-shirt re-emerges with an old man on her trail. Thomas puts the roll of duct tape back on the shelf and re-joins Karel at the counter.

"Good morning, gentlemen. I understand you are after some slivovice?" The older man's glance skips from Karel to Thomas and then back to Karel again.

Both men nod.

"Unfortunately, we don't have any," the older man says.

Thomas and Karel exchange glances, after which Thomas replies, "In that case, becherovka will do."

The bell tinkles behind them once again and all three men turn in unison to look at the door.

"Evka, look after that gentleman, will you?" the older man says to the lady in the black t-shirt, cocking his head in the direction of the newcomer. To Thomas and Karel, he says, "Come with me."

As Evka flits gracefully to greet the newcomer, Thomas and Karel move behind the counter to follow the older man through the door to the back room. They pass two doors in a narrow hallway, all three men walking in silence, accompanied only by the sounds of their footsteps until they arrive at a third door.

The older man reaches into his pocket and fishes out a ring of keys. Expertly, he picks the right one and jostles it through the keyhole. With a gentle twist, the door clicks open. Without a word, the two men follow him into a cool garage where a car sits quietly in the dimness. Before closing the door, the older man peers out into the hallway to make sure no one is around. In a distance, he hears murmurs of voices talking in the shop. Cautiously, he closes the door and bolts it shut.

"I have to say, I never thought this day would come," the older man says as he turns around to greet both men. "It's so good to see you again, Tomáš."

His business-like demeanour dissolves into a warm, broad smile and the two men slap their hands together in a handshake, which then turns into a hug.

"And you, Ivan," Thomas says, hugging his old friend tightly. After a few pats on the back, the two men separate from their embrace.

"Jan didn't make it," Karel says gravely, answering the question that isn't asked.

"I heard what happened to him. It's terrible but I know he wouldn't have had it any other way," Ivan says thoughtfully, his voice echoing faintly in the garage.

"We don't have much time," Thomas says. "We might be followed by a Kraut or two."

Ivan nods towards the car, picks another key from the ring and unlocks the car doors. The two men climb into the back seat without needing to be told. Karel and Thomas take turns crouching down, climbing into the empty space beneath the seats, custom made for the smuggling of contraband. With Karel's broad built, the space feels small and tight. His long legs jut out from underneath like a pair of prosthetic legs without an owner. Ivan throws a grey blanket over them and gets in the front seat. The front door slams shut and the engine revs to life, followed by the droning of the garage's roller door. Before long, the car is moving – slowly at first, turning onto the street and then rattling over uneven cobblestones. Once it hits the dirt road, the car picks up speed and glides away from the town of Iglau, into another stretch of countryside.

Hidden underneath the seats, in the cramped and stuffy compartment, Thomas loses track of time. All he notices is the stench of sweat mixed with mustiness, and the pain in his body from every jolt of the car when it runs over potholes or crunch over stones. Neither he nor Karel speaks. In the tiny confines of their hiding place, both men are content to remain silent, biding time until the moment they can climb back out again into the daylight and fresh air.

"Shit." Thomas hears Ivan swear.

Up the road ahead, men in military uniform wielding long, black guns are milling around a make-shift barricade. Two army trucks are stationed on either side of the road, from which spill out a few more uniformed men.

"There is a roadblock ahead. Krauts everywhere," Ivan hisses.

Thomas shrinks further, as does Karel. The grey lump that is his legs contract as the car slows to a halt in front of the barricade, its engine still running. "Good afternoon, officers," Ivan says coolly, winding down the window as two soldiers approach his car. "What's with the roadblock?"

"Never you mind," snaps one of the soldiers. "Kill the engine and open your trunk."

Ivan does as he is told. The car engine dies, in its wake is a hollow silence. He presses a button below the steering wheel and the trunk of the car pops open. The two soldiers leave his window, drawn to the opened trunk. In the rear-view mirror, Ivan sees only the trunk lid. He hears the clanging of tools being moved around and a few muffled words being exchanged, then the trunk slams shut and the two soldiers walk slowly around the car – one on either side – shining their torches into the inside of the car.

"That's a lot of tools you have back there, where are you headed?" The first soldier is first to wander back to his window while his colleague continues to examine the inside of the car from the outside.

In the rear-view mirror, Ivan sees the cone of light from his torch lingering on the grey lump on the backseat floor. The soldier is now pressing his face against the window, shading his eyes to get a better view. Ivan's pulse begins to race.

"I'm a plumber," he says calmly, stealing another quick glance at the rear-view mirror before turning to meet the first soldier's gaze. "I'm on my way to a job in Brno."

"Pfffft, Brno!" The soldier snorts. "It's not Brno anymore, old man. We're in the Reich, use the German name!"

"Yes, yes, of course, I'm sorry, officer. I meant Brünn, not Brno," Ivan says with fake compliance.

"Show me your papers," the first soldier demands. Ivan reaches into the glove compartment and pulls out his papers. He hands it over to the officer, who flips through it, carefully checking the information contained within. Ivan uses the opportunity to eye the rear-view mirror. By now, the other soldier has stepped away from the car window. He hears a click and the cone of light disappears. The first soldier hands his papers back and then taps the roof of the car twice as signal for him to go. He turns the ignition back on, nodding gratefully at the uniformed men. The barricade lifts slowly and Ivan drives through it, feigning a smile as he passes the soldiers by.

The car picks up speed once again as they drive through the countryside, the grey lump in the backseat floor fidgeting but not uncovered. The silence that ensues stretch for as long as the drive through the countryside. When eventually the car slows to a halt and the engine killed, Ivan announces they have arrived.

Karel kicks off the blanket and crawls out from underneath their hiding place, grimacing in pain as he straightens his stiff limbs. Thomas does the same.

"I'm too old for this shit," Karel mumbles in his deep, gruff voice. A joint cracks audibly as he flexes his neck.

They get out of the car, which is now parked on a patch of damp grass next to the dirt road, outside a low wooden fence that surrounds a cottage. In the front garden, a doe sits with its legs folded on its side next to a bed of flowers, unperturbed by the strangers who have just emerged from the vehicle. Behind the cottage, a forest of pine trees looms, covered by a thin blanket of mist.

Ivan leads the way, trudging through the muddy footpath, through the unlocked gate and then up the front steps. Karel – still stretching his arms and rolling his shoulders – follows closely behind. Thomas hangs back, taking in the picturesque scene before him. His long journey across the Atlantic Ocean, past the British Isles, over the mass of land now marked as Reich territory culminates in this moment.

Standing outside the low wooden fence of this cottage, the slip of paper safely tucked in his trouser pocket, Thomas is suddenly unsure. He watches nervously as Ivan knocks on the front door, his heart pounding heavily against his chest as he waits with baited breath.

The door opens a sliver and Thomas catches a glimpse of the shadow of a figure. His heart skips a beat. He hears words being exchanged between Ivan and the sliver of the shadow before the door widens further and a figure emerges. Watching the figure step out onto the front porch, Thomas feels his throat catch.

20. ANNELIE

He surveys the café uncertainly. Outside, on the pavement, he double checks the sign to make sure it is the right place before pushing the door open.

Annelie spots him the minute he enters. In a café filled with Europeans, his American-ness is jarring – the oversize shirt with his sleeves rolled up part way to the elbow, his baggy jeans, the white sneakers. All the little details that may seem trivial in his home country – inconsequential even – highlights his foreignness.

She raises her arm in a half wave and catches his eye. Casually, he weaves past the many round tables and bentwood chairs to get to her.

"What's the matter, Annelie?" Jack frowns when he sees her red, puffy eyes. He sits down without being asked, immediately placing a comforting hand on her shoulder.

"Jack, it's horrible... so horrible," Annelie breaks into another round of sobs, her shoulders trembling. His hand finds a home on the small of her back. He rubs it gently but she is inconsolable.

"Tell me what happened," he says, looking earnestly at her, his face merely inches away.

She pauses to study him. Through the tears in her eyes, she sees the tenderness in his gaze. With a deep breath, she dries her eyes and blows her nose with the handkerchief he proffers. Then, slowly, she begins to tell him about the delivery she accepted at the museum earlier that day.

"It's unimaginable," she says with a sniff when she comes to the end. Those images of death haunt her as she sits in the café, surrounded by life. "What have those people done to deserve such a punishment?"

When she looks at him, it is with a pained expression.

Jack is pensive. He studies her without answering immediately. When he finally speaks, it is almost in a whisper.

"It has nothing to do with what they did."

"What do you mean? They are prisoners, I saw the pictures of them in uniform. They must have done something to be put in a place like that." Annelie stares at him with watery eyes.

Jack is quiet when he looks away. When he looks back at her, it is with a grave face.

"Annelie, they were put there because of who they are. Not what they did."

"What are you saying, Jack? I don't understand." Annelie scrunches her brow.

A sharp intake of breath comes from Jack before he adds quietly, "Those people are Jews."

It takes Annelie a moment to register Jack's words. When she looks at him again, she shakes her head in disbelief.

"They can't be! The Jews died from typhus! Everyone knows that."

"*Some* of the Jews died from typhus," he says reluctantly. "The rest of them were… they were… *exterminated*."

Annelie stares blankly into space. Her mind goes quiet before a sudden realisation hits her.

"The Führer… he put them there?" She looks at Jack with wounded disbelief. Jack nods gravely.

"He and his men – Himmler and Heydrich," he says with a sigh.

Annelie stares emptily at the dregs at the bottom of her coffee cup, unable to find the words for her shock.

The Führer? A murderer? That's impossible! She shakes her head in disbelief.

"But the Führer gave us all this." She extends her arms in exasperation.

"Your Führer is not as saintly as you believe him to be, Annelie."

Jack's words cut into her like a knife. She stares at him with wounded eyes, suddenly guarded.

"I know this is a big ask," he says, taking her hand in his. "Do you think you can go back there tomorrow and make some copies of the documents?"

All around them, people are talking in the café, sipping coffees in between forkfuls of pastries. Despite the cacophony of noises, the silence between them stretches out emptily.

There it is, she thinks as her gaze traces the features of his face. *He is using me.*

It is disbelief that she feels first, then an anger she cannot explain. She stares at him, taking in his earnest face and his kind eyes. In that moment, it occurs to her that she knows very little about him, so little in fact it terrifies her to be near him.

When she doesn't speak, it is he who speaks first.

"You don't have to do it if you're not comfortable with it," he says, still holding her hand. "It's a very big ask. And I know it puts you in a very difficult position. I just think that the world needs to know the truth. These kinds of crimes against humanity should not be allowed to go untried and unpunished. No one should be allowed to get away for murdering people – war or no war."

She watches as he speaks, and a wave of admiration washes over her.

"The dead can't speak for themselves, Annelie. It is up to the living to do it."

Tears mist Annelie's eyes once again. Without a word, she leans in, touches his face and kisses him. The tenderness fills her with a new resolve. When their lips part, she opens her eyes and says, "I'll do it."

*

In the deathly silence of the museum, Annelie pads briskly past the many doors along the hallway until she arrives at the Archive Department. Looking around to make sure no one is around, she jostles the key into the keyhole and finds that it is still locked. Quietly, she opens the door to an empty office and gently closes it behind her.

Once inside, she puts her things away in her drawer and begins to find the key to the storeroom. She tries first the drawers of Helga's desk, and smiling, finds it in a box buried in the back of the bottom most drawer, behind a bunch of stapled receipts and wads of yellowing slips tied up with thick rubber bands.

The hour is still early – not even five minutes past seven. If she hurries, she might be able to make copies of all the documents before the others arrive.

She sets to work quickly, unlocking the storeroom door, getting the boxes out one at a time. As she spreads the files open on the desk, running each sheet through the sweeping band of light in the photocopier, she glances over her shoulder every so often to make sure no one is coming.

As the minutes tick by and the copier groans and churns out sheet after sheet, forming a neat pile on the plastic tray, Annelie gets progressively nervous. When she is finished with one box, she returns it to the storeroom and comes back with another.

"The photos are very important," Jack had said to her when they were in the café. "Make sure you get as many copies of that as you can."

While the copier groans and works, she hurriedly stashes the neat stack of copied documents into a box and runs it through the back door into the alleyway where unused cardboard boxes of all kinds lay in a messy heap, waiting to be carted away.

Half way through the photos, she hears voices of people talking echoing from the other end of the hallway, advancing towards the office door. With lightning speed, she sweeps all the photos back into the folders, shoves them all back in the box and runs it back into the storeroom.

She has only just managed to hide the copies when the door opens and both Helga and Klaus Müller appear. He pauses mid-sentence when he spots her standing in the middle of the office, face flushed and out of breath.

"Ah, Annelie, you're here already," Klaus Müller says. "You must be feeling better then?"

Annelie nods quickly, forcing a smile. A look passes between Klaus Müller and Helga. From the tightness around Helga's lips, Annelie begins to suspect something is wrong.

"There is something I would like to discuss with you. Come by my office in ten minutes," it is he who speaks next. The two exchange a brief conclusion to their conversation before Klaus Müller disappears back into the hallway.

"Bring your things with you," Helga remarks brusquely as Annelie gets ready to leave for Klaus Müller's office. Annelie is taken aback.

She knows? Annelie panics in silence. Heart pounding, she does as she is told, gathering her things and taking them with her.

As she walks nervously down the hallway, she spots two police officers standing on the opposite end, at the entrance of the museum. They seem engrossed in conversation, neither of them noticing her presence in the corridor. Her nervousness rises a notch as she knocks on the Museum Director's door and is told by the voice on the other side to come in.

She lingers on the threshold for a brief moment, eyeing the two police officers uncertainly before making her way into the office, closing the door behind her.

"You wanted to see me, Sir?" Annelie says in the absence of any appropriate words to say.

"Yes, please, sit down," he says distractedly, not meeting her eyes.

After she has found herself a seat in the chair in front of his desk, he gets to his feet, his hands slipping into his trouser pockets as he begins to walk around the desk. His footfall is slow and deliberate, heavy with hesitation.

"This is quite a delicate issue, Annelie," Klaus Müller says, looking at her for the very first time. The crease on his brow is pronounced. He looks away almost immediately.

Pulse racing, Annelie waits.

"You are a very bright girl, Annelie," he says with a sigh as he sinks down onto a corner of his desk, facing her. His hands are still tucked in the safety of his trouser pockets. "You are still very young. You still have many years ahead of you."

Here he sighs and swallows audibly before continuing, "Under the right... *circumstances*, you could have gone on to do much more... so much more."

He pauses for a moment, looks at her with a pained expression before exhaling loudly.

"Unfortunately, that is not to be," he says with complete resignation. Annelie frowns uncomprehendingly.

"I received a visit yesterday from the Gestapo," he explains as he straightens up. The desk creaks from being relieved of his weight. "Apparently, there is an issue with your papers."

"My papers?" Annelie's eyes widen as she echoes.

"Your father... he's not your birth father?"

It suddenly becomes clear to Annelie why she is there. The moment she has been afraid of her entire life, the moment her mother had cautioned her against – that moment has finally arrived.

It is the moment of reckoning, of squaring off with Fate. Annelie shuts her eyes and draws in a deep breath. She knows there is no running away from it. Not this time.

When she re-opens her eyes, her voice is small.

"No, he's not."

Her shame forces her to lower her eyes. With nowhere to hide, she sits resolutely still, staring at her lap until her vision becomes blurry.

"Eckhert is not your real name?" she hears Klaus Müller say, pronouncing it more like a statement and less like a question.

She doesn't answer. She doesn't even look up. As drops of tears fall onto her lap, she hears a rustling of paper.

"Your birth name is Anna K... Ka... Kava... Ka-vas-."

"Kvasnicková," she croaks, wiping her nose with the back of a hand. "My birth name is Anna Kvasnicková."

The silence stretches out uncomfortably. Neither of them move. Eventually, he sighs.

"You wanted an education," he says quietly. "A chance at a better life. I get it."

She sniffs without looking at him.

"This thing with the Labour Repatriation Program, it can't be helped," he says. In his voice, Annelie detects a measured regret. "The system is designed to keep the economy functioning. We need people in factories. We need people working in the fields. We need people in the mines. All that is necessary for this nation to be self-sufficient. This nation did not become great without the Labour Repatriation Program. Do you understand this, Annelie?"

Annelie doesn't answer.

"What do you think will happen when everyone is allowed to go to university, get white collared jobs, work for the government? Who will grow our food? Who will work in the mines? Who will make the everyday things we need – clothes, shoes, cars?"

Again, Annelie doesn't answer.

"The back bone of this great nation is its Labour Repatriation Program, Annelie. To you it may be pointless and oppressive but to this nation, it is not. You must see that we are all working for the greater good, not just a personal benefit. Do you see this, Annelie?"

Annelie sniffs stonily.

"The war was won by everyday people, Annelie. Folks who went to work in factories, folks who grew the food and supplies that fuelled the Wehrmacht, folks who kept production going while our soldiers fought for our rights to a better life. There is honour in toiling in the fields and working in the factories. There is honour in keeping this machinery of the Reich well-oiled and running. Surely you must see that?"

If there is so much honour in toiling in the fields, why don't you do it? Annelie thinks bitterly but does not say.

"What's going to happen now?" she asks, finally lifting her watery eyes.

"That's not for me to decide," Klaus Müller says. Her gaze follows him as he walks towards the door. When he opens it, the two police officers are already standing outside. Without another word, they march in. One of them pronounces her offence while the other takes hold of her arms.

Annelie doesn't resist when the handcuffs are placed onto her wrists. She doesn't protest when the officers take her by the elbow and guide her out of the room.

When she steps out into the hallway, her eyes fall on Helga and Marcus. Disdain and disbelief etch on their faces in equal measures as they watch her being shuffled away. With head hung in shame, she walks quietly, escorted by the police officers, out of the museum into broad daylight.

21. THE PAST

September 1941

"Have you heard?" Ivan asked the moment he and Thomas met on the street. "Konstantin von Neurath has been replaced." Without waiting for Thomas to respond, he pulled out a baton of rolled up newspapers and shoved it into Thomas' hands.

It was early morning. A thin mist shrouded the city as they find their way to the bus stop to catch their ride out to the munitions factory. The streets were still quiet ahead of the rush hour. At any moment, the loudspeakers the Nazis had installed at every street corner could crackle to life, announcing a new decree of some sort.

As they walked, their shoes crunching the gravel, Thomas unrolled the baton of newspapers. There, on the top fold of the front page, a picture of a uniformed man with a long face and prominent nose greets him solemnly. He read quickly, eyes glancing up every so often at the road ahead as he walked.

"What do you think? Do you think this Reinhard Heydrich will be like Neurath?" Ivan asked, his steps matching Thomas', equally brisk.

Thomas reflected on Ivan's question, casting his mind back to Jan Opletal's funeral procession from two years earlier.

What happened to Jan Opletal had been a profound misfortune. Everyone thought so. He was a medical student at Charles University who had called for the rise of the Resistance. Thomas didn't know him personally, only that he was at the wrong place at the wrong time. Like many of his peers, Jan Opletal was there at Wenceslas Square on what would have been the Czech Independence Day had they not been occupied by Hitler. The crowd protested the occupation, sang the Czech national anthem and shouted anti-German slogans. There weren't only students there that day, there were other civilians too. The demonstration gathered strength as more and more people joined in. When protestors began to throw stones at German shops, the police fired shots into the crowd.

Two people died. Jan Opletal was one of them.

After his death, Jan Opletal's coffin was laid out and driven through Prague. The funeral procession was a sea of solemn people clad in dark colour clothing. Thousands of students had shown up, and – in their gathering strength – morphed into an anti-Nazi demonstration.

The uprising was met with brute force. Soldiers piled into the streets, chasing down students with their gunfire. In the aftermath, Konstantin von Neurath ordered for all the universities to be shut down. Two thousand students were arrested. Nine student leaders were lined up against the wall and shot. More than a thousand were taken away, their final destination unknown, their fate uncertain.

Thomas and Ivan escaped by a hair's breadth. They were lucky. It all came down to that. Thomas knew then that they were no match for Hitler's army. If they were going to defy the occupation, they had to do it covertly, not overtly.

"If Heydrich is anything like Neurath, the best we can expect is for things to stay the same," Thomas said as they both reached the bus stop just as the bus came trundling down the road, coming to a halt. He rolled the newspaper back into a baton and handed it back to Ivan.

"Time for work, Janiček," he said. "Let's go make some bombs." He winked as the bus door swung open and they climbed in.

As the bus moved out of the city, rattling over the uneven road, Thomas smiled conspiratorially to himself. They may be working in the munitions factory, making missiles for Hitler's army but he knew something that the Nazis didn't – the bombs they make will never go off.

*

"Come sit with me, Tomáš," Grandfather said to him that evening, after curfew was in place. Mother and Sarah were in the kitchen, talking over the chinking of plates and cutlery being washed in the sink. Thomas followed as Grandfather led the way to his room. Once inside, he carefully shut the door and locked it behind them.

"What's going on, Grandfather?" Thomas asked, creasing his forehead. Grandfather did not respond immediately. He moved slowly towards a chest of drawers. There, he raised his eyebrows and pointed at the bottom most drawer. Thomas went over, crouched down and pulled it out.

"Take everything out," Grandfather said as he sank onto the edge of the bed. His knees creaked along with the springs.

Thomas did as he was told, lifting the neatly folded pile of clothes out and placing them on the bed. His hand reached further into the back of the drawer, pulling out rolls of socks before his fingers hit something hard. He crouched further, squinting to get a good look. In the back corner was a paint peeled metal case. Thomas looked up at Grandfather questioningly.

"Take it out," he said.

Thomas did as he was told. The metal case scraped the bottom of the drawer as Thomas slid it out. When he lifted it up, he found that it was heavy. With both hands, he handed the case over to Grandfather before sinking onto the edge of the bed next to him.

"I kept some of the jewellery from being handed over to Hadega," Grandfather said with a wink and a conspiratorial smile. Thomas watched as the lid lifted to the squeak of its rusty hinges. Inside, bulky envelopes were organised in neat compartments.

"There is enough money here for all kinds of emergencies," he said, looking first at the envelopes then at Thomas.

"Why are you telling me this?" Thomas asked urgently.

"Keep the gold only for the direst of circumstances," Grandfather said, patting a brown envelope tucked on the side.

"Grandfather, why are you telling me this?" Thomas creased his brow as he studied the contents of the metal case.

A sigh filled the space between them.

"Tom, I'm not that young anymore, you know that," Grandfather said, placing a warm hand on his. "I need you to be ready. For when I'm no longer here. Do you hear what I'm saying?"

Grandfather looked at him earnestly, waiting for a respond.

Under the orange glow of the halogen bulb, Thomas suddenly noticed the deepening lines and smattering of brown spots on his face. In his eyes, he saw a dimness he did not comprehend. A sour sensation rushed to the tip of his nose and tears began to well up in his eyes.

"There, there, Tom, no need to be upset," Grandfather said, placing a comforting hand on his shoulder. "It's the cycle of life. We are born into this world, we grow old and then we die. It's the natural order of things. There is no escaping it." His voice was paper-thin, almost a whisper.

In the curtain of blurriness that clouded his eyes, Thomas could not tell if Grandfather was smiling or crying quietly. All he knew was that he was not ready for what Grandfather was asking of him. This, he expressed in his heaving shoulders.

"You are much stronger than you believe, Tom," Grandfather said. "I saw it in you the first time I met you." Thomas nodded as he cried but he didn't believe it for himself.

Later, after he had dried his eyes, he returned to the bedroom.

"What's wrong, Tom?" Sarah came to him.

"It's nothing," he mumbled, afraid to meet her eyes. "I'm tired. I'm going to bed."

He peeled off his clothes in silence and put on his pyjamas. Without another word, he climbed into bed and pretended to fall asleep.

That night, when the entire apartment was covered in darkness, quiet with sleep, Thomas lay awake in bed, Sarah stirring next to him. Grandfather's words turned over and over in his head, filling him with a restlessness he could not overcome.

Days after the news of the appointment of Heydrich as the Reichsprotektor, the loudspeaker on the corner of the street announced that all synagogues and Jewish places of worship were now closed. After the announcement, Grandfather went into his room and did not come out for the rest of the day. When dinner time came, Mother knocked on his door and pleaded for him to come out but he refused. The tray of food lay untouched outside his bedroom door until the next morning. After that, he withdrew from life completely, diminishing little by little, until he was nothing but a faint shadow of his former self.

On a cool October evening, not long after the announcement, Thomas returned home from his shift, weary and grimy, to an apartment filled with strangers. A hushed silence fell when he entered the living room. All eyes were on him. He noticed first that they were all dressed in black, then he saw that their eyes were red and watery. When his gaze found Sarah's and he saw the pain in her eyes, Thomas knew immediately.

Without another word, he went over to her. Someone scooted over to make space for him on the sofa. As he sat there surrounded by loud sobs and heaving shoulders, Thomas didn't know what to feel. When the reality finally sunk in, he broke down and began to cry.

22. THE PAST

October 1941

"The funeral will take place before sundown at the New Jewish Cemetery," one of the elders from the defunct Chevra Kadisha said to Thomas after Grandfather's body had been washed and prepared for burial.

Thomas thought pensively, looking from him to the other elders. Within the cold morgue, his voice echoed slightly.

"I'm worried it might draw too much attention to us," Thomas said, a deep crease on his brow.

"What will you have us do?" another elder piped up. All eyes were on him.

Thomas glanced from one to the next. He took in their scraggly beards and their penetrating gaze, his conviction wavering with each passing second. With a crumpled face, he inhaled deeply before voicing his thought. As soon as the words left his lips, a chorus of gasps erupted.

"That's forbidden, Tom!" the elders protested, eyes wide with shock.

"Please forgive me," Thomas said with a small voice as he swallowed the lump in his throat, his eyes misting.

As the linen shrouded body was fed into the crematorium, a collective wail of anguish erupted. Thomas knew he had made the wrong choice as soon as he made it but he saw no other way. He only hoped that Grandfather could forgive him.

No one spoke on their way home. When they sat in silence in the living room afterwards, the grief in the room was palpable. As daylight disappeared and twilight descended on them, Thomas got up pensively, walked over to the wall and flipped the switch. Light sprung from the ceiling lamp, showering an orange glow onto everything in the living room.

"There is something important we need to talk about," he said uncertainly in a small voice. Three pairs of red, puffy eyes lifted in his direction. He walked back to where he was sitting and sank onto a chair. Their gaze followed him. In Amos' eyes, he detected a flash of contempt.

"The Krauts are starting to round people up," Thomas added bravely, looking at all three of them. "It's not safe for us to stay here anymore."

"What are you saying?" Amos was first to speak.

Thomas took his time searching for the right words.

"We...we should leave. Go somewhere safe. Somewhere where nobody knows who we are and... hide for a while."

Thomas looked from one face to the next before looking to Sarah for support. She nodded encouragingly, reaching over to take his hand. He pressed on.

"I found a flat somewhere out of town. It's not much but it will do for now. We can hide there while I figure something out," he said.

"But this is our home...," Mother protested mildly. Her voice came out in a thin whisper, cracking right before she burst into a fresh round of tears.

"I know, Mother." Sarah rushed to comfort her, wrapping her arms around her heaving shoulders. "It'll still be our home after the war. We just need to live somewhere else. Just... just for a while. Just temporarily."

"This is bullshit," Amos said. "I don't care what you say but I'm not moving. You can't make me."

"I'm doing what I think is best for all of us," Thomas said.

"I'm a grown man now, you can't tell me what to do," Amos said defiantly. "We are fine where we are. You heard what Grandfather said before he died, our people have always been seen as the enemy. People hate us and then they forget they hate us. Why can't we just stick it out and wait till this pass? Why do we have to move?"

Thomas inhaled deeply, shutting his eyes.

"Amos," he said, almost pleading when he re-opened his eyes. "We don't know what the Nazis are capable of. Hitler's army is taking over Europe. No one knows what they'll do to us next. Uncle Ludvik and his family have disappeared. We could very well be next."

The atmosphere in the room was growing tense. Thomas stole a quick glance at Sarah and found her watching them both carefully.

"What do you know about what's it like to be us, huh, Tomáš?" Amos cocked his head as he looked at Thomas with narrowed eyes. "Who do you think you are? Your father is a Kraut for goodness sake! You have no clue what our people are like, what we have been through. What gives you the right to think you know what's best for us?"

In Amos' contempt, Thomas heard the unsaid in what was being said. A shiver of guilt ran down his spine.

"Amos." Sarah placed a soft hand on her brother's arm. He shook it off immediately.

"No, this has to be said," he said sternly as he rose to his full height.

Thomas' gaze followed him.

"Amos, please. Don't," Sarah said coldly. Thomas watched quietly, almost cowardly.

"No, this has to be said," he fought back, raising his palm mid-air. Then, turning to Thomas, he gritted his teeth and said, "What you did to Grandfather was an abomination."

His words came out one at a time, punching Thomas in the gut.

"Is it not enough that our people have been humiliated in life? My grandfather had to be humiliated even in death. A CREMATION??? What were you thinking???"

The pain in Amos' eyes stung Thomas more than his words. Thomas turned to meet his wife's teary gaze. In her crumpled face, he saw her sorrow in a different light – one tinted with a shame that could never be erased, a wrong that could never be undone. All at once, Thomas felt like a fraud.

"Amos-" Thomas tried to speak but was instantly cut off.

"No, you don't get to speak this time. This time, you listen," with tears in his eyes, Amos pointed his trembling forefinger in Thomas' face. "You are not the boss of me. You don't get to tell me what to do. I bet you've been waiting for him to die so you can get your greedy hands on our money. Greedy Kraut."

A loud slap cracked the atmosphere. Shock gasps followed.

Thomas' eyes widened in shock. Mother stopped crying and stared in disbelief. Sarah clapped her mouth in horror.

"I'm so sorry, Amos. I didn't mean it!" She fell to her knees immediately, tears gushing from her eyes. Amos stared at her with wounded eyes, nursing his red, throbbing cheek with his hand.

"I knew you would turn on me!" he spat venomously. "You always take his side! ALWAYS!" He pointed to Thomas when he shouted, "I hope you're happy now! You may be the boss of this family but you will NEVER be the boss of me! NEVER!"

Like a gust of wild wind, Amos stormed out.

Thomas watched, in stunned silence, as Sarah ran across the room, her footsteps thudding across the carpet of the living room floor. Numb from the shock, Mother froze on the couch in a daze.

It happened quickly. The front door opened and then slammed shut. It opened again and slammed shut once more. Outside, a set of frantic footsteps circled down the staircase, closely followed by a second set, echoing in the stairwell.

"Amos!!!" Sarah's voice reverberated through the building.

When his common sense returned to him, Thomas got up and rushed out of the apartment.

"Sarah!" it was Thomas' turn to call out as he ran down the staircase.

Two flights of steps below, the main door of the building opened and slammed shut. When he finally reached the bottom, chest heaving with breathlessness, Sarah was on her knees on the street, screaming at Amos' shrinking figure in the distance. Watching her face contorting in anguish, tears running down her cheeks as she wailed in desperation, Thomas' own face crumpled in pain.

What have I done?

When there was all but a tiny speck of Amos left within sight, Thomas picked Sarah up by her elbows and helped her to her feet. With arms wrapped around her trembling shoulders, he guided her back into the building, up the stairs and into the apartment.

"Don't worry. Once he's calmed down, he'll come back," he said. She nodded as she sobbed, neither of them entirely assured.

For the next seven days, Thomas, Sarah and Mother sat in silence for Grandfather's shivah. Now and then, visitors came and sat with them, offering words of comfort during their time of sorrow but both Mother and Sarah were inconsolable. Grandfather was gone and Amos never came back.

"No one's seen him, Tom," Ivan delivered the grave news on the eighth day. "We've looked everywhere and spoken to every person we can possibly think of. No one's seen him."

The two of them were in the kitchen, speaking in low tones. Thomas sighed audibly, visibly in pain. Sinister scenarios taunted him, tormenting him with their multitude of possibilities.

Has he gone into hiding?
Did he go looking for Uncle Ludvik? What if he had been caught?
Worse yet, what if he had been shot?

Thomas felt nauseated as he imagined Amos lying in a puddle of blood on the street somewhere in Prague, stepped over by indifferent passers-by.

"Do you still want to do it or not?" Ivan asked, bringing Thomas back from his reverie.

"Yes," he said, uncertainly at first, then with more conviction. "Yes, let's do it."

Two days later, their suitcases were packed. When darkness fell, just before curfew was to begin, Ivan came with two others. Quietly, they ferried the bags out of the apartment, down the stairs into the back alley, into the trunk of a parked car. Then, the engine came to life and drove their bags off into the black night.

The next morning, after the breakfast dishes had been washed and dried, a knock came over the door.

"Time to go," Thomas said, cocking his head towards the door. Sarah nodded, taking Mother's hand as they hurried to leave. As he cast a final glance around the living room before leaving the apartment, Thomas silently bade their home goodbye. When the door was shut and the key turned in its lock, he knew then it would be the last time he would see that apartment in Josefov.

23. GUNTHER

"Never in my life...," Gunther grumbles as he fumbles through the dark hallway. His hand pats around on the wall for the light switch. When he finally finds it, he flicks it on but nothing happens. Perplexed, he flicks it off and then on again. Still, nothing happens.

"For heaven's sake, what did they think I was going to do? *Steal* the electricity?" he grumbles into the darkness. Begrudgingly, he meanders the length of the hallway towards the kitchen, guided by his memory and the feel of his outstretched hands.

The mansion is eerily quiet now that the officers are gone. He had remained in the garden the entire time the men were combing his home. What they were searching for, Gunther could only guess. He is hardly a suspect of espionage, much less a cohort of the Resistance. At this thought, Gunther chortles. Him – a member of the Resistance? He laughs bitterly. His laughter echoes through the cavernous hallway of his mansion.

"At least I got to watch the sun set," he mumbles to himself.

That afternoon, as his home was being ransacked behind him, Gunther sat on a bench outside, studying his well-manicured English garden. From his vantage point on the veranda, the acreage stretched out before him in symmetrical precision, as if someone upstairs had placed a stencil over the land and traced the garden into existence. All at once, Gunther was overwhelmed by its beauty – by the neatly trimmed hedges, the delicate roses in their bushes and the majestic stone statue of Neptune in the middle of the pond.

As he sat there in a pensive mood, Gunther regretted not spending more time in his garden. He could have enjoyed his tea there in the mornings or a leisurely after dinner stroll on warm summer evenings. It would have made a splendid place for a children's picnic or a festive dinner party. But he was always too busy for those flights of fancy so the garden was left idle – underappreciated and underutilised in all the years of its existence.

On this day, when the loss of his garden became imminent, Gunther suddenly felt the urgency to cherish his garden, to enjoy it and appreciate it for all its glory. There he sat, under the clear blue of the sky, taking in every detail of his magnificent garden, at the same time lamenting a future devoid of it.

When the sky turned a mélange of pink, orange and purple hues, Gunther realised he was only really seeing the sun set for the very first time. He marvelled at how quickly the sun sinks in the horizon and how orange it looks, like the yolk of the soft-boiled eggs he used to have for breakfast in the countryside of Moravia when he was a little boy.

He hadn't noticed when the last of the military trucks left, only the silence that filled their absence. When the sun finally retired for the day, taking along with it the last streak of daylight, and as twilight punched in its time card, Gunther got to his feet and turned to go back into the house. His home, once full of life with brightly lit windows was but a shell encasing pitch darkness and pin drop silence. For the first time since returning from the hospital, Gunther feels immensely lonely.

Inside the house, Gunther rummages through the kitchen drawers and manages to find a box of matches along with a few stumps of candles. He lights a candle and uses it to light a few more, twisting them into the holders of the candelabra. Candelabra in one hand, with a small circle of flickering orange light around his face, he walks back through the cavernous hallway.

"Ah, Van Gogh." He sighs as he stops in front of the painting Starry Night Over the Rhone. "Of all the things in this house, I will miss you the most." He holds up the candelabra, casting the circle of flickering orange glow over the painting to study it closely. He fingers the bumpy strokes of paint on the canvas, caressing it gently with his fingertips before withdrawing to the kitchen. When he returns, it is with a knife in hand.

"If I can't have you, neither can they," Gunther says, taking the knife to the canvas. He stabs it ferociously, slashing it this way and that, shredding the painting to bits. Like the pieces of a jigsaw puzzle waiting to be put back together, the mangled strips of canvas fall to the floor and land in a messy heap. When he finally stops to catch his breath, Gunther is stunned by what he has just done. In a matter of seconds, he single-handedly destroyed a painting that was over a hundred years old. A painting that he loved more than all the others.

His bewildered gaze surveys the damage, tracing the bronze frame and the carcass of what was once Starry Night Over the Rhone. His gaze falls onto the pile of debris on the floor, registering the scraps of canvas, its colours now muddled in a heap, beyond recognition.

At first, Gunther is shocked by his senseless act but this shock is quickly replaced by a nameless euphoria. Wiping the beads of sweat from his forehead, he feels the rush of adrenalin coursing through his veins. It feels good. For the first time since returning from the hospital, Gunther feels alive.

Like a drug addict in search of his next fix, Gunther looks wildly around for something else to slash. With the candelabra in one hand and the knife in the other, he finds his next victim in Rembrandt. Setting the candelabra down on the floor, Gunther takes his knife to the canvas, stabbing Rembrandt right in the heart of his huge canvas. With both hands on the handle, he drags the knife through the cloth, slashing it downwards and then sideways, left then right. Then left and right again. The sound of the cloth ripping fills him with glee and spurs Gunther to slash with gusto. When finally, the painting is mangled beyond recognition, Gunther stands back to admire his work while he catches his breath. He then proceeds to do the same with all the other paintings hanging along the hallway.

"Ah, job well done, Scholz. Job. Well. Done. That was one hell of a good work out." Gunther huffs in satisfaction after the last of the painting has been destroyed. He pauses to catch his breath, wiping the beads of sweat on his forehead with the back of his hand before picking up the candelabra and walking back to the kitchen to put the knife away, a path of littered canvas scraps in his wake.

Gunther hums all the way to the kitchen. All that physical exertion has put him in a good mood, and also worked up a great appetite. As he stands in the kitchen, patting a growling belly, Gunther tries to recall when was the last time he ate.

"Breakfast at the hotel," he mumbles to himself, recalling the piping hot omelette with a side of fatty sausages and buttered bread rolls. The thought of the morning's breakfast makes his mouth water so he opens the fridge to see what he can find.

With the aid of the candelabra, Gunther surveys the contents of the fridge. He finds an opened carton of milk and an opened packet of sliced cheese on the top shelf. Loosely wrapped in a butcher's paper are a few slices of ham – dry and hard around the edges – on the second shelf, followed by an apple and a small bunch of shrivelled grapes in the fruit bin. In the vegetable crisper, he finds scraps of wilted lettuce leaves stuck to the bottom.

"The scullery maid needs to do a better job at cleaning the fridge…." Gunther frowns at the scraps of wilted lettuce leaves as he shoves the crisper back in disgust. He reaches for the shelves and picks up the packet of sliced cheese, the package of ham and carton of milk before slamming the fridge door shut.

He sets all the food down on the counter and wanders over to the pantry to see what else he can find. When he opens the door, he is greeted by the sight of white powder scattered across the shelves and the floor. Jars and tins lay opened haphazardly, their contents spilling out, creating a big mess.

"What did they think they will find here? Gold bars in the flour jar?" Gunther huffs angrily as he spots the bootprints in the flour dusted floor. He surveys the chaos in the pantry, rummaging through the spilled sugar, beans and dry pasta for anything edible. His forage yields him a teabag, a tin of sardines and a stick of butter completely untouched in the butter dish. He returns to the kitchen counter and plonks it all down before going back to scrounge for more. From the bread bin, he finds a hunk of bread. Under the flickering candle light, Gunther finds spots of green mould around the edges. He brings it back to the kitchen counter, peels off the chunks of mould and takes a knife to cut two thick slices for himself. With the spoils of his forage, he slathers the two slices of bread with a generous knob of butter and then sloppily piles all the ingredients together to make himself a sandwich of sliced cheese, ham and sardines.

"Never in my life…," Gunther mutters to himself as he looks through the kitchen cabinet, opening and shutting doors until he finds the one with the crockery. He fishes himself a plate for his sandwich and takes a teacup for his tea. Then he remembers the electric kettle won't work without electricity and settles for a cup of milk instead.

When he finally sits down to dinner, darkness has completely engulfed the house. With only the flickering candles from the candelabra as company, Gunther eats in silence in the vast dining room. He sits at the head of the table, gazing down the long stretch of empty dining chairs on either side, wondering what his wife is doing at that exact moment.

The envelope with his name scrawled across it is still sitting on the table in the entrance hall. Gunther has no desire to read the letter inside. He already knows what to expect. Later that night, when he goes upstairs to get ready for bed, he will walk into the walk-in closet and see empty hangers where Lotte's blouses and dresses once hung. The drawers of her dressing table would be empty of her bottles of perfume and jars of cream. The jewellery in the safe would be gone too, he is sure of it.

"When do you think she made up her mind to leave me?" Gunther speaks aloud into the darkness, at no one in particular. "Was it when I was in the hospital? Or was it when I was in Krakau?"

His questions are met with complete silence. Staring blankly ahead, Gunther takes a bite of his sandwich, chewing it slowly and then swallowing it deliberately, audibly.

"She must be in Paris," he adds, taking another bite. The bread is stale and the cheese is dry and hard but Gunther pays no attention and keeps chewing. He imagines his wife sipping champagne within the opulence of La Tour D'Argent, sitting at the table next to the window affording the best view of the Notre Dame and the river Seine. When the Sommelier comes over to proffer her the wine list, she will flirt with him – a slight touch of his hand, a tilt of her head and some harmless banter. She throws her head back when she laughs, making him feel significant, like he is the only man in the world. The Sommelier had always taken a shine towards her, with her charming smile and perfect French (the French still refuses to speak German even though it is the official language of the Reich). With the husband out of the picture, there is no telling what he might try.

Gunther snorts at that thought.

When the waiter comes over to take her order, he knows she will order the pressed duck – not because she enjoys it (she eats like a bird) but because it is in keeping with appearances. When the dish arrives, she will pick at it and push her food around the gold-plated dinner plate with her fork, making a show of eating it when she is anything but.

"What a waste of a good pressed duck....," Gunther spouts. The juice from the sardines drip down his chin but he doesn't bother to wipe it away. He chews slowly, masticating his food in his mouth absently.

She wouldn't be dining alone, of course. Gunther knows this. Instead, she will be surrounded by her gaggle of Parisian girlfriends, each trying to outdo the other with their sparkly diamonds and flashy jewellery.

"As commoners do," Gunther says with spite. No woman of class would brazenly deck herself in all that jewellery, looking like a chandelier walking down Champs Elysees.

At the end of the night, when the bill arrives, Lotte will reach for her purse, playfully slapping away her friends' hands as they play-fight for the bill (they never really mean it).

Don't be silly, this one's on me. She will say. She makes a show of opening her purse and fishing out her black credit card while discreetly watching the envy on their faces.

"The bank accounts must be frozen by now," Gunther continues to direct his monologue at the emptiness before him. A sudden realisation flashes before his eyes, lifting the corners of his mouth into a sly smile. "I wonder how she is going to pay for dinner when she realises her credit cards have been cut off...." At this thought, Gunther laughs heartily and takes a celebratory drink from his cup, his laughter echoing in the high ceiling of the cavernous dining room.

"Serves her right for leaving me," he says as he sets his cup down, chomping into his sandwich.

"Serves her right for leaving me," he echoes with his mouth full and finishes the rest of his meal in silence.

*

In the small hours of the night, Gunther wakes to a commotion. He is still half asleep when he hears voices of people shouting coming from the street. Beyond his bedroom window, he can hear voices shouting unintelligible words. He sits up in bed, groggy and in a foul mood until the sound of glass shattering downstairs wakes him fully. In no time, he swings his legs out of bed, reaches for the revolver in the bedside drawer and dashes down the stairs in the darkness, two steps at a time.

Half way down the staircase, he is greeted by a cloud of black smoke. The thick fumes rush up his nostrils, choking him, making him cough. Gunther dashes back upstairs to his room and picks up the phone to call the emergency services. After that, he quickly grabs a blanket and runs into the bathroom, turning on all the taps, dousing the blanket in a gush of cold water. Then, draping the wet blanket over himself, he cowers and makes a dash down the staircase once more.

The plume of black smoke has thickened in the minutes he was away. The fumes sting his eyes and instantly make them water. Instinctively, Gunther pulls the corners of the wet blanket over his face, trying to stay as low as possible. When he gets to the bottom of the staircase, a searing heat forces him back. Out of the corners of his eyes, he sees the angry red flames ravaging the furniture in the parlour, crackling uproariously as they devour his prized possessions. In the far end of the room, on the feature wall, the corners of Emperor Hirohito's Japanese painting begin to curl as fire crawls over it. Gunther feels an urge to run to it, to rescue what is left of it but the flames block his way. The heat growls at him like a wild beast and his common sense returns quickly.

Through the thick cloud of black smoke and the deafening roar of flames, Gunther manages to find the front door and stumbles out onto the front porch. He coughs and splutters as he runs barefooted down the long, curved driveway, away from the house, whereupon he spots a few lurking shadows scampering off in the distance.

"Bastards!" he yells at the top of his lungs, punching the air with a clenched fist. "You will never get away with this!!!"

The shadows cackle with laughter as they disappear from view but Gunther has neither the desire nor the willingness to run after them.

"Bastards!" he yells once more, his face scrunched up in anger. When he turns around to face the house, his eyes widen with horror. On the outside wall of his home of twenty-five years, the arsons had sprayed red graffiti on the cream colour wall.

BURN IN HELL YOU DIRTY SLAV.

Those words send a rush of blood to his face and Gunther begins to shake uncontrollably.

"I AM NOT A DIRTY SLAV!!!" he shouts angrily, first at the wall, then at the phantom of the cackle of laughter in the distance.

The sound of sirens could be heard in a distance, growing louder as the fire engines fast approach him. When the first engine turns into his street, he stands at the bottom of the driveway, waving his arms high in the air to get their attention. When the headlights finally train on him, Gunther runs forward to meet the advancing fire engine.

"Over there! Over there!" he shouts as he points up the driveway. The engines are killed and the firemen leap from their trucks, getting to work speedily. By this time, lights begin to appear in the windows of neighbouring houses. Front doors open, and neighbours dressed in their pyjamas step out onto their front porch to witness the commotion. A handful even make their way out onto the street, gathering at the bottom of the driveway in a cluster, watching the plumes of grey smoke rising into the dark sky.

Gunther feels embarrassed by the graffiti on the wall. He wants to cover it with something so that the neighbours don't see it but the words are right in front of them, big and bold, in striking red paint while the orange flames rages against the backdrop of an inky sky.

BURN IN HELL YOU DIRTY SLAV.

They must think I deserve it, Gunther thinks as he looks at them sullenly, the shadow of the flames dancing on their faces. He sighs dejectedly, watching, along with the others, the firemen pointing the nozzle of their long hoses at the raging flames. The gush of water comes out in a magnificent spray, altogether deafening. Except for the loud exchanges between the firemen, no one speaks.

The fire is put out by the first light of day. The crowd disperses, leaving Gunther all alone, standing barefooted at the bottom of his driveway, forlorn and exhausted.

"There is a bit of damage but it's all contained to the two front rooms. Do you have somewhere you can go?" the fire chief asks as his men roll up their long hoses and prepare to leave. Gunther's glance goes from the blackened windows of the house to their soot-covered uniforms and tired faces.

"Yes," Gunther says distractedly, shaken by the events of the night. "I will go to my daughter's and stay with her for a while. Thank you for all your help."

They exchange a handshake and the fire chief goes on his way.

Gunther watches as the men pile back into their trucks, the engines rev to life and, one at a time, the fire engines pull out of his driveway and onto the street. As they drive off, he waves at them, his gaze never leaving the backs of the shrinking trucks until they move further and further away and disappear completely from view.

Surrounded only by silence, Gunther turns and walks back up his driveway. In broad daylight, the graffiti seems less menacing. If anything, the words are clumsily painted, like the scrawling of a child learning to write for the first time. Gunther takes one more look at it, sighs and then goes inside the house. The smell of burnt wires immediately stings his nostrils. His coughs a little but remains undeterred. A little worse for wear, he mills around the soot-covered hallway outside the damaged rooms, peering into the parlour to size up the extent of the damages.

All his possessions in the parlour are gone. In their places are blackened carcasses of what they once were. Shards of crystal from the broken chandelier litters the blackened floor. In the middle of the room, Gunther sees broken pieces of blackened glass and a burnt rag – the Molotov Cocktail that started it all. The souvenir of hate that the vandals gifted him in the small hours of the night.

Gunther gazes wistfully around the room, resting finally on the blackened feature wall where the Japanese painting once hung. All that remains of the painting are the charred edges of the bamboo frame. All at once, he feels an emptiness he has never felt before – a sense of overwhelming defeat.

When he is done surveying the damage, Gunther turns around and slowly makes his way up the soot-covered stairs, his bare feet blackened, his pyjamas catching the ash and the soot from the remnants of the fire all the way to the top.

He returns to his bedroom, greeted first by the sight of his unmade bed and then the revolver on the bedside table, its drawer still opened. Most of his things are untouched, covered only by sprinkles of black dust. Gunther proceeds to clean himself up as best as he can. He takes a shower with the cold water, then he finds some clean clothes in the drawers and puts them on absently. Afterwards, he fills a big suitcase with his uniform, his best suit, two dinner jackets, his favourite coat, two pairs of shoes, a few shirts, trousers and whatever else he can fit in. The rest he leaves behind – pressed shirts still hanging from hangers, silk ties rolled up in their individual boxes in his tie drawer, polished shoes made from Italian leather, glittering cufflinks, cashmere sweaters and merino wool coats. He sighs with resignation as he stands in his walk-in closet, staring at every item of clothing he owns.

"Such a shame," he laments. He will miss the cashmere sweaters and the merino wool coats the most. Winter in Germania can be unforgiving but he decides not to think about it for now. He proceeds to go through the drawers and cupboards thoughtfully, picking only the belongings he can't bear to part with. The others, he leaves them exactly where they are. Once he is done squeezing the two sides of his suitcase together and zips it shut, Gunther calls himself a cab.

The suitcase is heavier than expected and he spends an inordinate amount of time getting it down the staircase one step at a time. By the time he reaches the bottom, Gunther is severely out of breath. Beads of sweat cover his forehead, and his shirt stains in two patches under the armpits. He pulls out his handkerchief and wipes his face, his breath returning to him. Then, with a final glance around the house, he lugs his bag out the front door without much fanfare.

Standing at the top of the driveway in front of a singed window, Gunther watches the speck of yellow slowly approaching, growing larger and larger as it crawls up the driveway. When the cab grinds to a halt with its engine still running, Gunther opens the door and shoves his suitcase into the backseat. He then climbs in next to it, giving the driver the address. The driver notices the graffiti on the wall and casts a glance in the rear-view mirror. A look passes between them.

"I'm sorry, Sir, I can't take you to your destination," the man says politely, looking away from the rear-view mirror. "Please get out of the car."

"What?" Gunther frowns in disbelief. "I have money. Look." He reaches into his trouser pocket and pulls out a wad of cash, holding it up so that the cab driver can see it.

"I'm sorry but it's the law," the cab driver steels himself. "Please. Get out of the car."

"This is ridiculous! How am I going to get to Mitte from here?" Gunther wails in exasperation.

"There is a bus stop at the junction. That will take you into the centre of town. From there, you can catch the U-bahn to Mitte."

Unhappily, Gunther gets out of the car with his suitcase in tow, grumbling the entire time. He makes a show of slamming the door, to which the driver responds by stepping on the gas and speeding off, tyres screeching.

"I AM NOT A DIRTY SLAV!" he shouts at the back of the cab, at the trail of exhaust fumes in its wake.

"I am not a dirty Slav," to himself, Gunther repeats quietly, as if by convincing himself, he can convince the world.

After the cab disappears, he inhales deeply, his gaze falling on the mansion across the street. Hit by a sudden stroke of inspiration, Gunther wheels his heavy suitcase down the driveway, across the street and up the ramp to the Schneiders'.

The journey exhausts him, and, for the second time that day, Gunther finds himself all puffed out with sweaty armpits. When he has sufficiently recovered, he rings the front door bell and waits. On the other side of the door, voices murmur and footsteps thump in the hallway. He hears a shuffling and then the door opens a sliver. From behind it peers the housekeeper cautiously. When she sees that it is him, she opens the door wider.

"Good morning, Herr Scholz," she greets warmly.

"Good morning," Gunther says. His gaze follows hers, which falls on the suitcase by his feet. "I was wondering if Dieter and Emilia can spare me the driver for the afternoon?"

The housekeeper brings her gaze back to him and feigns a smile.

"I'm sorry, Herr Scholz," she says. "Master and Madam are not home."

"What about the driver?"

"Oh, he is out as well."

Gunther recalls seeing the car parked outside the garage on his way in. His brow crinkles with confusion. Then, it dawns on him. With mixed emotions, he forces a smile and says, "That's all right. It's not your fault."

"Good day, Herr Scholz," she says.

"Good day."

The door closes and Gunther's face falls. A sigh escapes him.

With slumped shoulders, he wheels his suitcase down the ramp. The wheels crunch the gravel noisily, catches a pebble and tips over. The suitcase falls in a loud crash, tumbling a few more times down the ramp. When he finally manages to catch up to it, Gunther looks up and catches a moving shadow in an upstairs window. Behind a ruffled curtain, he spots the shadow of a familiar face. At first, she shrinks away. Then, as if changing her mind, she steps out in full view, staring coldly at Gunther.

Madam is home after all, Gunther thinks.

He looks at her with a wistful smile then, with a resigned sigh, Gunther turns and walks away. He knows the life he is so desperately trying to cling on to is now a thing of the past.

24. THE PAST

February 1942

"Did you get any food?" Sarah appeared from the bedroom the moment Thomas closed the front door of their flat. Thomas smiled as he held up the bulging hessian bag in his clutch. Mother looked up from where she was sitting, her glasses low on the bridge of her nose, a threaded needle pinched between two fingers in one hand and an old coat in the other. She smiled briefly and then resumed her sewing.

"I got a loaf of bread, some jam, carrots and potatoes," he said. She wandered over and greeted Thomas with a quick peck. Placing a hand on her belly, Thomas added, "How are we doing today?"

The shape of a tiny foot poked out from underneath her sweater. A smile passed between Sarah and Thomas. Very soon, they would be bringing a new life into the world. Almost constantly, Thomas wrestled with his anxiety.

Ever since Heydrich became the Reichsprotektor, hundreds have been arrested, tortured, then shot or hung. In the wake of the executions, families were forced to cough up compensation to the Gestapo for the expenses and the inconvenience. Fear fell over the city. Everywhere, people went about their lives with frayed nerves, afraid that they would be next.

The moment they discovered Sarah was with child, Thomas was on edge. For the first few months, she was terribly ill. Out of fear of being discovered, they did not seek out a doctor. Thomas and Mother took turns nursing her, feeding her sips of water and dry biscuits, changing the damp towel folded over her burning forehead every so often. Then the worst passed and she began to mend.

"Baby's been kicking a lot today," Sarah said, eyes lowered as she stroke the bulge of her belly. "Do you think it's stressed?"

Thomas straightened to looked at his wife, at her sunken cheeks and the dark rings underneath her eyes. Her once shiny dark hair was tied back in a limp messy bun, her skin a pale dullness, not having seen sunlight for months. When she breathed, wisps of white fog blew from her nostrils. That sight cut into Thomas' heart.

He reached over to adjust the overcoat draped over her shoulder, too small now to wrap around her belly. Despite her growing bump, her shoulders were bony underneath the coat. The occupation was taking a toll on her, that much was obvious.

He exhaled silently, squeezing her shoulders as a measure of reassurance even though deep down, Thomas was less than assured himself.

He looked around the living room, at the basic furniture cramped in the small square footage. His gaze fell on Mother, who sat squinting in the dimness, her face so close to the old coat she was mending that it was almost impossible to tell where the old coat ended and her face began. They had run out of firewood for the heating stove the night before and the dampness in the flat meant that they were never quite warm enough.

Life could be much worse, couldn't it? he thought as he returned to Sarah. In her eyes, he saw that she had the same thought.

Their new home was in Žižkov, in a two-bedroom flat in the damp basement of an apartment building. There were two flats in that basement – theirs and another with a front door painted a dark green. Across the landing, the green front door creaked opened and closed several times a day. Occasionally, Thomas would press his ear to the door to the sounds of shuffling footsteps. As for voices of people talking, there were none.

His landlady had mentioned that a writer and two of his friends lived in the flat across the landing. Who this writer was, Thomas didn't know. Neither would he recognise his neighbours if he had seen them on the street in broad daylight. They moved around like phantoms, slinking in and out at all hours of the day, sometimes even during curfew.

The day they moved in, they had been careful to do it during the hours when most people were out. Since going into hiding, Thomas himself had stopped working in the factory. He went out only rarely – under the direst of circumstances when they desperately needed food, medicine or firewood for the stove. Otherwise, the three of them spent their days indoors, away from the public eye.

Weeks after they had settled in their new home in Žižkov, Ivan brought news that the Jewish Council had been knocking on people's doors, handing out notices to those on their list that they were to be rehomed. They had a few days to settle their affairs, and then to gather their things and assemble at the fair ground near Stromovka Park.

"They were there for ages," he said in almost a whisper. "All of them – men, women, children. No one knows what went on in that place. There were at least a thousand of them, all marching out of the fair ground, carrying their suitcases. The whole sidewalk was just a sea of people walking to Bubny station. Rumour has it that there, they were put on trains to go to Poland."

Thomas listened gravely without saying anything. He stole a glance at Sarah and Mother before returning his attention back to Ivan.

"What about Amos? Has anyone seen him?" Thomas asked. His question was met with a resigned shake of the head.

"Keep looking," he added, clapping his friend by the shoulder.

Then, Ivan was gone.

That night, Thomas lay in bed staring into the darkness at a ceiling he could not see. He felt a warm hand on his chest as Sarah snuggled up to him. He pulled her in with an arm around her shoulder while her head rested on his.

"Don't worry," she whispered, stroking his chest. "It will be over soon. Everything will be all right."

"Will it?" His question hung in the air, his tone full of doubt. He reached for her hand in the dark and clutched it tightly, fearful that if he fell asleep, she might be taken away in the dark of the night.

The next time Ivan visited, Thomas confided in him.

"I'm worried the Jewish Council will track us down here," he whispered as they sat in the kitchen. "We need to move somewhere where nobody will find us. Somewhere far from here."

Ivan watched him carefully, thought for a moment before saying, "There is a guy." He looked around first and then got up to close the kitchen door before lowering his tone further.

"He's part of the underground. He's helped a few people go into hiding. You will need to give him some money, for train tickets and stuff. He can get you false papers if you need them."

Thomas studied Ivan carefully as he listened. He had heard stories about people smugglers who turned out to be collaborators of the Gestapo's, trying to capture those on the 'wanted' list who were trying to escape. His suspicions were cemented at the mention of money. War did that to people – the opportunistic found ways to profit from others' suffering without the burden weighing on their conscience. If he had felt a shred of suspicion towards his old friend, he did not show it.

"Let me talk it over with Sarah and Mother," was all he said.

They never talked about it again.

Since then, more trains had been sighted departing from Bubny station, ferrying thousands of Czech Jews to a new destination – Terezín, an old military fortress built during the Habsburg dynasty some forty miles outside of Prague, known then as Theresienstadt. No one knew for sure what went on in Terezín and what actually happened to those people who left on the train. But wherever they were, Thomas was sure it was no better than their own home.

Later that day, to everyone's relief, Ivan came bearing some much-needed firewood for the stove.

"Tell me about this guy in the underground," Thomas finally said when the two of them were alone in the kitchen.

"Why don't you meet with him yourself?" Ivan said in a hushed tone. "There is a basement bar in Nové Město. He is there most days. I'll get word to him to expect you."

Curfew was upon them. In no time at all, Ivan was gone.

In the morning, Thomas woke up to find a note slid in from underneath the door. After reading it, he went into the bedroom where Sarah was still sound asleep. Quietly, he pulled out the suitcase from underneath the bed, opened it and removed the paint-peeled metal case. Kneeling on the floor, he lifted the lid to a loud squeak.

On the bed, Sarah stirred, rolled over and continued to sleep, snoring lightly. Very quietly, Thomas removed the wads of cash from the envelopes, thumbing through the corners, counting them quickly. He took only what he needed. The rest he stuffed back into the metal case, carefully closing the lid and putting it back into the suitcase under the bed.

That afternoon, he went out into the street nervously, the wads of cash stuffed in his coat pockets and the soles of his shoes. He moved discreetly, careful to watch out for any signs that he might be followed. A short distance away from the flat, he hopped onto a tramcar, which took him most of the way into town.

It did not take him long to find the address scribbled on the note. When he arrived, he found the small statue of the Madonna hanging over the arch of an old wooden door, as described. After looking around the busy street, he stealthily made his way down the stairs and disappeared into the basement bar.

Inside, the dimness gave no indication that it was daytime. Thomas looked around the room – empty save for a few men nursing half-empty glasses of beer. He approached the bartender and signalled for a drink.

"I'm here to buy Jan a slivovice," he said quietly. The bartender surveyed him briefly.

"Jan's out the back." He cocked his head towards the back of the room before returning to polishing glasses.

With nervous apprehension, Thomas surveyed the dark corners of the room. In one of them, he saw a man writing in a thin notebook under the dim orange light, a lit cigarette between two fingers of his left hand.

"Slivovice?" Thomas asked when he was standing over him.

"Who wants to know?" The man looked up, his eyes squinting as he draws from the lit cigarette. A cloud of smoke puffed in Thomas' face, making him cough.

"Tomáš," he replied after he had collected himself.

"I don't have any slivovice," the man replied dismissively, returning his gaze to the tiny words scribbled in his thin notebook.

"Becherovka then," Thomas replied.

"Have a seat."

As Thomas sat down, Jan signalled to the bartender. Neither of them spoke as they waited for the drinks to arrive. Jan studied him carefully, sucking on the cigarette now pinched between his thumb and forefinger.

"So, you're a friend of Ivan's?" he asked coyly. The drinks arrived – two small glasses filled to the brim with liquid. Thomas nodded. Jan was first to pick up a glass. Thomas followed suit. Without another word, the two men raised their glasses to each other, brought the rim to their lips and tipped them back with a swift flick of their wrists. The liquid burned all the way down his throat. For the second time in minutes, Thomas spluttered and coughed.

"Ivan tells me you need a passage," Jan said, setting down the empty glass. It hit the table with a loud chink.

Thomas nodded.

"For three."

"We have a shipment leaving in two days. Train to Hungary, then to Greece. Then by boat to Britain."

"Is it safe?" Thomas asked.

"Of course not. What do you think this is – *a holiday*?" Jan said evenly, drawing another puff from the cigarette. The orange ember curled the tip of the cigarette into grey ash. He tipped it into the small glass bowl on the table before adding, "But don't worry, we've never lost a cargo. Pick up at 3 p.m. inside the Hotel Fiser. Pack only the essentials. One suitcase per person."

Thomas reached into his coat pocket to pull out the cash but was immediately stopped by Jan.

"Not here," Jan whispered, stubbing out his cigarette. "Men's bathroom. In the cubicle closest to the wall, there is a tin in the water tank. Put it there." He signalled to the bartender again. Two small glasses of drink appeared. They drank, less ceremoniously this time.

After exchanging a final handshake, Thomas rose to leave. Jan reached into his coat pocket and pulled out a packet of cigarettes, slid one out and lit it.

The men's bathroom was at the end of a narrow corridor. When Thomas found it, there was no one in there. Under the dim orange light, Thomas locked himself in the only toilet cubicle and pulled out the wads of cash from inside his shoes and coat pockets. Carefully, he rolled them up in a tight bundle, secured it with a rubber band and stuffed it into the round tin in the water tank. For safe measure, he pulled the flush before he left.

When he passed the bar once again, Jan was nowhere to be seen. He made his way up the stairs two steps at a time. When he stepped out onto the street into broad daylight, something hard hit him on the back of the head. A blinding pain shot through him. He fell to the ground, hitting the cobblestone street face first. Then the world went black.

25. THE PAST

February 1942

Thomas awoke to a splash of cold water. The iciness shocked him, instantly rousing him from grogginess. He squinted into a blinding light and shook his head of the dripping iciness, altogether disoriented and confused.

When he came to, a voice barked unintelligibly at him. The loudness hurt his ears. He winced – both from the assault to the senses as well as from the aches in his body from being bent in an awkward position for too long – but he did not respond immediately.

After the initial shock of iciness had worn off, Thomas found himself sitting in the middle of a small room. His neck was sore on the nape and his head was throbbing with pain. He tried to move but discovered quickly that his hands were tied behind the back of the wooden chair, cuffed by cold metal. He tried anyway, tugging this way and that, finally relenting when the stubborn steel began to cut into his wrists. His struggle was accompanied by the sound of a haughty laugh. Then the laugh stopped abruptly and took on an angriness, barking at him again.

When his eyes had adjusted to the brightness, Thomas realised the room was in fact quite dark. The spotlight that shone on him was but a small circle of intense light, coming from a floor lamp. It was bright as well as hot, and Thomas could feel the light was beginning to burn his face.

A set of boots crunched on the cement floor. A silhouette stepped into the light. The stiff outline of a cap, a set of unmoving square shoulders and the rustle of starched fabric suggested to him that the silhouette in question was a Nazi officer.

"I ASKED YOU A QUESTION!" the silhouette shouted in his face, a smattering of spit landing on him. A blow landed on his cheek. A blinding pain shot through him. For a split second, Thomas saw a blackness studded with stars.

Then, it all came rushing back to him.

The exchange in the basement bar.

The burning sensation from the drink.

The wads of cash rolled up and sealed in a tin.

Thomas became immediately alert.

Where am I?

What day is it?

I need to get home. Now.

I need to talk to Sarah. Tell her she needs to get ready.

Hotel Fiser. We're leaving soon.

He shook his head and opened his eyes wide. His fuzzy vision came back into focus and, for the first time since waking up in that room, Thomas saw the face of the man shouting at him – a sallow face with a hooked nose, thin lips pursed in a straight line, a high forehead covered by a starched cap stitched with the skull insignia. In his eyes was a coldness that was reminiscence of a hangman.

For the first time too, Thomas became aware of another figure in the room. Standing a few feet away in the background, he was rounder, less foreboding, dressed in an entirely different uniform. His round cap gave him away as a Czech policeman. Thomas couldn't decide if the man was a Nazi sympathiser who volunteered for the job or a Nazi dissenter who was forced into it. Either way, he scowled at them both.

"Let me ask you again – what were you doing talking to Jan Novak?" the shouting descended a notch, the voice no less angry, firing in rapid German.

The man in the background translated into Czech – solemn and calmer – without the same effect.

Thomas looked first at the Czech policeman then at the Nazi officer, flexing his jaw before replying in perfect German, "We were having a drink."

A flicker of surprise flashed in the Nazi officer's eyes. Feeling much braver, Thomas added, "As a German citizen, I am fully aware that there is no law against having a drink in a bar. Why have you arrested me? My father works for Reichsprotektor Heydrich. Who is your Commanding Officer? I want to speak to him. NOW."

The Nazi officer stared at him, a hint of uncertainty flickering in his eyes. Thomas curled his lips into a smirk. Then, another blow landed on his other cheek, toppling him over sideways, sending him crashing onto the floor. Pain shot through him like a jolt of electricity. For a split second, Thomas' head spun with dizziness.

"You. Will. Pay. For. This," he mumbled feebly as he tried to sit up but a heavy boot kicked him in the side. A crack was audible as another sharp pain shot through him. He whimpered meekly. Before he could catch a breath, the boot kicked him again. This time, hard in the belly. He curled, face crumpling in pain. Then something hard whacked him on the shins and then his legs. Over and over again. Pain was shooting through him from all directions. He gasped and writhed, desperately sucking for air.

As he lay there, unable to move, Thomas could feel the chair being pulled out from underneath him. The chair scraped the floor, leaving him suddenly spineless. He slumped onto the floor in a heap as it crashed two feet away. The cold cement kissed his cheek when a rough hand grabbed him by his shirt collar. Like a rag doll, he felt himself being dragged across the floor, every muscle in his body screaming in pain. He tried to resist but found that his strength had deserted him. Then the dragging stopped and he fell in a crumpled heap.

The last thing Thomas remembered was the shadow of an object coming towards his face. Pain shot through his head. Then the world went black.

*

When he next woke up, it was in an unfamiliar bed in a room he did not recognise. The room was small, with a narrow window on one wall and faded floral wallpaper on the others. The ceiling sloped downwards like a wedge of cake tipped on its side.

Groggy and disoriented, Thomas nursed the pain in his head and tried to sit up. A sharp pain shot through his side, prompting a groan from him. Begrudgingly, he lay back down. As he lay there, face crumpling with pain, a thumping could be heard coming up a set of staircase, stopping just outside the door. A hinge creaked and the door opened a crack. The unfamiliar face of a girl poked around the door.

"You're awake," she said.

"Where am I?" Thomas asked, wincing as he raised his head to look at her.

"You are in Holešovice. My father found you lying on the street two days ago. He was the one who brought you here," she explained, moving around the door to reveal a small, wiry frame in a shabby dress. Thomas groaned yet again as he lowered his head back onto the pillow, overcome by the excruciating pain in his side.

"Try not to move too much," she said, rushing over. "You might have broken a few ribs."

"I have to go." He winced as he tried once again to sit up. "There is somewhere I have to be."

"Where?"

"Žižkov," he said painfully. "My wife. She is expecting a baby. I need to get home. Now."

The girl lowered her eyes before scurrying away. The thumping of footsteps descended the staircase. A muffled voice could be heard a floor below. Moments later, two sets of footsteps thumped up the staircase – one light, the other heavy. When she returned, it was with an older man with a leathery face. His sleeves were rolled up to his elbows. In his hands was a dirty rag covered in black grease.

"You want to get to Žižkov?" the man asked.

"Yes, can you help me get there?" Thomas replied hopefully.

A long pause followed, within which the man and the girl exchanged a glance.

"Young man, the Gestapo just swept through Žižkov. Caught a few Resistance fighters. And some Jews in hiding. Put them all on the train to Terezín. What's your address? Maybe I can go look in on your wife? Let her know you're all right?"

Thomas sank back onto his pillow. Stunned and deflated, he gazed at the ceiling, an inky darkness quickly closing in on him.

26. THOMAS

Thomas studies the man carefully. They are all sitting around a wooden table in the middle of the kitchen – Thomas, Ivan, Karel and the man who opened the front door. After the initial introductions, no one says anything. A clearing of throat and the creaking of chairs sagging under their weight fill the space meant for conversations. The silence stretches awkwardly, waiting to be rescued.

The man's wife busies herself by the kitchen bench. The electric kettle rumbles and then stops, followed by the sound of liquid being poured into mugs. The smell of coffee wafts tantalisingly through the air.

Thomas looks to either side of him, first at Ivan, then at Karel. Both men busy themselves studying the décor of the small kitchen. Thomas then looks back at the man – Mirek – but he merely looks anxiously at his wife.

When she brings over a tray of mugs and hands out the coffee, Thomas accepts one gratefully. Around the table, a murmur of thanks can be heard but Thomas' attention is on Mirek. He studies his jaw line, his nose, his eyes, even the curve of his lips. What he sees crinkles his brow. He remains silent, absently taking a sip from the mug, his eyes never leaving him. A plate of biscuits is set down in the centre of the table then the woman takes residence in the empty chair next to her husband.

"This place is as beautiful as I remember it to be," Ivan says, breaking the silence. Karel's hand is the first to reach for a biscuit, after which, the men follow suit – except for Thomas. Thomas is still watching Mirek.

"We love it. It's so peaceful here. We hardly ever get any of the officers come this way," Mirek's wife says, both hands hugging the porcelain mug on the table.

"There was an older couple who used to live here," Ivan adds. To which, Mirek nods slowly.

"Yes, they were my parents," he replies. "Sadly, they are no longer with us. They passed away some years ago."

A sombre silence follows, in which, the sound of biscuits being crunched between molars can be heard.

"Take off your shirt," Thomas says, nudging his head at Mirek. Around the table, eyebrows raise in stunned silence.

"What?" Mirek frowns at him.

"Take off your shirt," Thomas repeats, pointing to his shirt.

"Why?"

"Just take it off," Thomas commands, getting up. The legs of his chair scrape the floorboard noisily. Mirek does the same.

"Why should I?"

The atmosphere tenses in the kitchen.

"Gentlemen," Ivan says, looking at them both as he gets to his feet.

Thomas and Mirek are glaring at each other.

"If you don't do it, I will," Thomas says. Mirek huffs.

In a flash, Thomas grabs hold of Mirek's shirt collar from across the table, knocking over the plate of biscuits, spilling coffee out of mugs. Mirek resists violently, struggling to pry Thomas' hands away. Everyone leaps back in shock. Chairs are knocked over, crashing loudly onto the floor. Mrs. Mirek gasps and then screams as the two men entangle in a violent struggle, writhing around the kitchen, bumping into furniture, knocking things off the counter.

"STOP IT!!! Both of you! STOP!!!" Ivan shouts but no one is listening. He signals to Karel, who lunges at Thomas and drags him away while Ivan pulls Mirek to the side, breaking up the fight. A loud rip follows and a chorus of gasps erupt. As the men stare at each other with heaving chests, all eyes are on the ripped sleeve in Thomas' hand.

"Tomáš!!! What is the meaning of this???" Ivan shouts at his friend. Thomas shrugs off Karel's grip and tosses the sleeve aside.

"Tomáš!!! What is the meaning of this?" Ivan repeats when his friend does not answer but Thomas' attention is elsewhere. All eyes are trained on him as he moves slowly towards Mirek. The man eyes Thomas warily and starts to back away.

"Turn around," Thomas says to him quietly, his forefinger tracing a half circle in the air. Mirek hesitates at first but then turns around warily. Thomas gently peels away the torn shirt, revealing the bare skin of Mirek's back. He examines it closely and then, without a word, hands the shirt back to him.

"What is it?" Ivan asks, noticing the colour drain from Thomas' face.

"He's not it," Thomas mutters as he walks away.

"What do you mean he's not IT?" Ivan frowns. "He has to be IT. THIS is the place. THIS is the exact house I came to all those years ago. I handed everything you gave me to the couple who lived here. He has to be it!" He turns around and stares at Mirek in desperation. The man quietly slips his shirt back on and runs his fingers through his tousled hair. All the while, Karel and Mrs. Mirek look on in silence.

"Something went wrong somewhere, Ivan," Thomas sighs as he shakes his head, stopping in front of the window. He gazes out into the distance, at the forest of pine trees. "If he's not here, then he's out there. Somewhere." His voice comes out in almost a whisper, cracking right at the end.

"It's impossible," Ivan mutters in disbelief. "I remember it as clearly as it was yesterday. I was standing right here in this very same kitchen. I gave them the basket and handed them the letter. They said they would take care of it."

The mood in the room shifts.

"The package in that basket, where is it?" Thomas turns around abruptly, his tone suddenly urgent.

"A man came to retrieve it yesterday," replies Mirek.

"Did he say who he was?" A look passes between Ivan and Thomas.

"He said his name is Tomáš Marz," Mirek says. "Before my father died, he said that one day a man named Tomáš Marz will come to this house and ask for a package, so I gave it to him."

"No, No, NO!" Thomas wails in anguish. "He's not Tomáš Marz! I am!!!"

"I'm sorry, I didn't know," Mirek shrugs. "We didn't know what Tomáš Marz looks like."

When Thomas next looks out the window, it is with tears of anguish. He cannot believe that, after all these years, he is still trapped in this game of cat and mouse, in this cycle of running and hiding, trying to beat the Germans at their own game.

27. THE PAST

March 1942

It took Thomas several weeks and many attempts to find Jan. When he finally saw him again, it was within the quiet confines of St. Giles Church on a Thursday afternoon.

"I didn't pick you as the religious type," Thomas said quietly when he slid into the pew behind Jan. His whisper echoed into the high ceiling.

"I didn't think I would see you again," Jan replied without turning back. "I thought you were dead."

Before them, in the front pew, an older lady with a dark head scarf was hunched over, her shoulders heaving as she weeps into her hands.

"Spare me the bullshit. Where is my wife?"

The lady with the dark head scarf stopped crying for a moment and lifted her head. In the silence of the church, a trumpet of a nose being blown echoed, then the weeping resumed.

"How did you know I was here?" Jan looked at him from out of the corner of his eye.

"I have my sources. Where is my wife?"

"You're very lucky, I hope you know that," Jan said, staring straight ahead.

"Oh yeah?" Thomas stared at the back of his head.

"If it wasn't for your neighbour, your wife would be in Terezín right now," he hissed.

The lady with the dark head scarf lifted her head again, this time to wipe her eyes. A whimper escaped before she burst into a fresh round of tears.

"Then tell me where she is."

"She is safe," Jan said quietly. "So is her mother. They are both safe."

"Tell me where they are. Now." Thomas leaned forward and spoke into Jan's ear. His words came out in short hot breaths.

Just then, the door behind them groaned open. A sliver of light and a blast of chill burst in, followed by the noise from the street and a pair of footsteps. Thomas leaned back against the wooden bench and lowered his head. The sliver of light narrowed and disappeared as the door closed, shutting out the noise from the street. The church once again plunged into dimness.

The tramping footfall was slow and measured. It echoed within the high walls as it drew nearer, stopping when its owner took residence in one of the pews. Behind Thomas, a wooden bench creaked. He stole a quick glance out of the corner of his eye and saw that the new entrant was a tall middle-aged man dressed in a shabby coat.

At that very same moment, the wooden bench in front of Thomas creaked. Thomas' eyes followed as Jan rose from his seat and shuffled out of the pew. With his hands in his pockets, he walked past Thomas without so much as a glance, his shoes clacking against the floor all the way to the door. Thomas panicked. So as not to rouse suspicion, he forced himself to remain seated. As another sliver of light expanded and contracted with the opening and closing of the door, his hope of seeing his wife again crumbled rapidly as Jan's footsteps disappeared completely.

Now only the three remained – Thomas, the old lady and the tall man. Within the dimness of the church, the old lady continued to weep. Her sadness echoed within the cavernous chamber, rising up to the high ceiling like a pair of desperate hands reaching out to God. The tall man sat in his pew like a stone statue, gazing blankly into the distance at nothing in particular.

After two agonising minutes, Thomas slid out of the pew and quietly made his way to the door. He stole a quick glance at the tall man as he passed, but the man neither looked at him, nor even noticed he was there.

The Nazis had turned him into a paranoid wreck, Thomas realised as he stepped out of the quiet, dim church into the noisy daylight. He ran down the steps into the street, looking left and then right, his eyes frantically scanning up and down the cobblestone street for signs of Jan. But Jan was nowhere to be found.

Panicking, he took a punt and turned left, weaving himself in and out of the stream of pedestrians walking down the narrow sidewalk, cowering into their own bodies to keep warm on that chilly day. He scanned every face, looking at the men's faces hidden beneath the rim of their hats.

"Come with me," a voice spoke quietly into his ear from behind as a hand grabbed hold of the crook of his arm. Instinctively, Thomas tried to yank it away.

"If you want to see your wife. Come with me. Now." The voice was much hoarser now as the gripped tightened impatiently around Thomas's arm, fingers digging into his flesh. Thomas relented and allowed himself to be guided away from the street, down a quiet laneway. There, the man let go of his arm and they walked briskly in companionable silence for a few more blocks, neither looking at the other, until they reached a truck with an open back ferrying empty wooden crates parked on the side of the street.

"Get in," the voice commanded as he climbed into the driver's side. With one hand on the door handle, Thomas finally took a good look at the man. He was tall with broad shoulders. His shabby grey overalls peeked out from underneath his unbuttoned brown coat and his face was partially hidden underneath the rim of a tweed cap. From where Thomas stood, all he could see was an angular stubbled jaw.

"Who are you?" Thomas asked, narrowing his eyes.

"Just get in the truck. You can ask questions later," the man barked.

Thomas did as he was told. Inside the truck, a little boy scooted to make room for Thomas, his short legs dangling, barely able to touch the floor. He beamed at Thomas, baring two untidy rows of little white teeth. His innocent smile softened Thomas.

"Hi, I'm Tomáš. What's your name?" he said when he was finally seated in the passenger's seat with the door slammed shut.

"Karel," said the little boy before sinking his teeth into the apple in his hand, making a crunching sound.

The man jostled his key into the ignition. The engine squeaked without turning on. He tried a few more times before the engine finally roared to life.

The truck began to move, slowly at first as it manoeuvred out of the parking space onto the street, then picking up speed once it hit a quiet road and began to move away from town.

They passed through three road blocks along the way. Each time, all their papers were checked by the soldier on duty while two others examined the empty wooden crates in the back of the truck.

"Dropped off a shipment in town. Heading back to the farm now," the man replied with practised ease each time he was interrogated by the soldier checking the papers. "This is my son. That is my farmhand." He pointed first to the little boy then to Thomas. The officer glanced at both Karel and Thomas, then with a grunt, handed the papers back and waved for him to move along.

As the truck drove down the dirt road, slicing through the wintry countryside, no one spoke. Thomas fixed his gaze out of the window, looking but not looking at the same time as the empty meadows sped past. His mind was elsewhere, accompanied by his mounting anxiety.

Two-and-a-half hours later, the truck made a turn into a small dirt road branching off the main road. As it rattled over bumpy ground, passing by clumps of tall trees flanking either side of the small dirt road, Thomas straightened up. Without needing to be told, he knew they were close to their destination.

When they finally emerged on the other side of the clump of trees, an open field greeted them. Standing in the distance, at the end of the stretch of dirt road, was a two-storey farm house. It seemed small at first but as the truck advanced, moving closer and closer, the house grew bigger and bigger until there was no more road and all there was, was a big house painted the colour of pale yellow.

"Is this it?" Thomas asked as the man killed the engine.

"Come with me," he replied as he opened the door and climbed out of his seat. The little boy followed, scooting over before being picked up by the armpits and set down when his feet touched the ground.

Thomas followed as the man walked up the front veranda and pounded on the front door.

"I'm here to pick up some slivovice!" he said loudly. Thomas could hear a shuffling noise followed by the faint sound of footsteps advancing towards the door. Moments later, it opened. A wrinkly face and a head of wispy white hair greeted them quickly, beckoning them to come in. Thomas, Karel and his father stepped inside, and the door shut behind them immediately, cutting off the cold air.

"Pavel, this man is after some slivovice," the man said to the older man, cocking his head towards Thomas.

"Where is my wife? I need to see her," Thomas said anxiously, his words rushing out in their desperation to be heard.

The wrinkly face studied Thomas from head to toe before turning back to the truck driver. A look passed between them.

"I don't have any slivovice. Will becherovka do?" the older man named Pavel finally said, staring hard at him. Thomas looked blankly at the driver, who now cocked his head towards Pavel, signalling for Thomas to answer.

"Yes, yes, becherovka will do," Thomas replied clumsily, finally catching on.

"You, come with me," Pavel said with a sharp nod. To the little boy and his father, he nodded towards the other side of the house and added, "There's soup and bread in the kitchen. Milena will fix you up."

As the two thumped off towards the kitchen, Thomas followed Pavel up the stairs. Neither of them spoke as they made their way to the top. At the top of the staircase, they moved across the upstairs landing, the floorboards creaking here and there under their weight.

They past two closed doors on the landing before arriving in front of the third, whereupon Pavel reached into his pocket, fished out a key and jostled it into the keyhole. The door unlocks with a click. Inside, Thomas saw an empty wrought iron bed, a chair, a dresser with a wash basin and a cupboard. His gaze flitted around the room, taking in the faded wallpaper, the dated furniture and the naked bulb dangling from the ceiling.

"Where's my wife?" he turned to Pavel quizzically.

With a small smile, Pavel marched towards the cupboard in the corner. Thomas' eyes followed him as he opened the door, pushed apart the shirts hanging limply in the cupboard and rapped on the back a few times.

A sudden shuffling noise and a creak from the other side of the wall prompted Thomas to move closer. When he leaned in to peek into the cupboard, a hole in the back wall opened and Mother's face appeared. The crinkle on her brow instantly dissolved when her eyes fell on Thomas.

"It's Tomáš!" she squealed. "It's Tomáš!"

Thomas climbed into the cupboard, through the hole and stumbled out into a small windowless room on the other side. Lit only by a small oil lamp, the small circle of orange glow cast a shadow of the scant furniture against the wall.

"Oh, Tom! You're alive!" A squeal came from a corner of the darkness. Thomas turned and, in the poor light of the room, managed to see her, sitting upright on a narrow bed pushed up against the wall. He rushed towards her, tears filling his eyes as he folded her tightly into his arms.

"I thought I had lost you," he whispered into her hair, inhaling her familiar scent as tears fell from his eyes.

"I thought you were dead," she croaked, clutching him tightly. He held her, stroking her hair, her shoulders then her back, desperate to be assured that it really was her that he was holding, and not just a figment of his imagination.

When they finally parted and his eyes had adjusted to the darkness, he saw that Sarah's cheeks were glistening with tears.

"I was so scared, Tom." Her lips quivered as her hands clasped his tightly.

"I know. I was too. I'm sorry," he said, wiping a tear away with his thumb. He cupped her face with his hands and kissed her. The comfort and familiarity of her lips filled him with relief.

"From now on, I won't leave your side, I promise," he whispered.

Through her tears, Sarah's lips curved into a small smile. Thomas smiled too. He gathered her back into his arms, stroking her hair until he felt a jab in his rib.

"I haven't forgotten you either," he said to her swollen belly, stroking it gently. "I will never leave any of you ever again."

Thomas looked gratefully at Pavel before turning back to Sarah. With tears in his eyes, he hugged her and their unborn child tighter, afraid that if he let go, they might slip through his hands once again and disappear from his grasp forever.

28. GUNTHER

Gunther fluffs the pillow before putting it down on the sofa bed. It's just after nine p.m. Every muscle in his aching body is screaming for rest. After the day he has had, Gunther feels completely worn out. Never has he been more eager to go to sleep.

After he left the Schneiders' that afternoon, Gunther had lugged his heavy suitcase on foot all the way to the bus stop, which he estimated – while he was wiping beads of sweat off his forehead and catching his breath at the same time – was about a mile and a half from his house.

"Good thing this thing has wheels," he mumbled as he bent over to examine the plastic wheels, now heavily scuffed by the gravel on the road. He didn't need to wait long as the bus to the U-bahn station came trundling down the street within minutes.

As the bus slowed to a halt and the door fanned open with a hiss, Gunther looked to the young man behind him to help with the suitcase. With his headphones cupped over his ears, he walked past Gunther without a sideways glance and got on the bus, the queue behind him passing Gunther quickly.

"Are you getting on or not?" the bus driver yelled over the loud engine when he spotted Gunther frozen on the pavement, a scowl on his face. He took a look at the suitcase, pressed a button and the bus floor lowered a smidge.

"Come on old man, I haven't got all day," he bellowed, his hands on the big steering wheel as he watched Gunther struggled to get the suitcase onto the bus.

"Don't you have a ramp or something?" Gunther bellowed back. The bus driver looked him up and down, then he said, "Not today."

Gunther rolled his eyes.

While the bus engine groaned and choked intermittently, Gunther wrestled the heavy suitcase onto the bus all by himself. Then, awkwardly, he juggled between counting the coins into the bus driver's till and keeping his suitcase from sliding down the sloping bus floor.

When the door fanned close with a hiss and the bus began to move again, Gunther turned to the bus full of passengers, scanning for an empty seat. There were none. His eyes darted from one passenger to the next, hoping to catch the eye of a good Samaritan but they were too pre-occupied with their mobile phones to even notice he was there. In the end, Gunther managed by holding on to a rail with one hand while balancing the suitcase with the other, sourly holding his footing as the bus lurched forward and swerved a corner.

"What is wrong with the young people today?" Gunther complained loudly after he got off the bus with a huff, suitcase in tow. "And that bus driver, what a nightmare!" He shouted a few expletives at the back of the bus and received only a cloud of black smoke in return. It choked him and made him cough. Gunther's first thought was to ring the Transport Minister, then he remembered none of them wanted to have anything to do with him.

"Those bastards." Gunther coughed sourly as he made his way into the station.

He found the machine that dispenses ticket and spent a considerable amount of time trying to figure out how to work it. After fiddling with the buttons and feeding a handful of coins into the coin slot, the machine spits out a paper ticket. Gunther takes it and brings it up close to his eyes to examine it.

"Hey, can you hurry up? There's a line here." A hand tapped him on the shoulder at the same time as a voice speaking to him from behind. Gunther turned to find a sour face glaring at him. Behind her, three other commuters looked on impatiently. He grunted and shuffled along reluctantly.

"Why are there no escalators in this place?" Gunther scowled when he found himself standing at the top of a flight of dusty steps leading down to the underground platform. For the third time that day, he grappled with his suitcase, awkwardly negotiating the staircase one step at a time. Other commuters brushed past him. No one offered to help. A teenage boy with his eyes glued to the screen of his mobile phone accidentally knocked into him, toppling the suitcase down the steps.

"What is wrong with you???" he shouted when the boy did not apologise, his eyes still glued to the screen of his mobile phone as he descended the steps. No one paid Gunther any attention.

By the time he got to the bottom, Gunther was sweating and out of breath. What he found there appalled him. The underground station was a tunnel of dirty tiles for walls, lit by the weak light of ageing fluorescent tubes. Paint-peeled wooden benches sat on the dusty platform, from which a pervasive stench wafted. The smell stung his nostrils, making him wince. Gunther couldn't decide which he disliked more – the obnoxious bus driver or the underground station.

He found an empty spot on the platform and waited for the next train. All around him, people were busy staring at the screens of their mobile phones, their faces illuminated by a small rectangle of white glow.

When the train finally arrived, Gunther could not believe his eyes.

"THIS is the U-bahn?" He frowned as the string of metal carts rattled down the tracks before coming to a complete halt. When the doors slid open, his jaw dropped when he saw the inside of the carriages. The walls were covered with what looked like brown linoleum covering – like something out of a 1960s kitchen. The worn benches were upholstered in a vinyl-looking material in a similar colour. It was an assault to his senses.

"THIS is Germania's public transport system?" Gunther huffed incredulously. The sleek, air-conditioned modern high-speed train of his fantasy was crushed by the ghastly sight of what was in front of him. He stepped away from the platform, too appalled to get on. As people on the train pushed past him to get off and others around him brushed past him to get on, Gunther looked around in bewilderment.

When the doors slid shut and the train began to rattle again, Gunther's eyes followed it until it disappeared down the tunnel.

"THAT is the U-bahn," he mumbled to himself in stunned realisation.

It took Gunther three more attempts before he was finally able to bring himself to step into the underground train. Unlike the bus, the carriage he stepped into was scantly populated. Still, Gunther refused to sit on any of the empty benches, preferring instead to stand.

He leaned his suitcase against the back wall of the carriage and held onto a grimy metal rail for support. On the opposite end of the carriage, four rowdy characters were talking loudly. Gunther looked over and saw that they were boys rather than men. Their colourful tattoos peeked out from underneath their t-shirts, full sleeves of them on both arms. They were all wearing black t-shirts, faded black jeans, heavy boots, and spiky studs for earrings. Thick chains hung from their belts. Around their wrists, they each wore a variety of thick metal bracelets and black leather cuffs.

"Scum," Gunther muttered under his breath as he eyed them. He caught one of the boys' eyes.

"What did you say, old man?" he piped up. His friends instantly looked over at Gunther.

Gunther said nothing. He merely looked away, pretending not to hear him.

"Hey, you, old man! I'm talking to you."

The boy began marching up the carriage, his boots thumping heavily. His friends followed suit, narrowing their eyes gleefully. All round him, Gunther noticed that the few passengers in the carriage were looking elsewhere, afraid to meet his gaze.

"Didn't you hear me?" The boy was now inches from him, his breath hot on Gunther's face, reeking of the sour stench of beer.

"Hey, he's that guy in the newspapers," one of his friends piped up from behind. "That Minister who got sacked."

Gunther's face instantly felt hot.

"Oh yeah," the boy who was closest to him said. "You're that dirty Slav!"

"Yeah, dirty, filthy Slav!" the other boys chorused and cackled behind him. "Go back to where you fucking came from, you dirty Slav!"

"Or better yet, why don't you just kill yourself? Scum," the boy who was closest to Gunther spat in his face.

Gunther reached for his handkerchief and slowly wiped the spit from his face as the boys laughed some more. The corners of his mouth turned downwards. Then, screwing up his face, he began to shout.

"I. AM. NOT. A DIRTY SLAV!!!"

His voice shook the carriage, stunning all the passengers.

"I. AM. NOT. A DIRTY SLAV!!!"

"I. AM. NOT. A DIRTY SLAV!!!"

He kept shouting until he ran out of breath. When he finally stopped, his face was a deep shade of red. The entire carriage stared at him in stunned silence.

"You don't belong here, old man," the boy said to him before re-joining his friends. When Gunther turned around to look at the other commuters, he could tell they were thinking the same thing.

As soon as the train slowed to a halt at the next station, Gunther took his suitcase and got off. He didn't bother to read the sign on the station wall. All he wanted was to get out of that place, away from the gawking eyes and the pitiful stares. His eyes pricked with hot tears as he lugged his suitcase up the staircase.

"All I need is a break…," he muttered to himself, his nose tingeing with sourness. "All I need is a break."

He walked the rest of the way to Eva's house, pushing his suitcase against the noisy wind on the side of the busy main road. A few cars in the passing oncoming traffic honked at him but he paid no attention to any of them. When he finally arrived at her front door, his toes were sore with blisters.

"Papa, why didn't you just call me? I could have come pick you up!" Eva exclaimed when her eyes fell on his dishevelled appearance. He folded her into his arms in a tight hug, blinking back the tears that were threatening to fall.

When they parted from their hug, Gunther stepped into the house and the front door was closed behind him. For the first time that day, Gunther heaved a sigh of relief.

"Everyone, Opa is here!" she called into the empty hallway. Immediately, thumps and thuds thundered through the house. Hurried footsteps pounded down the hallway. The sight of his three grandchildren running towards him filled Gunther's eyes with tears once again.

He folded them all into his arms, peppering them with kisses, his tears a confused mix of relief and anxiety.

Later, after the grandchildren had scampered off, Eva led him into the study. When the two of them were alone, Gunther said gravely, "Your mother left me, you know that?"

"Oh, Papa." Her hand clapped over her mouth in shock as her face crumpled in pain. She went over to hug him, resting her head on his chest.

"But the credit cards are cut off," Gunther added. Eva burst into a laugh. The mood instantly lifted.

"They took the house back," Gunther continued. "Some punks set fire to it last night."

"Papa!" Eva straightened, looking at him with panic in her eyes.

"It's fine. It's only the front rooms." Gunther waved nonchalantly.

"Poor Papa," Eva sighed as she gave Gunther another squeeze. "I know things haven't been good lately but I'm sure it's only temporary. It'll get better, you'll see."

Gunther forced a small smile as he reached over to pinch his daughter's cheek, the same way he used to do when she was a little girl. In her eyes, he saw hope and optimism – something he wished he had. A small sigh filled the space between them.

"Get some rest, Papa. You must be tired. I'm going to get dinner started," Eva said, patting him on the arm before tearing away. Gunther's eyes followed her all the way to the door before she stopped and turned around.

"It will all be fine again, Papa. I'm sure of it," she said.

"I'm sure you're right, sweetheart," Gunther replied with a forced smile. Deep down, he wished he believed it himself.

After Eva left, Gunther sank onto the sofa and stared blankly into space.

How did I get here? he thought.

Where did I go wrong?

He remembered the morning of the day of the press conference, when he was getting dressed in front of the full-length mirror. He remembered looking at himself, at his sharp uniform buttoned all the way up to his neck, his prized medals dangling from his breast pockets. As he looked at himself, his life flashed before his eyes and he wondered what his father would say to him if he was still alive.

Would he be proud? he had wondered.

I was so close, Gunther thought as he exhaled quietly. So close to the top. The pinnacle was right in front of him, almost within his grasp, until that reporter showed up and sent him tumbling down.

Now, he was at the bottom of this impossible mountain, with neither the time nor the energy to climb back up to the top. Overnight, everything he owned was ripped away from him. His years of service wiped off unceremoniously. His friends were nowhere to be found. Every single person he knew avoided him. Like he was a leper.

How did I get here? Gunther wondered as he stared blankly ahead.

What did I do to deserve this?

Later, when he was in the bathroom, tiptoeing around the yellow rubber ducky and other brightly coloured plastic toys on the bath mat, it dawned on him that that was his new reality. That bathroom – with its many coloured toothbrushes in the blue plastic cup, the different towels hanging from various hooks with names written above them, and the plastic basket holding the many different bottles of moisturiser, shower gel, shampoo and conditioner – that was his new reality. He imagined an extra hook on the bathroom door, above which his name was written in black marker ink, his damp towel hanging from it. That notion forced a bitter laugh out of him.

After his shower, wiping away the steamed-up mirror with one hand, Gunther stared at his own reflection. Standing over the sink, his towel wrapped around his waist, Gunther leaned in to examine his face. He studied the colour of his eyes (blue), the contour of his nose (sharp), his jaw line (masculine), his ears (ordinary) and his teeth (perfectly straight, stained by the copious amounts of tea and coffee he drank on a daily basis).

After he was done examining his face, he stood back. In the bathroom mirror, he saw only an old man with silvery hair, a double chin, a web of fine lines around his eyes, and deep wrinkles above his brow.

"I don't know what they are talking about," Gunther muttered to himself. "I look every bit as Aryan as the rest of them. I am exactly the same person as I was before."

Before Anna Weiss.

But nothing in his life was the same as it was before.

Gunther got dressed and went to dinner.

To lighten the mood at dinner, Gunther asked his eldest grandson, Erik, what he was planning for the summer break.

"Erik, Opa asked you a question," Eva piped up when no answer came.

Erik pushed some food around on his plate, not really eating but not really looking at anyone either.

"I was thinking of going to summer camp," when he finally spoke, it was in a small voice. "There is a good military program for boys my age."

"That sounds good." Gunther nodded approvingly, putting another forkful of vegetables into his mouth.

"But he didn't get in." Martha, who was sitting across the table from Erik, chomped on a mouthful of bread. "The counsellor told him not to bother with the application."

"Shut up! Nobody asked you!" Erik scowled at her.

"Is that true?" Eva said, looking first at Erik then at Martha before looking back at Erik again. The knife and fork in her hands were set down.

Every pair of eyes around the table fell on Erik. He shrank further, concentrating on pushing a pea around his plate with his fork.

"Is that true, Erik?" his father asked with a frown.

A small grunt came.

"Why not?" Gunther asked.

As soon as the words left his mouth, Gunther knew the answer. He stopped chewing as a shadow passed his face. The adults exchanged glances around the table but no one spoke immediately.

"Erik, what exactly did the counsellor say?" Gunther was the first to speak.

No reply came.

"Erik, Opa asked you a question," Eva prodded.

The silence stretched out uncomfortably before a small voice could be heard.

"He said the program is only for boys from... umm... elite... umm... Aryan... families."

Gunther's heart sank as he took in the pained look on his grandson's face. He was merely a child! Why was he a victim of the politics of race?

Gunther's face darkened.

"I'm sure it's just a misunderstanding," he heard Eva say with false brightness. "I'll ring the school tomorrow. I'm sure the Headmaster will sort it out."

They finished dinner in complete silence.

Gunther turns off the table lamp and lies down on the sofa bed, staring into the darkness at a ceiling he can barely see. The conversation at dinner time weighs heavily on his mind but he has had an exhausting day. His eyelids feel heavy and he doesn't fight it. Very soon, he falls into a deep sleep.

Sometime in the middle of the night, Gunther wakes up to a dry throat. He climbs out of bed groggily and fumbles through the darkness into the hallway. Halfway towards the kitchen, he sees a narrow sliver of light across the carpet. The door to the sitting room lay ajar and the lights are still on.

Absently, he moves towards it. When he reaches the door, he sees that Eva is in there, sitting next to Friedrich on the couch, talking very quietly. Gunther stops in his tracks but doesn't move away immediately. Instead, he remains hidden behind the door, listening in on their conversation.

"What are we going to do?" Gunther hears her say in a teary voice.

"Surely they can't do that?" Friedrich says.

"They can and they have," Eva weeps.

"But you've worked there for almost twenty years! You work harder than anyone else there and they know it. They can't just fire you like that!"

"Fred, you and I both know *why* I got fired."

"This whole scandal with your father's identity is ridiculous. Why are we being dragged into this? The whole thing about Erik's summer camp is pure madness! He's just a boy! Why he is being dragged into this politics is beyond me."

"You're one to talk. I don't remember you complaining when *'this politics'* gave you all your opportunities. Have you forgotten who you were before you met me? Have you forgotten it's because of my father that we have this house and this life??? Have you forgotten that it was my father's connections that got you your job???" Eva's voice rises.

Gunther smiles, silently pleased that his daughter has come to his defence.

"Look where he's gotten us now!" he shoots back.

"It's not his fault he wasn't born into the right family!"

"Then whose fault is it, Eva? Whose fault is it that our son doesn't have the same opportunities as the other boys? Whose fault is it that you got fired from your job after working there for twenty years? I could be next in line to be fired, have you thought of that?"

"You think I don't know that? You think I haven't thought about what would happen to this family? I don't decide these things, Fred! I DON'T!!!"

"I don't want your father living with us. You heard what he said. Some punks tried to burn his house down. I don't want that kind of threat hanging over our family."

"We can't kick him out. He has nowhere to go!!!"

"He got himself into this mess. He can get himself out of it."

"FRED!!!"

Gunther can't bear to listen any longer. Quietly, he slips back to his room without his glass of water. There, he lays in bed, unable to fall asleep as he listens to the muffle of raised voices coming from down the hallway.

Eventually, the voices reduce to murmurs. A door creaks open and then shut. Then, the house falls into complete silence.

I'm going to fix this, Gunther thinks as he stares into the darkness. *I'm going to fix this Goddamn mess even if it kills me to do it.*

Turning over on the sofa bed, Gunther falls into deep sleep.

29. ANNELIE

It seems like a lifetime ago – her father's death. Annelie recounts as she sits on the cold cement floor, leaning against the concrete wall as she hugs her knees to her chest. She looks around the narrow cell – three feet wide and four feet long, with a small slit for a window where the wall meets the ceiling. If she was any larger, she would not have been able to sit down. She imagines most of the inmates would have been men, in which case, the experience would have been even more claustrophobic.

A small sigh escapes and echoes in the narrow chamber. In that small, dim room, Annelie has lost all sense of time. How long has she been sitting there? Three? Maybe four hours? She can't be sure.

It's all Mama's fault, she thinks as she buries her face into her knees. She was so young – only four years old – when it all happened. How was she to know something like this would come back to haunt her later in life?

Another small sigh escapes.

She adjusts herself in an attempt to save her back from going numb. As she stares at the grey slab of the iron door right in front of her, she tries to remember her father. His face appears as a blurry image, a patch of skin colour paint in a roughly sketched outline, hardly recognisable.

Did he use to sing to her? What did his voice sound like? She couldn't remember. Not remembering frustrates her.

Another string of sigh echoes in the narrow chamber.

She remembers a time when they were living in the village – her mother and her – in the house her mother grew up in. They slept in Mama's old room – the one where she spent her nights daydreaming as a child, and then as a teenager, before she met her father and fell in love with him.

In that house in the village, she and her mother shared a narrow bed, sleeping on a thin mattress. For a long time, she remembers her mother crying. When Mama held her in her arms, singing her to sleep at night, she would cry.

"Your mother has a lot of sadness in her," Babička had said to her one day when she took a brush to Annelie's long, strawberry blonde hair.

"Why, Babi?" Annelie asked curiously.

"When two people's lives are as intertwined as your father's and your mother's, one of them is bound to feel a lot of sadness when the other is gone."

Her father had died in an accident at the factory, Babička told her.

"It was quick," Babička said. "At least he didn't suffer."

She remembers waking up in the middle of the night once to find that her mother was not next to her in bed. Instead of turning over and falling back to sleep, she decided to get up and look for her. There, under the orange light of the ageing bulb dangling naked from the kitchen ceiling, her mother sat by the shabby kitchen table, weeping. Babička's back was to her, and she had her wrinkly hand on her mother's.

Annelie remembers standing in the doorway, witnessing the sadness expressed by her mother's heaving shoulders.

"This is your chance to change your life," Babička said. "Think of Anna. Think of the future she could have. Think of the life she could have that we couldn't."

"Maminka," Annelie called out sleepily, breaking the spell that bound the two women together. Hurriedly, her mother dried her eyes and came rushing to carry her back to bed.

After that night, her mother changed.

"I'm going to Prague for a week," her mother said to her a few days later. "You will stay here with Babička, you hear me?" The suitcase lay opened on the bed. She was getting ready to fill it.

"Why can't I come with you?"

"I'm going to be doing grown-up stuff. It will be very boring. Here, you get to play with all the other children. Babička will take good care of you, you hear me?"

Annelie watched with a pout as her mother filled the suitcase with her best dresses, high heels and a bottle of perfume. Then she ran off to throw a tantrum to Babička.

"Your mother is going to give you a better life, you'll see," Babička said to her as she cradled her in her arms.

When her mother finally returned after an agonisingly long absence, Annelie could see that she had been completely transformed. She began the day by sitting in front of the mirror, doing her hair as she hummed a tune to herself. Then, she would apply her make-up, pressing the powder onto her face, brushing rouge onto her cheeks and then curling her eyelashes. The ritual was carefully completed by the application of red lipstick. A few new dresses appeared in the closet – ones made from soft, slinky fabric, some of them without shoulders, only thin straps anaemically holding on to the hanger.

After that, her mother went away more and more often and her absences seemed to stretch longer and longer each time.

One night, not long after her fourth birthday, when her mother was brushing Annelie's hair right before going to bed, it happened.

"You are going to have a new father, Anna," she said softly as the bristles ran through her hair. "Herr Eckhert is a wonderful man. We are very lucky to have him. You must learn to love him like your own father, you hear me?"

Annelie listened without saying a word.

"We won't be living here much longer. Our new home will be in Prague," she continued dreamily. "Herr Eckhert has a very nice apartment. You will have your own room, with lots of toys and dolls to play with. You'll be very happy there, you'll see."

"But I want to stay here," Annelie protested. "I want to stay here and live with Babi."

"This is not about what you want, Anna," her mother replied sharply, shaking her by the shoulders. Annelie could see, from the tight lines around her mother's lips, that she had angered her.

"I'm doing this for your own good. It's already decided. We will be moving to Prague next week. When we get there, you will address Herr Eckhert as your Papa and you will call me Mama, you hear me? We are going to live a different life now. We are going to be real Germans."

Annelie made no further protest. She pouted silently and went to bed with angry tears.

A week later, they wore their best dresses and got on the train to Prague, bringing with them suitcases and carefully labelled boxes stuffed with their belongings. Babička waved to them from the train platform. She waved back. As the train began to pull away, Annelie saw there were tears in her eyes. Whether they were happy tears or sad tears, she could not tell. She didn't know that would be the last time she would see her Babi. If she did, maybe she wouldn't have left.

When the train pulled into the station in Prague, her mother said to her, "When we get off this train, we will be starting our new life. You hear me?" She shook Annelie when no answer came. Obediently, Annelie nodded.

"From now on, we are starting over as different people. From now on, you will be known as Annelie Eckhert. You hear me?"

After they got off the train, Annelie watched her mother as she waved brightly at a strange man dressed in a suit. She rushed forward to kiss him, already so comfortable in her new identity. When moments later, Annelie met Herr Eckhert for the first time, he had smiled, bent over and offered her a new doll. Obediently, she accepted it – the same way she accepted her new name, her new father and her new life. Little did she know, years later, that moment would come back to haunt her.

In time, she came to love Herr Eckhert like her own father, but not without much despise towards herself. When she thinks back to the day she first arrived in Prague, Annelie feels only a sense of foreboding. She knew she would always remember that day, though not for the reasons her mother had hoped. She atones for it by vowing to spend the rest of her life making amends but she knows it would never be enough. That moment she accepted the new doll from Herr Eckhert would forever be etched in her mind as the moment she betrayed the memory of her own father.

As she sits hugging her knees in the cold cell, Annelie feels a strange sense of relief. Her mother had been right. They did start over as different people, only not in the way she had hoped. Since getting off the train in Prague all those years ago, they had been living their lives like fugitives on the run, walking the tight rope between who they really are and who they wished they were. The moment she stepped off the train as Annelie Eckhert, she had not known a moment's peace. Now, as she finds herself confined to the cold, uncomfortable chamber of the prison cell, the relief of finally being able to shed the pretence fills her with unfathomable lightness.

Outside the cell, down the far end of the corridor, a heavy door opens and then clangs shut. The sound of tramping footfall follows, getting louder and louder as it approaches, until it finally stops outside her cell. Annelie looks up. A key jostles in the lock. A click echoes then the door swings open, letting in a shaft of light. The light hurts her eyes. She squints, making out the silhouette of a tall man.

"Get up!" he barks.

With some difficulty, she climbs to her feet. Her stiff knees creak audibly in the chamber. His big hand grips her by the forearm and yanks her out of the cell. She is pushed first, then pulled down the corridor until they arrive in a different corridor lined with closed doors.

The man opens one of the doors and pushes her inside before he himself enters, closing the door behind him. The room is windowless, lit only by a desk lamp, bare except for a table and a few chairs. Two men are already sitting on the other side of the table, the circle of light ending just under their chins.

"Sit," a voice comes from one of them. Annelie does as she is told, sinking onto the only empty chair in the room.

"I presume you know why you are here?" another voice pipes up.

Annelie turns to look at the tall man standing guard over the door. When she turns back to the two men whose faces she cannot see, she nods.

"Falsification of identity and class," the first voice says. There is shuffling of paper as a file is flipped open and the first voice thumbs through the sheaf of documents. The folder is thick. He soon loses patience. Huffing, he shoves it onto the desk, its contents slide out like a cascading paper waterfall.

"What tipped you off?" Annelie asks stonily.

The two silhouette turns to face each other, then break into a laugh that echoes in the emptiness of the room.

"Oh, you think we've just found out?" the first voice jeers. To his partner, he echoes, "She thinks we've just found out!"

Annelie endures yet another peal of laughter.

"Do you honestly think you and your mother – two country bumpkins under the Labour Repatriation Program – can outsmart a system of sophisticated computer programs and a network of highly trained intelligence officers?"

Annelie bites her lip but does not answer.

"Anna Kvasnicková, when we are done with you, you will be put away for a very, very long time," the second voice says.

"Why are you detaining me now?" Annelie asks, staring past the circle of light. "If you've known this whole time, why are you only detaining me now?"

There is a brief silence. The two silhouettes turn towards each other again before turning back to face her.

"You are obviously a very bright girl, Anna Kvasnicková," the first voice says. He pauses before continuing, "Here's the deal. There is a man you seem to be very close with. A certain... *American* man."

Annelie scrunches her brows.

"I barely know him," she snaps.

"Oh? You seem pretty close to him the other night... when... you know...," the voice mimics hers in a pleasurable moan. Annelie tenses up immediately.

"We got it on tape, you know," the second voice says smugly. "You put on quite a show that night."

The second voice mimics a few more whimpers and moans. The two men laugh.

"What is it you want?" Annelie snaps angrily, her face turning hot.

"We don't care for that man. We want his accomplice – Tomáš Marz. Give us Tomáš Marz and we will make this whole thing with the false identity go away."

Annelie does not answer immediately. Instead, she lowers her eyes. A deep silence follows, within which only the sound of breaths being inhaled and exhaled can be heard.

As she sits in silence, Annelie can feel the two sets of eyes burning into her. When she finally lifts her eyes, she says, "There is something I want."

BANG! A hand slams on the desk, simultaneously startling Annelie while sending the smattering of documents flying.

"Listen, you little punk!" the first voice snaps as he leans forward for the first time, his stubbled chin stepping into the circle of light. "You are this close – (he pinches with his thumb and forefinger) – to being banished into oblivion. YOU don't get to make demands."

"Do you want Tomáš Marz or not?" she asks haughtily.

Her question hangs in the air. The stubbled chin withdraws into the darkness. The silhouette turns to face the other.

After a brief silence, the second voice answers, "What is it you want?"

Annelie stares hard at the two faces she cannot see.

"Here are my terms," she says. "And this is how it's going to happen."

Without waiting for the two silhouettes to respond, she begins to spell them out. When they remain motionless, she adds impatiently, "Why are you still sitting there? Write it down!"

She sits there, dictating the terms of the exchange to the scratching sound of pen scribbling on paper.

30. THOMAS

When Thomas returns to his rented flat, he finds Jack sitting on the sofa with a young woman, their knees touching, his hands holding hers. It takes him a moment to place her – the young guide from the museum. He wasn't aware that they were friendly. He himself had been pre-occupied with his own hunt for the past, and had not seen much of Jack in the past week.

The young woman is mid-sentence when he enters the room, her bewildered eyes turn towards him warily. She stops talking immediately, lowering her eyes to avert his gaze.

"Jack, what's going on?" Thomas frowns, glancing from one to the other. "Why is she here?"

"It's fine," Jack says. "She's here to help us."

"With what?" Thomas looks at her again and then back at him. The young woman sits quietly, staring into her own lap. Upon closer examination, he sees that her cheeks are glistening.

"She's been helping me gather evidence for the story about the Jews who disappeared in Europe during the war," Jack says, rising from the sofa. "And she knows where the package is."

"She does? You do?" Thomas' eyes light up, looking first at Jack then at her. For the first time since entering the room, she meets his gaze, nods and wipes the streaks of tears from her face.

Thomas stares hard at her, suspicion rising. He pulls Jack aside, tearing them apart. She merely stares at him, blinking her watery eyes as she sits motionless, folding her hands in her lap.

"Are you sure about this, Jack?" he hisses, stealing a glance at her. "Can she be trusted?"

"Do you have a better plan?" Jack whispers back.

Thomas steals another glance at her staring at her own hands, looking altogether young and naïve. When he returns his gaze back to Jack, Thomas sighs audibly. Retrieving the package has proven to be more difficult than he originally thought. Time is his enemy. He knows the longer he waits, the harder it will be for him to find it. Reluctantly, he shakes his head.

When the two men return to where Annelie is sitting, Thomas says quietly, "Jack tells me you have some information that can help us with what we are looking for." She looks at him and nods earnestly. Thomas pulls up a chair and sits down while Jack takes residence next to her on the sofa. The three of them sit in a semi-circle, and Annelie repeats to Thomas what she told Jack.

That night, after Jack has gone to bed, Thomas sits by himself in the darkness in the living room. Despite being sufficiently exhausted, he is sleepless. Something about that museum guide makes him uneasy.

As he sits staring into the darkness, questions swirl around his head unanswered. To Jack's satisfaction, she produced copies of some classified military information from the war, which made her seem credible enough. Yet, something about the serendipitous nature of the whole affair plies him with doubt.

How did his unidentified, less than remarkable brown paper package end up in the Archive Department of the museum?

Only three days ago, the package was still in Mirek's custody. A man falsely identifying himself had known where it was and collected it the day before Thomas himself could get to it. For reasons unknown to everyone, it somehow miraculously turned up at the museum.

The holes in her story have 'Gestapo' written all over it.

Is he being too cynical? Thomas wonders as he ruminates in his own thoughts.

Jack, usually the cynic of the two, seemed entirely convinced that her intentions were pure. Thomas can tell by the way he looks at her that he is smitten, maybe even in love.

"His judgment is impaired," Thomas mutters into the darkness, letting loose a small sigh.

His own judgement had been impaired too, all those years ago. Love blinds people to the most obvious truth, he realised. And yet, from within love emerge an impossible strength and courage, inexplicable and irreplaceable by anything else.

This, he discovered when he held his child for the very first time.

*

1942

One night, in the middle of spring, Sarah woke Thomas up with a shake. They were all camped within the narrow space in the annex – Sarah on the narrow bed, Thomas on the floor next to her, and Mother on a mattress rolled out on the other end.

"Tom, something's happening," she said, panicking, her flailing hand shaking him violently by the shoulders. He rubbed his eyes and sat up sleepily.

"What's the matter?" he yawned.

"I think the baby's coming," she squeaked, a slimy hand gripping his arm. Sleep deserted him instantly. In the dark, he shot to his feet in a panic.

"Mother!" he called in the darkness. "Mother, the baby's coming!"

Within minutes, the entire house was awake. Milena rushed into the room, rolled up the sleeves of her dressing gown and began firing orders. To Mother, she instructed for towels to be fetched from the laundry downstairs. To Pavel, she called for a basin of warm water.

"Tomáš, you help me get Sarah out of this place. She needs to be in a proper bed," Milena said, taking hold of Thomas' arm. Everyone scurried off on their respective missions.

When finally, Sarah had been moved out of the annex into the bed in the room, and the towels and warm water brought up, Milena instructed the menfolk to leave the room.

"Mother and I will take it from here. I have delivered a few babies in my time, rest assured that Sarah is in good hands," she said perfunctorily, guiding Thomas out of the room by his elbow. Uncertainly, he cast a glance at Sarah. Her face was scrunched up in pain as beads of sweat formed on her forehead. She whimpered without looking at him.

"I want to stay," he protested but Milena shook her head.

"And what will you do?" she scolded. "If I need you, I will call you."

With a final push, he was out on the landing, the door shutting in his face.

"Sarah, I'm just outside!" he called out anxiously, pounding on the door. Inside, muffled voices spoke urgently. Mixed in amongst them were Sarah's whimpers.

"Don't worry, Tom. Sarah will be just fine." A comforting hand landed on his shoulder. With an earnest smile, Pavel clapped him on the back, guiding him away from the door.

They sat on the floor on the landing for what felt like an eternity, their backs leaning against the wall, their heads resting on the nape of their necks such that their eyes were lifted skyward. From behind the closed door, Thomas heard Milena's voice coaxing Sarah gently. Groans of pain burst intermittently, making Thomas tense up.

"Relax, it's normal," Pavel said, patting him on the leg. "There's a human being coming out of Sarah, there is bound to be some pain."

There they sat, the orange glow of an oil lamp at their feet, the farmhouse quiet in the deep of the night except for the murmurs and groans coming from behind the closed door.

"You are about to be a father, Tom," Pavel said without looking at him. "It will be the scariest thing you will ever do. But also the most wonderful."

Thomas could hear the smile in his voice.

"I was a father twice," he continued. "Both sons."

"What happened?"

"They went and fought in the Great War. For the Austro-Hungarian Empire," he replied quietly. "They never came home."

In the moments that followed, a blood-curdling scream pierced through the silence of the night. Thomas shot to his feet but Pavel's reassuring hand calmed him.

"It's only just starting," he said. "There will be more before the baby comes."

Hesitantly, he sank back down. They sat and waited while groans of pain came through the door.

"It's a terrible thing, losing your children," Pavel said. "I hope you never have to experience it, Tom."

A long silence ensued. The only sounds to be heard in the deep of the night were the screams of agony coming from behind the closed door. Thomas wrung his hands as he waited, glancing at the closed door every so often, his foot tapping anxiously.

Sometime before the first light streaked across the sky, a baby's cry pierced the pre-dawn silence. Thomas shot to his feet immediately. He paced outside the closed door, waiting impatiently as sounds of feet shuffling emanated from the other side.

When the door finally opened, he rushed in, eyes falling first on Sarah then on the wrapped bundle in her arms. She smiled weakly, wet hair plastered around her face. In the crook of her arm, a tiny face peeked out from beneath the layers of towels. It was then that he saw his child for the first time.

"It's a boy," Milena said, placing a gentle hand on his back. Thomas looked at her first, then at Mother, and finally at Pavel. Everyone was smiling. Then he realised he was smiling too. His heart was swelling so fast he thought it might burst.

"Here, say hello to our son," Sarah said as the tiny bundle exchanged hands. Thomas held it uncertainly. The baby's head flopped this way and that before he finally found a home in the crook of his arm.

"Hello, little one," Thomas whispered as his eyes misted, swallowing the lump in his throat. He stroked the soft cheek on his tiny face with a finger, counted each tiny finger and toe, and gently touched the small birth mark on his left foot. The baby gurgled and pawed his own face. Tears began to fall from Thomas' eyes.

"I'm your Táta," he said, pressing his lips to the soft skin of his tiny forehead. The baby squints, his eyes disappearing into tiny slits on his face.

"I've thought of a name," Sarah said. "How do you feel about Miloš? After Milena."

"Miloš," Thomas echoed, looking first at their child and then at Milena. She was smiling.

"I love it," he said to Sarah. "Miloš Marz."

Overwhelmed with feelings of love, Thomas turned to Sarah and kissed her. Then, they both stared silently at the tiny bundle in his arms with tears in their eyes.

As light streaked across the sky, Thomas held his son carefully, gently rocking him to sleep.

Finally, they were a family.

31. GUNTHER

The last time Gunther waited for someone was at that fateful press conference. Even then, it was for the Chancellor – someone of higher rank than he was. He has been waiting around a lot lately, he realises. That thought turns the corners of his mouth downwards.

Almost two hours have ticked by since Gunther first sat down on one of the three chairs lined up against the wall outside the Headmaster's office. He counted that seven people had come and gone from that office since he sat down – five of them students, two of them staff. Each time the door opens and closes, Gunther sneaks a peek and catches only glimpses of a bookcase against the wall and one corner of the desk. He hears murmurs of voices, none of which calls out his name.

Gunther sighs as he shifts his weight around in the chair. Unwittingly, the twinge in his back prompts a groan. He stretches in his seat and lets out another groan, reminding himself never to carry heavy objects up and down the staircase again.

At five minutes to 1 p.m., the Headmaster's door opens. Out of the corner of his eye, Gunther sees the gleam of a pair of polished black shoes in the doorway. He lifts his eyes to look at the man fully, starting with the pair of pressed grey trousers, then the maroon knitted vest, a navy-blue tie and a crisp white shirt with the sleeves rolled up to his elbows.

"Herr Scholz, so good of you to visit," the Headmaster says with a strained smile. "Sorry to keep you waiting."

You're not sorry at all, Gunther thinks to himself. He uncrosses his legs and rises from his seat.

"You must be doing really well, Joseph. You seem more... *prosperous* since the last time I saw you," Gunther says, raising his eyebrows at the Headmaster's paunchy mid-section.

The Headmaster merely laughs and beckons for him to come in. Gunther steps into the office and takes residence in one of the two chairs facing his desk.

"To what do I owe this visit?" the Headmaster says as he closes the door. He walks briskly around Gunther's chair and sits down behind his own desk.

You know exactly why I'm here, Gunther thinks but does not say aloud. Instead, he takes his time looking around the Headmaster's office, at the many plaques hanging on the walls.

"The school seems to be doing well," Gunther says as he brings his gaze back to the Headmaster's face. "How many years has it been? Seven? Eight?"

"Well, yes, we have been ranked number one for eight years," the Headmaster replies with a proud smile.

"How interesting," Gunther remarks, stroking his chin. "That's exactly the number of years Erik has been in this school. What a striking coincidence."

"I suppose you could say that...."

The ensuing silence stretches uncomfortably as Gunther studies the Headmaster from his vantage point.

"Joseph, do you remember when you came to me all those years ago?" When Gunther speaks again, his voice lilts in a sing-song tone. The Headmaster tenses up, staring awkwardly at him but does not reply immediately.

"Do you remember what you asked me to do?" Gunther adds, raising both eyebrows.

When no reply came, he continues to speak.

"Well, let me refresh your memory. You came to me... what was it... twenty-five? Twenty-six years ago? You were just a lowly teacher in a small village at the time. Do you remember that? Desperately, desperately underpaid. Completely insignificant. With no prospects whatsoever in life. Ring a bell?"

The Headmaster merely stares at him. A hint of disdain flickers in his eyes as the corners of his lips tighten.

"Odd, isn't it? How quickly one forgets one's struggles when swimming in success?" Gunther's mouth curls into a sly smile.

"I remember, you know," he adds when the Headmaster does not speak. "You tried to see me several times. Called the office and asked my secretary if you could make an appointment to meet me. I thought you were pathetic, I really did."

Gunther pauses to swallow his saliva audibly. The Headmaster sits stonily behind his desk, his eyes never leaving Gunther.

"Then you showed up outside my office building. Hanging around waiting for me to come out. You were like a fly that wouldn't go away. Buzzing around. So annoying."

Gunther stops talking and begins to play with the Rubik's cube that sits weighing down a pile of documents on the Headmaster's desk. He is momentarily distracted as he fiddles with the cube.

"I have to give it to you, Joseph. You're smart. You know how to motivate someone into doing what you want." Gunther glances up at him. "The lead that you gave me for my case turned out to be a pretty good one. I rewarded you, didn't I?"

Still, the Headmaster does not answer.

"Do you know how difficult it was to get someone like you into a school like this?" Gunther sits the Rubik's cube back down – every square of colour in the right place – and leans back in his chair.

"I gotta tell you, it was bloody difficult," Gunther adds. "You? A Class Two in the Labour Repatriation Program. In a place like this?" Gunther expands his arms at the interior of the Headmaster's office.

"Pffft, impossible!" Gunther says, folding his arms back onto his lap. "But I did it, didn't I? I got you into this dig. This elite, private school in Germania. The best of the best in all of Europe. The Headmaster at the time could easily have filled the position with any other candidates. One who is of the right stock and definitely more qualified for the job than you were. But he didn't. He took you in. Have you ever wondered how I managed to persuade him to do that? Hmmm?"

Gunther raises his eyebrows at the Headmaster, waiting for a respond but none came so he continues to speak.

"Joseph, did you know there are only two ways to motivate people into doing what you want?"

He looks at the Headmaster again but receives only a cold stare in return.

"Pain," Gunther says counting out his thumb. Then, unfolding his forefinger, he adds, "And Pleasure."

There is a pause, during which Gunther inhales loudly, his chest rising as he does.

"Did you know, Joseph, that your predecessor was a homosexual? He was. He didn't know I knew. Of course, I knew. It was my business to know everything about everyone."

Gunther swallows his saliva audibly, his Adam's Apple bobbing up and then down.

"The laws are not too kind to the likes of him, he knew that. He also knew that if he didn't submit to my... *wishes*, I could easily make him disappear. Poof!" Gunther snaps his fingers. "Just like that, he would be wiped off the face of this earth. No one would ever know what happened to him. No one would care, to be honest. As far as the law is concerned, he is vermin. He is bad for this country."

A sharp intake of breath punctuates his monologue.

"I still remember it," he continues. "He was sitting in that very same chair, the one you are sitting in right now, and he stared at me. His eyes were so wide, they were like golf balls. He could not believe I would do that to him. I said to him, 'Hans, the law is the law. I'm merely upholding it.' He got desperate. So desperate that he did everything I told him to. He took you in. You – a teacher in a small, insignificant school in a tiny village in Moravia. I have to give it to you. You didn't waste the opportunity. Now, look at you, a Headmaster in the most prestigious school in Europe."

Gunther leans in and looks hard at the Headmaster. Then, he adds, "But you forget. You forget that if I gave this to you, I can also take it away from you."

The Headmaster's face darkens.

"What do you want?" he spouts.

"Erik is having a bit of... how shall I put it... *challenge*... getting into summer camp," Gunther says, leaning back.

"With all due respect, Herr Scholz," the Headmaster says quietly. "The law is the law. I am the Headmaster of this school. I have to be seen to be doing the right thing. I cannot possibly allow him into that camp in your current... *situation*. And if you care about that boy, you wouldn't let him go either. It's bad enough that all the other kids are picking on him in school now. It will be worse when he goes to camp."

Gunther narrows his eyes. If he is surprised by the Headmaster's revelation, he does not show it.

"Handle it," he says. "I don't care how you do it. Just. Handle. It."

The Headmaster stares at Gunther, who in turn, stares back at him. Neither of them speaks. Then the phone rings, breaking the spell. Reluctantly, the Headmaster picks up the receiver from its cradle.

"Ah, Mrs. Zimmerman, what a pleasure to hear from you. I was just showing your father out," he says with false brightness as Gunther rises to leave. "Yes, yes, we have been catching up on old times. Yes, he did raise Erik's predicament with me. Not to worry, I will look into it. Rest assured that it will be resolved very soon."

After a few more moments of pleasantries, the Headmaster bids farewell into the phone and hangs up. Gunther stands at the doorway and waits for him to place the receiver back on the cradle before saying, "I trust that by the time I get home this afternoon, it will all be sorted out."

"Herr Scholz," the Headmaster says, plucking his glasses from the bridge of his nose as he rises. Gunther's eyes follow him. "If I were you, I would be very careful about making demands in your current... *situation*."

"I can take care of myself, Joseph."

"I'm sure you can," says the Headmaster. "It's your family I'm worried about."

A look passes between them, then Gunther steps out into the hallway, closing the door behind him. Through the ceiling-to-floor windows, he sees a horde of students huddled in a tight ring in the courtyard some distance away. Their backs are facing him, some of them are punching the air, hooting and shouting like hooligans.

"What is this place coming to?" Gunther frowns, shakes his head and walks off.

32. THOMAS

Thomas knew it was a trap the moment he walked into the back room of the museum. His eagerness to retrieve his lost package blinded him to all the earlier signs – an unmanned guard post, the unlocked doors, empty hallways, but most of all, the anxious look on Annelie's face as she led him into the trap.

Looking back, all the signs were there, he just didn't pay enough attention to them. When he stepped through the doorway, the door flung shut behind him with a loud bang. Immediately, he was sprung by a chorus of clicks. Five barrels of guns pointed at him from all directions. Before he could do anything, two men pounced on him, pinning him down onto the concrete floor. In the commotion, he saw Annelie scurrying away through the back door. His eyes met hers when she threw him a backward glance. In them, he saw tears of fright. He forgave her instantly.

Every man for himself, Thomas thought as the men pushed his face down onto the floor until all he could taste was cold concrete. The only thing within his field of vision was a pair of gleaming black shoes. Thomas whimpered when the men manhandled him with brute force, pulling his shoulders backwards until the handcuffs clicked shut around his wrist. He didn't struggle. He made no attempt to fight back. It had all happened quickly but somehow, time seemed to be moving slowly, the seconds stretching out like long minutes. Before he knew it, he was pulled up onto his feet, an officer on either side of him, grabbing him by the arm, pushing him into the hallway and then into an empty office.

Now, strapped to a wooden chair, Thomas glances around the empty office disinterestedly. He hears shuffling of footsteps in the hallway followed by a faint murmur, then the door hinges squeak as it opens.

The tramping footfall breaks the silence within the room. The door hinges squeak again and then the doorjamb clicks shut, shutting out the voices of people talking in the hallway. Now, they are alone.

"So, you've decided to come back after all," the voice comes from behind but Thomas does not turn around to see who it belongs to. He knows the kind of men who belong to the Nazis. They are men of bravado. Pompous and arrogant, devoid of any shred of humanity. All they care about is winning. At any cost.

"I'm disappointed," Thomas says as he stares at the floor.

"Oh? You're disappointed?" the voice behind moves around him in tandem with the tramping footfall, until the man is standing right in front of him. Thomas recognises the gleaming black shoes. He looks up and recognises the face as belonging to the man he spotted in the basement bar in Nové Město.

"How so?" adds the man, bemused.

"Your men have lost their edge," Thomas says, his gaze never leaving the man's face. "I've been here one week and they've only just managed to catch me now. Not as sharp as they used to be."

"I'm not too happy about that either, trust me," the man says as he walks behind the desk and plonks himself down in the chair. The cushion lets out a hiss as it sinks under his weight.

For a while, neither of them speaks. Accompanied only by the rhythmic ticking of the wall clock, both men study each other dispassionately.

"You know what I've been asking myself this past week?" The man is the first to speak when he is done studying Thomas. Thomas' eyes follow him as he leans back in his chair, his fingers interlaced over his belly.

"I'm sure you will tell me even if I don't want to hear it."

"Yes, that is true," he says. His chair creaks as he gets up slowly and walks around the desk with his hands in his pockets until he is standing right next to Thomas. Thomas does not bother to meet his gaze. Instead, he stares blankly ahead, catching only glimpses of the man's gleaming shoes out of the corner of his eye.

"I think to myself… what does an exile have here that is so important that he just absolutely has to come back to get it?"

The pair of gleaming shoes steps beyond Thomas' field of vision. The man walks slowly, his pace deliberate as he encircles him.

"Then I asked myself, why now? Why not earlier? Why not ten years or twenty years ago?"

His question hangs in the air unanswered.

I tried, Thomas thinks but does not say. *But the borders were closed.*

"We eliminated every single member of the Resistance on our list," the man says now, sounding distant. "They didn't stand a chance." He scoffs, sounding pleased with himself.

"But we couldn't get you because you were outside our jurisdiction," he says with an audible sigh. The pair of gleaming shoes reappear in Thomas' field of vision on the other side.

"But not anymore."

Thomas hears a smile in his voice. He looks up and sees the smug grin bearing down on him. He grits his teeth and narrows his eyes, struggling to get out of the chair. The man merely laughs.

"You see, your romanticism is your weakness, Tomáš Marz." The man steps away from Thomas and walks slowly back to his seat behind the desk.

"I always knew you would come back. It was only a matter of time," he says, lifting his trousers before sitting down. "And I knew the first place you would come to is this museum. You are so predictable." The chair cushion hisses again as his weight sinks onto it.

Thomas watches him lean back, his chair creaking one more time as he takes up his previous position. The clock on the wall keeps ticking but he sits there idly, watching Thomas with disinterest.

"I got the package, you know?" he says with raised eyebrows after a spell of silence. Thomas grits his teeth and squirms in his chair. The chair legs scrape the floor noisily but does not give way.

"I haven't opened it yet though," he continues, fiddling with a paperweight, his eyes flicker with annoyance. "I wanted to but the War Office wouldn't let me. They said I would be tampering with evidence, or something like that."

He puts down the paperweight and waves a hand nonchalantly. "Too much bureaucracy if you ask me," he adds.

"Tell me, what's in it? The package?" He looks coyly at Thomas as he straightens up.

"Nothing of consequence," Thomas says, catching his breath.

"Surely it must be something precious? Why else would you risk your life for it? Doesn't matter. I will find out soon enough," he mutters to himself eventually.

The clock on the wall continues to tick away. Beyond the closed door, faint sounds of footsteps advance and recede down the hallway.

"They call you Werewolf," Thomas speaks after he stops trying to break free from the straps.

"Hmm? Yes. I've been known by that nickname." The man looks at him with boredom in his eyes.

"So, it's true then?" Thomas raises his eyebrows.

"What's true?"

"The story about the wolves."

The man throws back his head and laughs. His laughter reverberates within the walls of the room, making a faint echo.

"It's a good story, isn't it?" he says when his laughter subsides. "A little boy got lost in the woods and came face to face with a pack of wild wolves." He mimics the voice of a newscaster.

"The wolves stood no chance against his bravery and skill. He wrestled each of them and, after a Herculean effort, made the wolves run deep into the woods with their tails between their legs. Amazing." He chuckles, slapping his thigh as he laughs.

When he finally stops laughing, the man stares blankly into space, suddenly deep in thought.

"To be honest, I don't remember any of it," he says quietly, bringing his gaze back to Thomas. "All I have is a scar."

At the mention of the scar, Thomas raises his eyebrows slightly.

"Do you want to see it?" he asks, almost giddy.

Without waiting for an answer, the man gets up, sheds his jacket and unbuttons his shirt. Thomas feels his throat catch as the shirt comes away, revealing a pale stretch of skin on the man's shoulder. Thomas' eyes begin to mist as he stares at the scar.

"It's quite magnificent, isn't it?" the man says, catching him staring. He parades his scar this way and that before pulling his shirt back on and re-doing his buttons with practised ease. "My mother told me it's a cut. If you ask me, I think it's more than that."

Thomas says nothing as he watches, through the curtain of blur, the man pulls his jacket back on. His eyes train on his face, taking in his jaw line, his nose and his eyes. Looking at this man now, he asks himself why he did not notice them before.

"Tell me about your family," Thomas' voice quivers when he speaks next. "A high-ranking army officer like you must come from good pedigree."

"There's not much to tell, really," the man says, looking up at Thomas as he absently reaches into the back pocket of his trousers, producing a comb which he expertly runs through his hair. Once he is done, he puts it back into his back pocket and wanders around his desk to where Thomas is sitting.

"Let's see… grew up in a military family. Father was an officer in the air force. He was stationed here actually, in the Protectorate of Bohemia and Moravia," he replies with a frown. Then, smiling, he adds, "My mother was a wonderful woman. The kindest, most loving person I've ever known. She loved me very much, you know. Passed away not long ago. A shame, really."

"I'm sorry to hear that," Thomas croaks, unable to meet his gaze. A sour sensation rushes to the tip of his nose.

"That's life, isn't it? You are born into this world, you live and then you die. There are no two ways about it, you know?"

Thomas sniffs.

"And that scar, that… *cut*, how did you get it?" Thomas looks at him with glistening eyes.

"I've always had it, ever since I was a little boy," he replies, looking at the patch on his shoulder where his scar is. "My mother told me I cut myself while playing in the woods when I was very little but I don't remember any of it."

"You have a birth mark," Thomas mumbles. His eyes are on his own feet now, staring as drops of tears fall onto his shoes.

"What did you say?"

Thomas looks up with a crumpled face, tears streaming down his cheeks.

"You have a birth mark... on your left foot...," he says, almost whispering.

"How... how did you know?" the man stares at him in disbelief. "I've never told anyone about it."

Thomas hunches over and begins to weep, his shoulders trembling violently.

"You were right," he says as he stifles a sob. "Your mother was a wonderful woman. The kindest, most loving person I've ever known."

"You... you knew my mother?"

In the stunned silence, Thomas continues to cry but he does not answer.

33. THE PAST

1942

The farmhouse was the perfect place to hide. Away from the main road, hidden behind thick clumps of trees, visits from outsiders were rare.

Jan came to visit once, in the first week of June. He came in the same truck Thomas had arrived in months earlier. Krystof drove while Karel rode shotgun. Jan came cloaked under a dark blanket, crouching on the floor, under Karel's short legs.

Thomas spotted the truck coming down the dirt lane from an upstairs window before anyone else did. By the time the engine could be heard approaching the house, he was already downstairs. The truck slowed to a stop, its engine killed, then the truck doors opened and slammed shut. Through the downstairs window, Pavel saw that there were three of them. He opened the front door and they piled in noisily. Greetings and handshakes were exchanged before Krystof and Karel followed Pavel into the kitchen, a trail of shoe prints in their wake, leaving Jan and Thomas in the living room.

"See this?" Jan said, brandishing a folded newspaper as he ran his fingers through his tousled hair. "The assassination of Reinhard Heydrich!" He poked at the headlines on the top fold of the newspaper. Thomas' brows crinkled as he took the newspaper, unfolded it and began to read.

"And this," Jan pulled another folded piece of paper from his back pocket, unfolded it quickly in a noisy rustle and shoved it into Thomas' hands. On the top fold was a picture of a Mercedes Benz 320 Cabrio Special with a tattered back tyre, crumpled soft top and a dismembered car door. At the bottom of the page were pictures of two men not much older than Thomas. The picture of Heydrich, Thomas dismissed without even a fleeting glance.

"Have they found them?" Thomas said, pointing to the pictures of the two men.

"The posters went up that afternoon after Heydrich was ambushed. The Gestapo and the SS are searching all the homes in Prague. There's a hefty price on their heads, I won't be surprised if someone sings soon. We're doing the rounds, making sure all the radios are stashed away."

Thomas thought for a moment, rolled the newspapers up into a baton and handed it back to Jan.

"I've been thinking," he said pensively. "How quickly can you get us out of here?"

"You can't be serious?" Jan frowned. "Tom, you have a baby now. The journey is too long and too dangerous for a grown man, let alone a child!"

Thomas was about to speak when Krystof marched in, Karel hot on his heels.

"Time to go," he said to Jan, pointing at the watch on his own wrist. "We still have two more stops to make. Let's go." He cocked his head towards the front door.

Under Pavel's watchful eye, all three piled out of the house into the truck. Thomas returned to his perch by the upstairs window. From behind the curtain, he watched anxiously as the vehicle made a turn and drove off, kicking up a cloud of dust in its wake.

Weeks later, news came from Jan in the form of a brown envelope. Nobody saw him arrive or leave. It was Milena who found the brown envelope on the floor, slid in from underneath the door. They gathered in the upstairs bedroom, Mother and Sarah sitting next to Milena on the edge of the bed while Pavel took residence in the only chair in the room. Thomas parked himself next to the cupboard, leaning against the wall with both hands in his trouser pockets. No one said a word as Pavel tore open the brown envelope and fished out the folded piece of paper inside. After placing his reading glasses on the bridge of his nose, he unfolded the letter, cleared his throat and began to read out loud.

"Hitler is furious about Heydrich's death," Pavel read. "We are all being punished for the assassination. The Krauts hunted the assassins all the way to Lidice. All the men and older boys were rounded up, lined up against a wall and then shot to death. The women and children were put on trains, sent off to Poland. The entire village was burned to the ground. Then they did the same to Lezaky. No one survived."

"Tell Tom now is not the time," Pavel finished reading and plucked the glasses from the bridge of his nose. A grave silence fell. No one spoke as Jan's words echoed in the privacy of their own thoughts.

"What a waste," Pavel sighed, shaking his head. "Hundreds of Czechs' blood, maybe even thousands, just to pay for one German's death." He shook his head a few more times, his face crumpling with pain.

"It could have been worse," Milena said quietly, her eyes fixed on a spot on the floor. "There could have been much more."

Thomas looked over at Sarah, humming a lullaby at the baby cradled in the crook of her arm. He then looked over first at Mother, then at Milena and finally at Pavel. A string of sighs followed, the creases on their forehead deepening with worry. Thomas knew there was only one thought on everyone's minds.

That could have been us.

It could have been anyone, Thomas wanted to say but didn't. Deep down, he was secretly relieved that the Nazis headed northwest instead of coming south. They could have been found out. Thomas gulped nervously. Never had he felt more anxious to leave but they were trapped, with no means of getting out.

For that entire summer, neither Thomas nor Sarah left the house. With not a soul in sight for miles, they still could not risk being seen. They fell into a lull, filling the long days with books, playing with Miloš or listening to the gramophone. The only radio in the farmhouse was broken, cutting them off from the outside world. Save for the snippets of news that came with their visitors, they knew nothing of what went on beyond the front door.

Mother kept to herself more and more, and was often found weeping on the narrow bed in the annex. After the baby was born, Thomas and Sarah took the bed in the bedroom. Pavel brought in an old cot for Miloš and they all made a quilt for him out of scraps of fabric Milena had stashed away from dresses made over the years.

The days turned into weeks, and weeks into months. Every so often, they received news from Ivan through Krystof. His letters were often short, hurriedly scribbled on scraps of paper. He spoke sparingly of the trains ferrying human cargo out of Prague, and sent them rations when he was able to. He never signed any of the letters, and made no mention of Amos.

The warm weather came and went. Like a changing watercolour painting, the colours of the woods around the farm house began to change as the seasons turned. The warm wind turned cold and the nights became longer. Autumn crept into their lives, bringing with it the harsh reminder of yet another winter under a hostile occupation.

Late one night in November, Thomas woke up to the sound of engines revving in a distance, slicing through the silence at high speed.

"Sarah, wake up!" he whispered urgently, shaking his sleeping wife. She stirred and rubbed her eyes.

"What is it?" she mumbled. The revving of the engines grew louder, closing in on them rapidly. Sleep deserted her instantly. They both leapt out of bed and fumbled through the darkness to reach the cot. By now, the engines were roaring right outside the front door. A panic look passed between them.

"Quick! Get in there!" Thomas whispered urgently. She picked Miloš up and padded hurriedly towards their hiding place. The cupboard door flung open, the hole appeared and Mother's anxious face peered out.

"Mother, get back inside!" Sarah whispered. Mother ducked back in. They took turns climbing in, and, very quietly, Thomas closed the cupboard door and replaced the false wall.

The house shook when a banging came over the front door.

"OPEN UP!" a voice shouted. "OPEN UP NOW!"

Crouching in complete darkness, Thomas could feel Sarah next to him, shaking like a leaf. Her hand fumbled in the dark and found his arm, clutching him so tightly that her nails were digging into his flesh. His own heart thumped hard in his chest as the banging on the front door became more urgent. Within the tiny confines of the annex, a small whimper escaped from Mother's direction.

"Mother, I need you to be very. Quiet," Thomas hissed. "Don't make a sound. And Don't. Move."

In the inky darkness, Thomas sat very still, listening carefully to every sound in the house.

On the other side of the wall, floorboards creaked in the upstairs landing. Pavel's familiar footfall padded towards their room. The hinge squeaked as the door opened and then shut before the set of steps padded back. Two sets of footsteps walked down the staircase, one slow creak at a time.

"OPEN UP!!!" The shouting became louder and the banging more urgent. "OPEN UP!!!"

When the footsteps stopped at the bottom of the staircase, the front door creaked open. Thomas held his breath as he gave Sarah's hand a squeeze. She cowered closer to him, shaking uncontrollably.

Downstairs, a muffled exchange took place. Then a loud voice spoke angrily, followed by the drumming of heavy boots filing into the house, dispersing in all directions. Doors flung opened, banging into walls. Cupboards were opened and then slammed shut, drawers slid out and then banged close. Over the commotion, voices spoke urgently, barking orders. Boots trampled heavily in and out of rooms. Noises of things crashing and glass shattering made them shrink further.

"Did you say it's only you and your wife here?" Another voice came from the bottom of the staircase. A murmur replied. Right at that moment, Miloš let out a whimper. Within the annex, a gasp followed. A hand clasped over a mouth. Another whimper came out in a stifled muffle.

"What's that?" the stern voice wafted up the staircase.

Thomas stopped breathing.

A mumble came in Milena's voice. A loud slap followed. Then a whimper.

The voice fired orders angrily. Immediately, boots drummed from all directions in a stampede towards the staircase, thumping up the steps urgently. An orchestra of creaks came as boots trampled heavily on the landing. Doors creaked opened and boots stamped into rooms. Hinges squeaked as cupboard doors were opened and then shut. There was shuffling, fumbling and sounds of drawers being slid opened and then slammed shut. Taps and knocks came over walls and wooden furniture. Unintelligible words were exchanged in urgent tones. Then the thumping moved out of the rooms back onto the landing.

When the door to their room squeaked open, Thomas held his breath. Boots stamped into the room. The floorboards creaked and then went quiet. A squeak of the hinges told him that the cupboard door was opened. A rustle followed the scraping of coat hangers against the metal rail. A voice came from the doorway, interrupting the scraping sound. Through the thin wall, Thomas heard a quick exchange of words.

Nothing in the bedrooms.

There was a brief pause, then the voice nearest to the cupboard spoke.

"Tell the men to wait outside, I'll be down in a minute."

Thomas sat very still, waiting for the squeak of the cupboard door closing. Next to him, Sarah was trembling. She pressed Miloš' face into her chest and held him tightly. The baby squirmed but did not make a sound.

A set of footsteps thudded out of the room, onto the landing and down the staircase but the creaking of the cupboard door closing never came.

He knows. Thomas thought, alarmed.

A thin wall away, the officer stood outside the opened cupboard door, staring at the wall between the parting of clothes hanging from the coat hangers. The bed in the room was unmade. Its rumpled sheets were still warm. The cot in the corner also did not escape his attention. He looked around the sparsely furnished room – at the wrought iron bed, one wooden chair, a dresser, and the wooden cupboard sidled up against the wall. *Someone is hiding in that room, he can smell it.*

A voice called out from the bottom of the staircase, urging him to hurry. He did not reply. Instead, he pulled the revolver from its holster on his waist belt, pointed the barrel at the wall and fired rapidly, punching neat holes across the wall. The loud bangs and the thudding of bullets through the boards cracked the deep silence, reverberating through the house, rippling through the woods in the small hours of the night.

Thomas cowered as the splinters of wood showered on him in the deafening explosion of gunfire. His face was still buried in his knees when the explosion stopped. The smell of burnt ash hung in the air. In his ears was an incessant ringing. Then, two more shots were fired downstairs. A car door slammed shut, then a fleet of engines roared to life, speeding away as quickly as they had arrived.

When all was quiet, Thomas looked up to find rays of faint light shining into the annex through the bullet holes, casting a steady constellation against the wall. He drew a deep breath and swept the splinters away from his shoulders.

"They're gone," he whispered as he nudged Sarah. A loud thud fell onto the floor. A baby's cry erupted within the annex.

"Sarah?" Thomas called out shakily. No answer came. The baby went on crying. "Mother?"

Still no answer came.

Something warm touched his feet. When he looked down, Thomas saw a pool of dark liquid, slowly spreading around him. Heart thumping, his eyes followed the viscous pool until they finally fell on two lumps slumped against the wall.

Thomas stopped breathing.

He doesn't remember screaming, only that the guttural sound of his voice erupted within the tiny confines of the annex in a long, pained howl.

When all the air had been sucked out of his lungs, Thomas collapsed on the floor and began to cry. Within the narrow confines of the annex, surrounded by Miloš' desperate wail, he crawled over the pool of blood weakly. With trembling hands, he pulled Sarah's limp body towards him. She flopped lifelessly as he gathered her neatly into the crook of his arm.

"Sarah, wake up! Please... please wake up," Thomas cried, his face wet with tears. His quivering hand cupped her chin, lifting her face up close to his own. Through the curtain of tears, he could see that her eyes were wide open but there was no longer any light in them. His face twisted in pain as he let out another howl.

"Sarah... my sweet... please... please... please wake up...," he sobbed into her hair as he cradled her limp body, rocking back and forth, back and forth until he could no longer feel his legs.

"Please... don't leave me... don't leave me...."

He howled and pleaded to the heavens, at a God he could not see. When finally, no answer came and the baby continued to wail, Thomas flew into a fit of rage, cursing and shouting until there was no more air left in his lungs.

Eventually, the baby stopped crying. Within the silence of the annex, Thomas knelt in numbness. He no longer felt anything, only a deep emptiness where his heart used to be. Planting a kiss on Sarah's lips, he wiped his eyes and gently lay her down on the floor. Then, he picked up a whimpering Miloš, held him to his chest and gingerly climbed out of the annex, through the cupboard and into the bedroom.

Under the silvery moonlight, Thomas placed Miloš on the bed and removed the blood-soaked wrap from around him. The baby lay quietly, staring at him meekly. Fresh blood oozed from his tiny shoulder, quickly seeping into the sheets. Thomas wiped the snot from his own nose with the back of his hand before examining the wound. The gash was shallow but long.

He went over to the dresser and began rummaging through drawers. When he didn't find what he was looking for, he left to go downstairs.

As he hurried down the staircase, Thomas was met by a gust of cold wind. He saw first that the front door was wide open. Then, his eyes fell on two bodies sprawled on the floor in haunting stillness. He felt his throat catch and hot tears began to fill his eyes.

"Pavel? Milena?" he croaked even though he knew they would not answer. At the bottom of the staircase, in front of the wide-opened front door, they lay completely still, dressed only in their night clothes in the chill of the night.

Thomas broke into another loud sob as he stepped into the puddle of blood. When he went to close the door, his gaze fell on the tyre tracks on the quiet dirt lane. With an angry sniff, he shut the door, cutting off the chill of the wintry night.

He found half a bottle of vodka in the liquor cabinet and took a swig out of it. The burning sensation in his throat made him wince but the liquor soon calmed his frayed nerves. He took the bottle with him, went into the kitchen and began looking through cupboards and drawers. In a bottom drawer, he found a metal tin with some gauze and bandages. From Milena's sewing basket, he found a small needle and some thread. Then, grabbing everything, he climbed back up the stairs.

Between steadying his trembling hands and wiping his nose, Thomas tended to Miloš carefully. He began by uncorking the bottle and splashing some vodka onto the wound. The baby let out a blood-curdling shriek, his little mouth stretching wide on his tiny scrunched-up face. Tears fell from Thomas' eyes faster than he could wipe them away.

"Shhh… shhh…," he hushed through his tears, his face crumpling in pain. The baby's wail deafened him, cutting deep into his heart. With trembling hands, Thomas began to stitch the wound. The moment the needle punctured his shoulder, Miloš let out a sickening shriek. Pained, Thomas bit his lip and pressed on. Every puncture of the needle to his delicate skin made both Miloš and Thomas cry. Thomas didn't think he had the strength in him to keep going.

Eventually, he finished dressing the wound. When he was done, he held Miloš to his chest and began to rock him. With a hoarse, broken voice, he hummed the lullaby Sarah used to hum until the crying stopped and Miloš fell asleep.

Sometime later, after he had placed Miloš back in his cot, Thomas wiped the tears off his slippery face and got dressed silently. He went downstairs, through the back door and into the stables where he found a shovel. In the crisp night air, under the silvery moonlight, he went out into the open yard, struck the shovel into the cold, hard ground and began to dig. He went at it, throwing himself into the task, wisps of white fog blowing from his nostrils as he worked the shovel into the ground, scooping up chunks of the hard earth, tossing it into a mount on the side and repeating it all over again.

When he had dug a trench big enough to hold a body, he climbed out, wiped the sweat from his brow and began to dig another one.

He dug into the early hours of the morning, tears falling from his eyes as the shovel hit the ground and came back out with a scoop of the earth. Every so often, he stopped to wipe his eyes with the sleeve of his coat before he went on digging. In the hard, physical labour, he found an outlet to vent his rage. For his grief, there was no consolation.

By the time he was done with the trenches, light had begun to streak across the sky. As he caught his breath, Thomas stood back to survey his work. Then, he threw the shovel down and went back inside.

Back in the annex, Thomas stared emptily at the two bodies lying in the darkened puddle of blood. In the eerie silence, he scooped Sarah up, sniffed and carefully climbed out of the annex. Her small frame folded in his arms, its limpness brought on a fresh round of choked sobs. Thomas struggled to breathe.

When he gingerly placed her down in the bathtub in the downstairs bathroom, Thomas dried his eyes and began to speak.

"Do you remember that day when I first saw you outside the synagogue?" he croaked as he turned on the tap. A loud gush of water rushed out. He sank onto his knees on the cold tiles of the floor and began scooping water over her face and hair. Slicks of red streaked down the tub, running in a squiggly stream down the drain hole.

"I knew, from the first time I saw you, that we were meant for each other."

He swallowed hard when he removed her nightdress and saw the two bullet holes punched into her chest. Crying quietly, he took a wet sponge to her body, gently scrubbing her clean in between wiping his eyes and nose. Then he held her, inhaling the familiar scent of her hair.

He knelt there until his legs lost all feeling, tracing a finger over the shape of her face, the crook of her nose and the petals of her lips, memorising every detail of her face. Then he pressed his trembling lips to hers and kissed her for the very last time.

He found her favourite dress and dressed her in it. Then, with an empty heart, he scooped her up, carried her into the backyard and gently laid her down in her final resting place.

When all four bodies were laid to rest in their graves, Thomas stood over them and said his final goodbye. His nose stung with sourness as he picked up the shovel and began to scoop from the mount of soil.

As he heaped soil over his beloved Sarah, tears could not stop falling from his eyes. The dark soil fell on her, covering her like a blanket one shovel at a time until eventually, all that was left was a mount where she lay buried.

By the time the sun was high in the sky, Thomas had buried all four bodies. Staring at the mounts of freshly heaped soil, he wiped the snot from his nose with the sleeve of his shabby coat and dried his watery eyes. Then, he took one last look at the graves and, with a solemn finality, turned and went back into the house.

Upstairs, he found Miloš wide awake in his cot, staring at him with lively eyes. For the first time that day, Thomas smiled in spite of his pain. He peeled back the quilt and saw that, underneath the crusty gauze, the wound had stopped bleeding. Relief washed over him instantaneously. He drew in a deep breath, feeling a sudden injection of strength.

Thomas fed his son, then washed and changed him before washing himself. After changing into some clean clothes, he took a rucksack and went around the house collecting things he knew he would need.

When he came across Sarah's things, a lump formed in his throat. In a small box, he found the flower motive hair comb and the well-thumbed copy of The Good Soldier Švjek he gave to her all those years ago. Beneath the movie ticket stubs and other mementos of their life together, he found a picture of their wedding day. It brought tears to his eyes.

Carefully, Thomas put the box into his rucksack. Then, strapping his son tightly to his chest, he pulled on his coat, strapped the rucksack to his back and headed into the woods.

34. ANNELIE

Annelie stops running and hides behind a garbage tip. In a quiet back alley with nothing but crushed boxes, empty crates and industrial size garbage dumpsters, she bends over, hands on her knees as she catches her breath. Her heart pounds furiously against her chest. She looks over her shoulders, relieved that no one is on her tail. There, she slinks down against the side of the garbage tip until she is hugging her knees. Then, she starts crying.

It had all happened so fast. One minute she was leading Thomas down the hallway to the back room, the next minute, they came face to face with barrels of guns. The men were fast. In no time, they had Thomas pinned down on the floor, kissing the cold concrete. In the commotion, she made a mad dash for the back door. The last image she registered before dashing out was the picture of Thomas being brutally manhandled, the men forcefully cuffing his wrists behind his back. Their eyes met. In his, Annelie saw only sadness.

"That wasn't how it was supposed to happen…," she sobs to herself, wiping her wet face with the sleeves of her blouse.

The officer – the Werewolf as he was called – assured her that he only wanted to talk to Thomas, to ask him questions.

"Nothing sinister," he said as Annelie eyed him suspiciously.

Now, crouching in the dirty back alley, Annelie is terrified. She is terrified of what will happen to Thomas. To Jack. And she is equally terrified about her own fate. The chaos and confusion leaves her trembling. Her immediate urge is to return to the flat to seek Jack out.

She begins running in that direction, her long legs striding down the streets, carrying her as fast as they can. Her heart thumps furiously in her chest. Her lungs are burning but she does not stop. Instead, she keeps running. She needs to get to Jack before the police gets to him. She must warn him.

What have I done? Annelie's face crumples with pain as the picture of Thomas being pinned to the ground flashes before her eyes.

"What have I done?" she mutters to herself desperately as she speeds past shops and buildings, past the early morning commuters getting on their way.

When she is finally across the road from the flat, she sees Jack emerging from the front door, his hands behind his back, an officer on either side of him, shoving him out onto the street towards the opened door of a car parked just outside. For a split second, his eyes chance upon hers, then with a final solemnity, he disappears into the car. One officer climbs in after him. The other walks around to the other side of the car. When he opens the door, Annelie catches a glimpse of Jack before the officer climbs in and the car door slams shut.

He merely sits there, staring straight ahead, his hands cuffed behind his back, not looking at anyone.

"He must think I've betrayed him," she mumbles to herself, her face crumpling with despair. Her eyes follow the car as the engine starts and begins to drive off.

They might be hunting me next, Annelie thinks as she looks around in panic. Then, she begins to run.

Before the car is even out of sight, she has covered the length of two blocks in the opposite direction, glancing over her shoulders every so often to see if she might be followed.

She stumbles into a deserted back alley, and finds a spot to hide behind another a grimy garbage tip. There, she sinks down onto her knees, shaking like a leaf. As she catches her breath, she wonders about her fate. She knows she can't go home. She also knows she can't stay there. Her job at the museum is as much as gone, of that she is certain. She thinks of the little bit of money she has saved up. It wouldn't last her long – a few weeks at best. Beyond that, her future is uncertain. Annelie's face crumples in desperation.

What am I to do? She whimpers.

When her nerves calmed, Annelie remembers something. Quickly, she wipes the last of the tears off her face, and climbs to her feet. Breaking into a run, she exits the alley and turns into a small street that snakes further out of town. The day is still young. The streets are quiet. If she hurries, she might make it to Pavlina's before she takes the bus out to the factory for her shift.

35. GUNTHER

It's been a long day for Gunther. As he walks out of Modenschau Magazine's office into the warm afternoon sun, beads of perspiration begin to form on his forehead.

The meeting with Frau Fischer did not go as well as Gunther had hoped. He had spent 45 minutes sitting in the foyer, waiting for his appointment. When he was finally called in, he had only ten minutes to make his case.

"Herr Scholz, we run a very tight ship here at Modenschau," Frau Fischer said, looking at him from behind the reading glasses perched low on the bridge of her nose. "Unfortunately, the magazine business is not doing as well as it used to, what with the internet and all. A lot less people are buying magazines now that they can find things online. It's nothing personal against Eva. We had to let her go because she is simply too expensive."

As she surveyed the glossy runway photos wedged between the crevices of her carefully painted fingernails, flipping backwards and forwards as she made notes on the margins, she added, "I can assure you this is not an isolated incident. We have gone through three waves of downsizing in the last twelve months alone. It was bound to happen."

"Surely you can make an exception, Frau Fischer? Eva is a great asset to the magazine. Good talent is hard to come by, you said so yourself," Gunther said.

"Eva is a very talented editor," Frau Fischer said without looking at him. "I'm sure, with her credentials, she will be snapped up by another publishing house in no time. Besides, didn't she say she's always wanted to write a book? This would be the perfect opportunity for such an endeavour. Now, if you don't mind, I have an awfully full schedule I have to get back to. You can see yourself out, can't you?"

She smiled wryly at Gunther. The meeting was over in five minutes.

As he stands outside the glass office building, the heavy traffic passing him by on the busy road, Gunther decides to pick up some of Eva's favourite Bregenwurst from the delicatessen around the corner.

The bell tinkles when he enters the shop. The rush of cool air from the air conditioner overhead is a welcomed relieve from the heat. Three pairs of eyes turn to look at him – one belonging to the young woman working behind the counter, the other two to the ladies she is attending to. The older of the two ladies eyes him from head to toe, unable to hide the disdain on her face but all three soon resume what they were doing before he entered the shop.

Gunther waits his turn as the ladies are being served. He takes the opportunity to survey the generous selection of sausages, cured meats and cheeses behind the glass counter, making a mental list of the things he would like to buy. The three ladies cackle in cheerfulness as meats and cheeses are fetched and then wrapped up in brown paper. Crisp bills exchange hands at the cash register and the wrapped packages are handed over before the ladies bid each other farewell.

As the two ladies pass him by on their way out of the shop, the older of the two snaps at him, "You're in the wrong shop."

"Excuse me?" Gunther crinkles his brow.

"You're the in wrong shop," the lady repeats sourly, the wrinkly corners of her thin lips curling downwards. "This shop is for Aryans only. You shouldn't even be allowed in here."

Gunther's gaze darts between the three women, all of whom stare at him with obvious disapproval.

He inhales deeply. Without restrain, he barks, "How dare you speak to me like that? I served in the armed forces in Greater Germania for fifty years! I have the same right to be in this shop as you do!"

The tension in the shop is palpable. The old lady glares at Gunther, clicking her tongue noisily.

"Let's go, Mama," the younger of the two ladies says, placing a hand on her elbow. "Let's not pick a fight. It's not worth the hassle."

Gunther stares at the older lady indignantly as she shuffles towards the door. When the door opens a crack and the bell tinkles gaily, she turns around, hawks noisily and spits in his direction. With narrowed eyes, she raises her crooked forefinger at Gunther.

"In my time, there was a place for people like you," she says. "It's called Auschwitz."

Gunther's glare follows her until she is out of the shop. In no time, the door closes to the tinkling of the bell and the two ladies re-join the bustling city sidewalk, leaving him standing in the middle of the shop, his face a deep crimson.

"What a quack," Gunther mutters, rolling his eyes skywards. As he turns around to place his order for the Bregenwurst, the bell tinkles once again. A sharply dressed middle-aged man in a suit enters, flashing a dazzling smile.

"Ah, Herr Schubert! So good to see you!" the young woman beams as she flits eagerly towards him, pulling a fresh pair of latex gloves over her dainty hands.

"HEY!!! I was here first!" Gunther shouts, pounding his fist on the cool stainless steel counter. The middle-aged man frowns, eyes him warily but does not say anything.

"Sir, please wait your turn. I will be with you once I'm done serving this gentleman," the young woman behind the counter chides.

"What??? I WILL NOT wait my turn. I WAS HERE FIRST!" Gunther slams his palm down onto the counter once again, his face flushed with rage. "Where is Hans? I want to see Hans. NOW!"

Gunther's big voice fills the small confines of the delicatessen, startling both the young woman and Herr Schubert. When the young woman does not respond immediately, he shouts again.

"I. WANT. TO. SEE. HANS. NOW!" he pounds his fist on the counter – once for each word, rattling jars of pickled cucumbers out of their rightful place.

"Hey, there's no need for this bad attitude, all right, old man?" Herr Schubert raises his voice to match his. "She's doing her best, okay?"

"Where is Hans? HANS!!! HANS!!!" Gunther continues to shout.

"Sir, may I suggest the deli in Spandau?" the young woman too raises her voice. "Perhaps it might have the kinds of food that are more suited to you?"

Gunther glares at them both, nostril flaring.

"SPANDAU??? SPANDAU???? What do you think I am? A DIRTY SLAV??? I WILL NOT go to Spandau! FOR THE LAST TIME – I. AM. NOT. A. DIRTY. SLAV!!!"

Gunther storms out of the deli, banging the door behind him. Standing on the sidewalk, chest heaving, Gunther glares through the shop window at Herr Schubert and the young woman. They both stare at him, deep frowns on their foreheads. Herr Schubert shakes his head in disbelief. With every muscle in his body, Gunter shouts through the glass window, "I. AM. NOT. A. DIRTY. SLAV!!!"

The shouting has strained him, he realises as he stands on the sidewalk. Feeling suddenly weak in the chest, Gunther clutches at his heart and stumbles his way to the underground station. A train arrives within seconds. He gets on hurriedly and sinks gratefully onto an empty bench.

As he catches his breath, he mutters angrily, "How dare they? Bunch of ingrates. Have they forgotten what I did for them? ALL of them???"

He is still angry when he arrives at Eva's house, cursing under his breath as he walks through the door. Once inside, he throws the keys into the bowl on the buffet in the entrance hall and calls out, "You will not believe the day I've had! The service at Hans' was an outrage!"

When no reply came, he wanders down the hallway, glancing into rooms until he arrives at the living room. He sees Eva first, sitting on the couch with red, watery eyes. Then his eyes fall on four uniformed men – Reichsmarschall Schmitt, the Constable and two Privates – standing before her.

"What's going on?" Gunther frowns as he slowly steps in. His glance darts around the room, skipping from one face to the next. No one responds immediately. It is Eva who speaks, after first having blown her nose into a scrunched-up tissue.

"Erik's been detained," she sobs, wiping her red nose.

"What? Why?" Gunther's frown deepens.

"He's been in a fight in school. Another boy is seriously hurt. He's in the hospital as we speak."

Gunther looks over at Reichsmarschall Schmitt.

"Schmitt, you and your men came here just to tell her this?" he asks, confused.

"The Constable was the one who came here to break the news," Reichsmarschall Schmitt replies perfunctorily. "I'm here for an entirely different reason."

Gunther looks at him quizzically. There is a sharp intake of breath before the Reichsmarschall speaks.

"We recently recovered an item that had been missing from the War Office. We believe it was... *stolen* some time ago. Somehow, it had turned up in your home."

"What?" Gunther's eyes widen in disbelief.

"Maybe this might jog your memory," the Reichsmarchall says, gesturing to one of the Privates. Gunther's eyes follow the young Private as he reaches into the satchel slung over his shoulder and pulls out an object wrapped in crinkled brown paper. He recognises the package immediately.

"That's impossible," he mutters in disbelief. "I didn't take that."

"We recovered it from your home during the raid the other day," Reichsmarschall Schmitt says. "Scholz, I'm afraid I have to take you in."

"That can't be right. Schmitt, I didn't take it! It wasn't me!" Gunther protests as the two Privates march over to him. He is still protesting when they seize him by the arms, clicking the cold steel of the handcuffs around his wrists.

"As with protocol, you will get a hearing," the Reichsmarchall says dispassionately, nodding to the Privates. They grab him by the armpits and march him out of the room.

"This is a mistake! I didn't do it! I didn't take the package!" Gunther yells as he struggles to break free. The Privates tighten their grip around his arms, dragging him, kicking and screaming out of the room.

When Gunther turns around next, he sees Eva paralysed on the couch, bursting into a fresh round of tears, her shoulders heaving violently. Two feet away, the Constable stands watching quietly with his hands behind his back.

Ahead of him, the front door opens and a jeep pulls up, ready to ferry him to a life of incarceration.

36. THOMAS

It happened quickly.

There was no hearing. Thomas made no plea. One moment he was crouching on the cold floor of a small windowless cell, bare footed and dressed in a prisoner's uniform, the next he was standing in a walled compound in broad daylight, the sun in his face, his hands tied behind his back.

When a guard stepped forward to blindfold him, he had said, "No. Leave me be."

The young man – no more than a boy – looked uncertainly at him first then at his superior. The man nodded perfunctorily and the boy retreated, blindfold in hand. And so Thomas was left standing there, facing his executioners in broad daylight, surrounded by the high walls of the compound.

The sky was a bright blue. There was not a cloud in sight. A light breeze blew gently, caressing his silvery hair. It was a beautiful day. Thomas couldn't ask for a more beautiful day to be outside. He squinted in the sunlight and gazed wondrously at the vast expanse of blue above him. It reminded him of his childhood, of a time when he was just a boy perched on the windowsill of his bedroom, looking out at the orange rooftops of the city, admiring the many spires that graced the skyline.

The firing squad was some ten feet away. There were eight men altogether. All young, all of them no more than mere boys. They stood at attention with their rifles straight by their side, waiting for a command from their superior.

It's not their fault, Thomas thought, despair and pity filling him in equal measures. He knew these men were merely trained soldiers. They were products of their environment, the fruit of their upbringing.

They don't know any better.

He felt the urge to sit them all down and to tell them of a time – a time long before the idea of them was even conceived, let alone their physical bodies – when people were merely people. Irrespective of their skin colour, their faith and their bloodline, they all belong to one race – the human race.

He felt the urge to tell them that their appearance – their fair hair, light eyes and even lighter skin – was merely a chance of nature.

A game of probabilities.

Just as they were born into Aryan families, they could easily have been born into non-Aryan families.

It was all luck. Russian Roulette. There was nothing more to it.

The rules that define supremacy are all man-made. He wanted to say. A long time ago, someone got it into his head that white people of Aryan heritage are the most superior of the human race. He got enough people to believe it so much that they failed to see that he himself had dark hair and brown eyes. He himself was a contradiction to his own conviction.

People are like that, Thomas learned in the long years of his life. Once they believe something, they latch onto it feverishly without regard for the truth. They defend it vehemently, without reason or rational thought. At the core of every conflict lies a difference in beliefs. It was as simple as that.

Nothing could be more obvious.

Thomas sighed.

Perhaps, in a parallel universe, in a world completely different to their own, the Aryans might be considered the inferior race, the lesser man. The tables would be turned, and he wouldn't be the one standing in that compound with his hands tied behind his back. In that parallel universe, he would be the one holding the rifle.

Perhaps even, in a different parallel universe, every human being is considered equal, regardless of their faith, their skin colour and heritage. And people lived in harmony all across the world, without fear, without oppression and without hatred.

I would have liked to have been born into that universe, Thomas thought.

As he resisted the urge to preach this sermon before his last breath, he was reminded that all over the world, across all time, human beings have habitually ostracised their own kind based on superficial differences.

Once upon a time, the Catholics murdered the Protestants despite both praying to the same God.

White-skinned races crossed oceans to colonise and enslave darker-skinned ones, labelling them as inferior and primitive.

Even tribes of the same land fought each other over territory and supremacy.

The cycle of faith-based and race-based hatred continues despite the colossal deaths and destruction in creates. One generation after another, it is perpetuated in different forms and shows up in different ways. But whatever form it takes, it still finds its roots in the human psyche of tribalism. Of people banding together against those who are not like them. Of staking their territory against those they consider the alien. It is a primal emotional response that defies logic, rationality and facts, easily incited by fear mongers and hate peddlers.

Thomas sighed as he looked into the eyes of every single one of the young men who stood before him. He felt sorry for them. He felt sorry for the miseducation they have received. He felt sorry that they did not have a mind of their own – one that deigned to question and think – *is this true? Is what I've been taught true? Is what I believe based on the truth? What is the truth?*

He felt even more sorry that each time they pull the trigger and a man dies at their hands, they lose a sliver of their humanity. Over their lifetime, they will be committing more heinous acts – ones far worse than what they were about to do. And each time they dehumanise a fellow human being, another sliver of their humanity is chipped away, until eventually, all that is left is their cold, empty hearts.

But it's not their fault, Thomas thought as he looked at them. They have not been taught that lives are precious, regardless of what package they come in. They have not been shown that every life exists only once. It gets only one chance at leaving an impression on human history. Once it is gone, it is gone forever.

Once it is gone, it is irreplaceable.

As they stood under the blazing sun – Thomas alone in facing his eight executioners – a metal door scraped open. From behind it, a man emerged.

It was the Werewolf.

Thomas looked over at him. He did not recognise this man in his army uniform. He did not tell him that the same men he now identifies with gave him the scar on his shoulder. Nor did he tell him that, if chance had not favoured him, his rightful place in the Reich would be in slavery, not superiority. More than anything else, he did not tell him he was his real father.

When his shame had passed him by, Thomas looked up at the sky and felt only a sense of peace. Then, he looked back at this man – this Werewolf – and said languidly, "I'm glad life turned out well for you. I'm sorry I didn't come back for you sooner. I tried. But it just wasn't meant to be."

The Werewolf did not flinch. At his command, all eight men raised their rifles in unison, their barrels aimed at Thomas.

Thomas closed his eyes at the sunlight and smiled. Underneath the red brightness of his eyelids, he saw Sarah's face smiling at him. After the long years of being apart, he was finally reuniting with his beloved. That thought filled him with peace.

At the Werewolf's signal, the men pulled their triggers. A loud explosion of gunshots filled the air. Thomas lurched about and fell onto the ground with a thud. Blood oozed out, seeping into the dirt. He died instantly.

The men stood back in attention, putting their rifles back by their side. Upon order, the compound emptied with the drumming of the boots. All that was left was Thomas' corpse. Everything else vanished the moment the bullets punched into him, taking along with them the life force within him.

37. THE PAST

November 1942

By the time Thomas spotted Krystof's house, daylight was fast disappearing from the sky. The cold grazed his cheeks, casting wisps of white fog with his breath. His fingers had lost all sensation in the hours he spent trudging through the icy slosh in the woods. His trouser cuffs were a darker shade of damp and his shoes squelched noisily through the slippery mud. He had lost track of time, guided only by the pale rays of sunlight shining through the branches of the tall trees as he made his way through the forest.

He stopped only once, when Miloš' whimper turned into an incessant cry. He fed him quickly, from a jar of homemade jam he found in Milena's pantry. He ate nothing himself, taking only a deep drink from his water canister. As the scant hours of daylight began to rapidly slip away, he became more anxious about being in the woods.

Thomas paused to catch his breath. The house was as described by Krystof – the wall the colour of daisy, one round window facing east, and rust coloured shingles for roof. It stood in a corner of a meadow – now barren from frost, a picture of drab isolation. Thomas imagined it to be beautiful in the spring time, when the grass is green and the daffodils bloom. For now, he could see it looming in the distance from between the tree trunks. The sight of it gave him an injection of new strength.

"We're almost there, Miloš," he said to the tiny bundle strapped to his chest. A pair of lively eyes stared curiously at him. Miloš gurgled and then smiled, prompting a smile from Thomas. He inhaled deeply, adjusted the straps on his shoulders and continued to walk. Under the darkening sky, he hiked out of the woods into the open meadow, guided only by the small rectangles of orange light coming from the house in the distance.

"Tomáš! What in heaven's name are you doing here?" Krystof's eyes were wide with shock when he opened the front door to find Thomas standing there, a small bundled strapped to his front, a rucksack on his back, shivering.

"Quick, come in," he beckoned hastily, peeling the rucksack from his shoulders. Thomas relinquished it gratefully as he stepped into the house. In the welcoming warmth, the door shut behind them, cutting off the evening chill.

In no time, a woman appeared, wiping her hand with a tea towel, Karel by her side. She broke into a smile when her eyes fell on the baby strapped over Thomas' chest.

"This is my wife, Dagmar," Krystof said. Thomas smiled wearily at her.

"Let me take him," she said, rushing forward, her arms outstretched. Thomas unwrapped Miloš from his chest and handed him to her by the armpits. His lively eyes moved from his father to the unknown woman, his little legs kicking in mid-air. Once he was firmly ensconced on Dagmar's hip, his tiny fingers reached out to touch her face, to which she responded by blowing raspberries at him, prompting a cackle of giggles. Thomas watched with a lump in his throat.

"He needs food," he said to Dagmar after he had swallowed the lump. She nodded at him before briskly disappearing into the kitchen.

A chair was pulled up next to the fireplace and Thomas was made to sit there. He sank onto it gratefully, relieved to be able to rest his aching feet.

"What happened?" Krystof asked as he took residence in his armchair by the fireplace. To Karel, he said, "Go get Tomáš a bowl of soup and some bread."

The boy scampered off to do as he was told.

Thomas swallowed hard, feeling the hot tears pricking his eyes.

"They came in the middle of the night," he said, voice trembling as he furiously blinked back the tears.

Krystof's face sank. He leaned forward, placing a comforting hand on Thomas' shoulder. Thomas was now biting his own fist, choking back the sobs, unable to utter another word.

"Here, eat something," Krystof said when Karel reappeared bearing a wooden tray containing a bowl of steaming soup and a hunk of bread, balancing the tray unsteadily as he walked. "You'll feel better after you've had some food in you."

Thomas wiped his tears and accepted the tray gratefully. He sat it down on his lap and began to sip his soup under Krystof's watchful eye, his eyes lowered the entire time.

"What now?" Krystof asked when the last of the soup had been mopped up by the bread, and the final crust eaten. Thomas lifted his eyes to meet his gaze.

"I need your help," he said quietly.

Just then, Dagmar reappeared with Miloš in her arms. Thomas could see that he now had a wooden rattle in his hand, which he shook and waved vigorously, giggling. Karel buzzed around him, taunting the child with a game of peekaboo.

"I need both your help," Thomas said now, looking from Krystof to Dagmar and then back at Krystof again.

"I am going to try to make my way to Britain," Thomas said. "I need you to keep Miloš safe until I get there."

A look passed between Krystof and Dagmar. In the silence, Thomas' eyes darted back and forth between the two. With each passing second, he grew anxious watching the expressions on their faces change.

"We can't keep the baby here," Krystof said finally, shaking his head at Thomas. "It's not safe for Miloš. And it will put us in harms' way."

Thomas' heart sank.

"Krystof!" Dagmar glared at him. Thomas' eyes followed her as she stamped across the room. She handed Miloš back to him, then taking Krystof by the hand, dragged him out of the room. Their tramping footfall ended in the next room where a door was first opened and then shut. Behind the walls, voices began to talk urgently.

"Do you know what I want to be when I grow up?" Karel's voice drew Thomas' attention away from the muffled voices in the next room.

"Tell me," Thomas said as he held Miloš to his chest. The baby yawned and blinked sleepily at him. Before long, he was fast asleep, the rattle slipping from his tiny hand.

"When I grow up, I want to be a pilot," Karel said, beaming at Thomas.

"And what will you do after you become a pilot?"

"I'm going to fly my plane and shoot the Krauts down!"

Thomas forced a smile but said nothing.

When the muffled exchanges in the next room stopped, both Krystof and Dagmar returned to the room. Thomas drew in a deep breath, looking at them hopefully.

"Here's what we are going to do," Krystof said as he walked over. Thomas' eyes followed him until he was once again in his chair by the fireplace. "Dagmar has a cousin living just outside Brno. She and her husband have no children of their own. They can take Miloš and look after him until you return. I will make the necessary arrangements."

Thomas exhaled loudly as relief washed over him.

"Thank you!" he replied with misted eyes, looking from Krystof to Dagmar and then back at Krystof again. "Thank you both so much. I don't know what I would do without you."

For the second time that evening, Thomas began to cry. Dagmar rushed to him, relieving him of the sleeping child in his arms as he sobbed uncontrollably, his body trembling with grief.

"There, there, Tom." Krystof clapped him gently on the back. He found no words for Thomas' grief, only a grave silence. There they sat, neither spoke a word as Thomas wept, accompanied only by the sound of fire crackling in the fireplace.

*

Three days later, on a frosty morning, a truck drove up the dirt lane leading to Krystof's doorstep. Krystof, Dagmar and Thomas piled out of the house as their visitor approached. When the truck slowed to a halt, the engine killed and the truck door opened, Thomas saw that it was Ivan.

"I'm so sorry," Ivan said with a pained look as he hugged Thomas tightly. Thomas' nose stung with sourness as he hugged him back, grateful to see his old friend. Then, without another word, they parted.

Silently, he turned to Dagmar and took Miloš from her arms. Standing on the front veranda, he held his son for a long time, breathing in his milky scent as he stroke his tiny back. Then, with glistening eyes, he gingerly placed him in the wicker basket lined with a quilt that Dagmar had prepared for the journey. The baby stared at him with lively eyes, gurgling and waving his tiny arms. Thomas felt a lump in his throat.

As Dagmar ferried a packed bag into the truck, Thomas pressed an envelope and a small box wrapped clumsily in brown paper into Ivan's hands.

"Take good care of my son, Ivan," he said, voice breaking. Then, he turned to look at Miloš for the last time, memorising every detail of his face before planting a soft kiss on his delicate forehead.

"I love you," he croaked, furiously blinking back the tears that were threatening to fall from his eyes.

Then, they were gone – Ivan, Dagmar and the wicker basket holding his son and the promise of his future, all bundled into the truck. The engine roared to life and the truck began to back out before turning around to head back in the direction it came from.

As the truck drove away, Thomas ran after it, waving his arm at a son he could no longer see. His eyes filled with tears as wisps of white fog blew from his sour nose. Within him was an emptiness he knew he could never fill.

As the truck sped off on the dirt track, putting more and more distance between Thomas and his child, Thomas stopped running. His eyes never left the truck as it shrank further and further, until all that was left was a tiny speck in the wintry horizon.

That was the last time Thomas saw his son.

That afternoon, Thomas slung the rucksack over his shoulders, hugged Krystof goodbye and began his journey to freedom.

38. GUNTHER

A loud banging startles Gunther, waking him from his nap.

"Scholz, you have a visitor!" the guard announces as he bangs on the bars of the cell. A key jostles in the keyhole and the iron grill slides open, rattling noisily on its tracks. Gunther squints, rubs his eyes and sits up slowly.

"Hurry up, I haven't got all day!"

Gunther takes a look at the guard – a tall, broad young man with a bored disposition, not much older than thirty, he guesses. He doesn't hurry. Instead, he takes his time to roll over to his side and slowly swings his legs over his narrow bed. When he is finally up, he shuffles languidly out of his cell, glancing at the guard disinterestedly as he passes him on his way out.

"Get moving, I haven't got all day."

The hard tip of the baton prods his back, nudging him along the shiny cement corridor.

"Hey punk, I'll get there when I get there, okay?" Gunther shot him a look and then continues to mosey down the empty corridor. The guard raises his baton mid-air and then puts it down again, his eyes flickering with hesitation. The other inmates are now peering out from behind their own bars, jeering and hooting.

"Yup, I didn't think so," Gunther says smugly.

When he arrives at the room lined with Perspex partitioned visitation booths, his eyes fall on a woman he least expected to see – Anna Weiss.

Dispassionately, he sinks into the chair in his booth, staring across the Perspex partition at the young reporter. Her face is emotionless when she picks up the phone on her side, gesturing for him to do the same. Reluctantly, Gunther follows suit.

"You should be dead," Gunther growls into the phone.

"As you can see, I'm not," Anna Weiss replies perfunctorily.

"What do you want?" Gunther says.

"To show you this," Anna Weiss says, putting down the phone on the table.

Gunther's eyes follow her as she reaches into her satchel and fishes out a few sheets of folded newspapers. She unfolds the top one first, plastering it across the Perspex window so that Gunther can read it, before picking up the phone again and putting it to her ear.

Gunther stares at the newspaper and squints a little with his poor eyesight. It's an American newspaper, that much is obvious. He slowly mouths the headline, one word at a time.

Vanished... The. Truth. About. The. Missing. Six. Million. Jews.

In the by-line are two words he detests more than anything else – Anna Weiss.

"Pffft, the Americans will publish anything just to sell some papers." Gunther snorts with derision, leaning back.

"The matter is being investigated by both the English and the American courts," Anna Weiss says. "They want to bring justice to the crimes committed by the Reich against the civilians of Europe."

"It will get nowhere." Gunther snorts dismissively.

He watches curiously as Anna Weiss folds the newspaper, puts it aside and picks up another newspaper, yellow with age. She unfolds it gingerly and then plasters it against the window once again. This time, Gunther recognises it immediately. A smug grin comes over his face.

The newspaper is a special edition of the Panzerbär from twenty-five years ago celebrating his heroic achievement saving the Reich from Western invasion. In bold print, the headline shouts - American Spies Caught Stealing Army Intelligence!

Gunther smiles as he remembers the jubilance that swept across Germania. There was a huge celebration in his honour. Parties were held everywhere and the state gifted him a beautiful mansion as his reward. It was the glorious prime of Gunther's career. What he wouldn't give to relive it again.

"That was some great times...," he reminisces.

"You remember him?" Anna Weiss asks, interrupting his reminiscing.

"Remember who?"

"This man," she says impatiently, pointing to one of the two smaller monochrome pictures.

"Oh, him," Gunther says after another squint of his eyes. "Of course, I remember him. His name was Tomáš Marz. He was with the Resistance. I was the one who caught that son of a bitch."

Another smug grin comes over him. Anna Weiss raises her eyebrows first and then shakes her head next.

"That son of a bitch was your real father," she says.

A flicker of horror flashes across Gunther's face.

"You lie!" He slams his palm onto the table, his face contorting with rage. "You lie!" He pounds the Perspex window angrily. It rattles and shakes but does not shatter.

"SCHOLZ! Keep it down!" the guard bellows from where he is standing. Gunther pays no attention to him and keeps pounding the Perspex window angrily.

"YOU LIE!" he shouts, his crimson face scrunched-up in a knot. But Anna Weiss does not say a word. She mere places the phone down on the table, reaching once again into her satchel. Gunther watches with wide eyes as she pulls something out – a withering brown paper package. He recognises it immediately.

"It was YOU!" he shouts, eyes flaring up with rage. "You framed me! It was YOU who planted the package in my house! You bitch! You'll pay for this!!!"

Anna does not say anything. Gingerly, she places the brown paper package on the table where Gunther can see it. Then, without another word, she picks up the phone and replaces it in its cradle. Gunther stares at her in incredulity as she rises and turns to leave.

"Who are you? Why did you do this to me???" Gunther shouts to her back but his voice echoes only on his side of the partition. Not being able to hear him, Anna keeps walking. When she reaches the door, she turns around and looks at him. Through the glass, she sees his contorted face, his fists pounding silently on the Perspex window as he shouts words she cannot hear.

"I don't deserve this!!!" he mouths angrily.

"Neither did Tomáš Marz," Anna says quietly to herself. "And all the innocent people who died in the war."

Turning around, Anna signals to the guard standing on the other side of the door. The door swings open and she walks through it without a backward glance.

Behind the Perspex window, Gunther watches in anguish as Anna Weiss walks through the door, shrinking smaller and smaller until she is only a tiny dot. When the door shuts completely, he lets out an exasperated bellow, and begins to cry.

39. ANNELIE

"It's not much but it'll do for now," Pavlina says as she jostles the key into the keyhole and unlocks the front door. The door swings open and they are immediately greeted by the high ceiling, intricately carved alabaster beams and generous shafts of sunlight streaming through white muslin curtains draping from the rails above the long windows.

They cross the threshold, Pavlina carrying a suitcase in each hand, setting them down to the side of the door. Annelie's eyes are shining as she looks around the apartment, taking in the two high-back armchairs by the fireplace – one on each side of the hearth. A small dark coffee table sits between the chairs on a grey rug. A floor lamp inhabits a corner of the room. In the opposite corner, a square stained wooden dining table with matching chairs are pushed against the wall.

In a sweeping glance, she imagines the home she's always dreamed of. A large Christmas tree by the window, a fire burning in the fireplace on a cold winter's night, family dinners of roast goose and fried potatoes, served with freshly baked bread around the dining table. She imagines the music that will be played within the four walls, the laughter to be had, the books to be read and the many memories to be made – away from the prying eyes of the authority. Away from the shackles of the Labour Repatriation Program. Those images dance vividly right before her eyes, bringing a wide smile to her face.

"It's perfect," she marvels. "I love it."

Pavlina smiles satisfactorily, squeezing her friend's shoulder before leaving the apartment to begin unloading their belongings stowed in the trunk of the car parked downstairs.

Beckoned by the tall windows, Annelie wanders over to take in the view. The gigantic Victory Arch looms in the distance, a large glass dome building a short distance behind it. The wide roads were lined with trees on either side. Cars move in an orderly fashion, crossing the vast city expediently. The city is a bustle of life. Her eyes sparkle at the grandeur but only for a moment. A part of her still misses her home – its medieval charm and uneven cobblestone streets now hundreds of miles away.

When Pavlina returns moments later carrying a large cardboard box, Annelie looks at her friend with tears in her eyes.

"What's the matter?" Pavlina asks, hurriedly setting the box down before rushing over.

"I don't know what I would have done without you," Annelie says as she breaks into a sob. Pavlina envelopes her in a tight hug, rubbing her back soothingly. They stand there for a long time, seeking comfort in each other's familiar company in the big, unfamiliar city.

"We're a family now," Pavlina says when they part from their hug. In her eyes, Annelie sees tears of gratitude. "You, me and Anna, we're a family now."

Annelie nods, smiling through misted eyes. They both look at the tiny face sleeping in the bassinet Annelie has set down on the floor. The baby stirs and paws her face before falling back into deep sleep.

"She looks so much like Jack," Annelie croaks, feeling a sour sensation rushing to the tip of her nose. "What will I tell her when she grows up and asks about her father?"

Pavlina shifts her glance from the baby to Annelie's face.

"You will tell her the truth," she says gently, squeezing Annelie's hand. "You will tell her that her father was a brave man, that he died trying to uncover the truth." They both gaze silently as the baby sleeps, each embroiled in their own thoughts of the past.

It's been a year since Thomas and Jack were executed. The Panzerbär had published a full front page with pictures and a jubilant headline.

American Spies Caught Stealing Army Intelligence! The headline screamed in bold lettering. Beneath it, two small monochrome pictures were lined up side by side – one of Thomas as a young man, another of Jack unsmiling. Across the text that separated the villains from the hero was a larger colour picture of a decorated army officer in full military gear. He was smiling – a patriotic, heroic icon – the epitome of German-ness.

Before news broke of the arrests and executions, Annelie knew the man only as one of the voices in the interrogation room. The front-page news had identified him as an army officer of pedigree heritage, a fine soldier in a family of long lines of decorated war heroes. His name was Gunther Scholz. As newsreel of the arrests took over every channel on the television, glorifying the superiority of the Reich's intelligence task force, Annelie wept. The nation celebrated Thomas and Jack's executions as though they were public enemies but Annelie knew better. More importantly, she knew the truth.

In the weeks following the executions, Annelie hid in Pavlina's flat, curled up in a ball under the blanket and wept. The officers in the interrogation room had reneged on all the terms of their agreement save one – that she and Pavlina's family would be permanently removed from the Labour Repatriation Program. She had been too naïve, thinking that she had the wherewithal to spare Thomas and Jack from execution. Her demands proved to be too far-fetched.

When the bodies had been cremated and the cardboard boxes containing the ashes lay unclaimed in the War Office, she had plucked up the courage to pick up the phone and dialled for Thomas' kin. Her hands were shaking when she was cowering over the payphone, unsure of what to say.

The woman who answered was equally distraught.

"I suppose it was bound to happen," the voice said after she first wept upon hearing the news. "Thomas was already dying before he got there. It was only a matter of time."

Terminal cancer.

The doctor said he had but a few months to live.

Annelie continued to weep into the phone.

"Where would you like me to send the package?" Annelie asked when she had collected herself sufficiently.

"What package?"

"The one he came to find," Annelie said. "It's a small box wrapped in brown paper."

"He didn't say anything about a package," the voice replied. "He went there to find his long-lost son. The one he left behind when he escaped the occupation."

"Do you know what he looks like?" Annelie asked, wiping her eyes.

"Fair hair, blue eyes. He has a scar on his shoulder. From a bullet wound he got as a child," the voice said. "And he has a birth mark on his left foot."

Annelie found a pen and a scrap of paper, furiously scribbling down every detail.

"He might have," she replied uncertainly as snippets of the front-page news came back to her.

"Then he would have died in peace," the voice said. "That's all he wanted to do. See his son for the last time."

There was a pause when the line crackled, prompting Annelie to feed more coins into the coin slot.

"Where should I send the ashes?" Annelie asked as their conversation neared the end. The woman gave her an address. She turned over the scrap of paper and scribbled it down on the remaining blank space.

"Jack's too?" Annelie asked bravely as her nose tinged with sourness.

"You can send those to his parents. I'll give you the address."

"You mean he's not your son?" Annelie's eyes widened.

"Heavens, no," the voice replied. "Jack is a reporter at the newspaper Tom used to work for. He's like a son to us but he's not our son."

So he had come to uncover the truth after all, Annelie thought after she hung up the phone.

As she stood by the payphone, stunned by the discovery, it finally made sense – the tour at the museum, the questions, the copies of the documents and the photographs that he had asked for – that was what he was there for. Annelie just didn't see it. She let out a sob and began to cry.

Weeks later, when she was hunched over the toilet bowl, hugging the cool ceramic basin, retching incessantly, a strange thing happened – she realised she was pregnant. For the first time since the executions, Annelie found an injection of strength. A new life was growing inside her, bringing a new sense of purpose to her existence.

A year on, the pain of the loss and the guilt of the betrayal weigh on her conscience. She needed to make things right. How she would do that, she didn't know.

"I'm going to get the rest of the boxes," Pavlina says, squeezing Annelie by the shoulder, pulling her back from her reverie.

"I'll start unpacking," Annelie says with a forced smile as she wipes a stray tear from the corner of her eye. A small gurgle emanates from the bassinet, drawing her attention. When she bends over to check on Anna, the baby squints, yawns and opens her tiny eyes.

"One day, Anna girl," she says to her daughter. "The world will know the truth. They will know that the entire race vanished because of one man's hatred. And they will see that only the weak attack those who are different, and the fools are the ignorant who follow the masses. One day, when the tables are turned, they will finally understand what it feels like to be on the wrong side of their own prejudice."

Then, gazing out the window at the glass dome in the distance, Annelie whispers to herself.

"The dead can't speak for themselves. It is up to the living to do it."

EPILOGUE

The kettle in the corner of the kitchenette whistles. The dumpy woman in the grocery store downstairs swears. Through the opened window, the noise of the street rises into the dingy flat.

The heat is stifling on that warm afternoon. The only reprieve comes from the slow whirring of the small table fan, its cage rusty with age, its blades caked with a thick layer of furry dust.

Not two months ago, Helena Svobodová received the stately minister in that little flat in Krakau. A heated exchange could be heard from the street. Even the dumpy woman in the grocery store downstairs stared at her ceiling, paying careful attention to the shouts coming from the flat upstairs. Neighbours in the building across the street witnessed – from their windows – Helena Svobodová tipping a kettle out her window. A gush of steaming hot water showered down onto the pavement, narrowly missing the stately older gentleman.

Not long after that gentleman left, a black car turned into the street and pulled up in front of the grocery store. Two men in grey uniforms with the double lightning bolt insignia on their collars exited the car, surveyed the neighbourhood before banging on the collapsible iron rail next door to the grocery store. Helena Svobodová came dawdling down the stairs, swearing under her breath. When the gate fanned open, the two men grabbed her by the arms – one on either side – and dragged her, kicking and screaming into the car. As swiftly as it had arrived, the car sped away.

No one saw Helena Svobodová again.

Not two months later, the stately gentleman returned, greyer and older, dragging a suitcase with him. He was seen clambering up the stairs with some difficulty, cursing in impeccable German. The dumpy woman in the grocery store downstairs stepped out of her shop and curiously poked her head into the dingy stairway. When the door of the flat upstairs slammed shut, she shook her head with a sigh and clapped the iron rails of the gate shut before returning to her shop.

Sometime later, the older gentleman came down to the grocery store to pick up a few things. A loaf of bread, a carton of milk, a box of teabags, half a dozen eggs, some cheese and apples. The dumpy woman rang them through the cash register as she eyed him up and down. He counted the bills onto the counter, picked up the bagged provisions and left without so much as a word. A few days later, he returned and picked up the same list of items, paid and left. He never spoke a word. Barely looked at anyone. Hardly ever left the flat.

He was like a phantom whose existence manifested itself in the form of thumping footsteps and the scraping of chair legs against the upstairs floorboard.

No one ever came to visit him.

The kettle in the corner of the kitchenette continues to whistle but no one is attending to it. A fuse trips and turns off the hot plate. The kettle stops whistling. On the shabby rug on the floor of the tiny living room, the stately gentleman lay crumpled with his cheek to the floor, his hand clutching at his chest, his face twisted with pain. He feels his breath leaving him. He struggles to summon it back. Faintly, he hears a tune from a distant memory. A woman's voice hums to him. Then, the pain in his chest is no more. He dies alone in the little flat, without anyone knowing. Without ever knowing who his real mother was.

Three days later, when the dumpy woman in the grocery store downstairs begins to complain of the stench coming from upstairs, her husband takes it upon himself to bang on the flimsy iron rails. He calls out into the stairway, his voice echoing faintly but no answer came. Then he returns with a plier cutter and forces the iron rails open.

Upstairs, behind the unlocked door of the flat, he discovers the decomposing body sprawled on the living room floor. A swarm of flies dances around it. He claps his hand over his nose and mouth, and, without a word, finds a blanket and covers the body with it. Then, he picks up the telephone and calls the police.

"No, he has no relatives that we know of," the man answers into the phone.

After a few moments, he hangs up and goes downstairs, back into the grocery store and continues to stack the shelves.

*

1945

The car engine spluttered and died. The wheels slowed to a halt. From the passengers' seat, a voice called out to the driver, "What's the matter?

VANISHED

Why have we stopped?"

The driver replied uncertainly, "Something is wrong with the engine." He turned the ignition off and then on again. The engine let out a squeak then a weak groan but struggled to fire up. The driver tried again, turning the ignition. Once again, the engine let out a squeak and then a weak groan but still refused to start. After a few tries, the engine went silent.

"Well?" the voice in the backseat called out impatiently.

"I'll have to have a look at it, Sir."

"Then why are you still sitting there? What are you waiting for? Fix it," the voice in the backseat remarked impatiently.

"Yes, Sir."

The front door opened and the driver climbed out. He took with him a metal box of tools. Under the blazing sun, he pried the hood opened and began examining the engine. A short while later, he returned and poked his head into the car.

"I've figured out what's wrong with the engine, Sir," he said.

"And?"

"It'll take me a while to fix it. About an hour or so," he said.

"Get to work then. I need to get to Prague before sundown," the voice in the backseat said.

As the driver set to work, tinkering with the faulty car engine, the back door of the car opened.

"I'm going for a walk," the voice said. "I won't be long."

"Yes, Sir."

They were on a quiet road in the countryside in Moravia, surrounded only by miles and miles of land and woods. The man looked around his surroundings and decided on a direction to walk. Under the blazing hot sun, he removed his cap and unbuttoned the collar of his uniform, walking along the road until he came to a small path branching off the main road.

On a whim, he decided to follow it. What he found at the end of the small path was a little cottage surrounded by a picket fence, set against the woods. From the dark soil of its front garden, colourful flowers bloomed in the flower beds.

He was immediately struck by an inspiration. Fixing his cap back on and buttoning up his collar, he pushed open the low gate and made his way up the path to the front porch of the little cottage. After several knocks, the door opened a crack, behind which the face of a man peered at him warily.

"H-how can I h-h-help you, Off-off-officer?" the man stammered.

"Open up," he said. "This is a routine inspection."

The door opened wider. Behind the man, he could see a woman standing nervously in the room, one hand on her protruding belly, a small child standing by her side, holding onto a corner of her dress.

"Is this your house?" he stepped into the cottage and began looking around as he paced in the small living room.

"Y-y-yes, it is," the man stammered.

It did not take him long to look around as the cottage was indeed quite small. When he was done, he returned to the living room to find the couple and the child gathered together like a little unit, watching him nervously. His eyes fell on the child – the little boy who was holding onto a corner of the woman's dress. He studied him, taking in his fair hair and his blue eyes. Then he looked up at the couple, registering no similarities between the child's appearance and theirs.

"Is this boy your child?" he looked at them with raised eyebrows.

"Y-y-yes, he is."

The flicker of fear in both the man and the woman's eyes did not escape him.

He took a few steps forward and crouched down to look at the child closely. The boy hid behind the folds of the woman's dress, peeking only when he was brave enough. His lively eyes fixed on the officer, shyly at first, and then more boldly.

A stab of nostalgia came over the officer. A memory from a not-so-distant past rushed back to him, filling him with a sudden insatiable yearning.

"Pieter…," he found himself whispering, staring at a face that wasn't there. He was suddenly overcome by an urge to hold the little boy but he caught himself just in time, and his common sense returned to him. This boy was not his son. His son was dead. His son had been dead for four years. Killed in an explosion in an air raid on Berlin by the RAF.

He straightened up and cleared his throat. Struck again by another flash of inspiration, he said to the man, "This child has been selected for Germanization."

A gasp escaped from the woman as her eyes widened in horror. Her hand shot up and clapped over her mouth. Her eyes began to water instantly. From the man, a clear speech sprouted.

"There must be a mistake, Officer," he said, pleadingly. "Your men have come by before. This child is not part of the Germanization program."

"This is an order from the Reich! Are you questioning the order?" the officer raised his voice. "How dare you question the Reich's order?"

The man cowered and said no more. To the boy, the officer asked softly, "What is your name, child?"

The little boy looked at him, enchanting him with his blue eyes.

"Miloš," he squeaked.

"Well, from this moment on, your name is Gunther," the officer said. "Do you know what chocolate is, Gunther?"

The little boy shook his head.

"Well, chocolate is a sweet treat. Do you like sweets?"

The little boy nodded.

"Where I'm going to take you has plenty of this chocolate. You can eat as much of it as you want," the officer said now, taking him by the hand.

The little boy looked uncertainly at the woman, whose face was now wet with silent tears. He frowned with confusion.

"Miloš, go with the Officer," she croaked, barely able to utter the words. He could see that she was trembling. From what, he wasn't sure.

"Yes, Miloš, g-g-go with the Off-off-officer," the man stammered. In his eyes, the little boy registered a sadness he could not understand.

"Come with me, Gunther," the man in the uniform coaxed as he led him to the front door.

"No! I don't want to! I want to stay here!" he said defiantly, trying to pull his hand back.

"Gunther, come with me!" The tone in the officer's voice hardened as he tightened his grip around the boy's arm. A struggle followed.

"No! Let me go! I don't want to go! I want to stay here!" The boy finally wriggled his arm free, slipped from the officer's grasp and ran to hide behind the woman's dress.

"You're coming with me whether you want to or not!" barked the man in the uniform, his face scrunched up in anger. He stamped across the room, picked the little boy up by his waist and slung him over his shoulder, carrying him kicking and screaming out of the cottage.

"Maminka! Táta!" the boy cried, his arms flailing desperately in the air, his face scrunched up in agony. "Maminka! Táta!"

The man and his wife watched mournfully as the boy was taken away. Then, as if changing their minds, they dashed after the officer, the woman running down the path, the man behind her.

"Meeelossshhh!" she cried out tearily, her feet pounding the dry earth.

"Maminka!!!" the boy screamed, his little hands stretching out at her.

"Meeeeeeeeeelowwwwwwsssssssssshhhhh!" the woman shrieked as she ran, her face crumpling with anguish, tears leaking from the corners of her eyes. A sharp pain in her belly stopped her in her tracks. She bent over, one hand holding her belly, the other supporting her back. With tears running down her cheeks, she watched helplessly as the little boy was carried off, his desperate cries piercing through the empty sky.

THE END

ACKNOWLEDGMENTS

The following people provided insights that went into the writing of this book:
- My guides in Berlin, Kraków and Prague – the two Chris', Dmitry and Václav – for providing historical context, which subsequently went into the construction of Thomas' past.
- Daniela Bartáková from the Shoah History Department in the Jewish Museum in Prague – for providing clarification on Jewish funeral rites in Prague during the German occupation.
- Václav Zahradník for lending Annelie his term of endearment for his grandmother.

Many thanks to Amy E. Freeman, who was the first person to have read the manuscript, and also to all the early readers who generously provided feedback and encouragement.

My family deserves a medal for enduring my writing fever for the last 27 years.

To friends who have continued to support me throughout the ups and downs of life, thank you.

Last but not least, my deepest gratitude goes to Alexander and Jiap, without whom, this book would not exist.

ABOUT THE AUTHOR

C.K. Lim was born in Malaysia, where she lived until age 19 before moving to Australia.
She now calls Melbourne home.

To find out more, visit:

www.authorcklim.com

Made in United States
Orlando, FL
26 September 2024